A Duke in Disguise

Also by Cat Sebastian

The Regency Impostors Series

Unmasked by the Marquess

A Duke in Disguise

COMING SOON

The Duchess Deception

The Seducing the Sedgwicks Series

It Takes Two to Tumble

A Gentleman Never Keeps Score

The Turner Series

The Soldier's Scoundrel

The Lawrence Browne Affair

The Ruin of a Rake

A Duke in Disguise

A Regency Impostors Novel

Cat Sebastian

AVONIMPULSE
An Imprint of HarperCollins*Publishers*

This is a work of fiction. Names, characters, places, and incidents are products of the author's imagination or are used fictitiously and are not to be construed as real. Any resemblance to actual events, locales, organizations, or persons, living or dead, is entirely coincidental.

Digital Edition APRIL 2019 ISBN: 978-0-06-282066-2
Print Edition ISBN: 978-0-06-282161-4

Cover art by Christine Ruhnke
Cover photograph © romance novel covers (couple); © AndreySkat/PinkyWinky/Shutterstock (two images)

FIRST EDITION

19 20 21 22 23 HDC 10 9 8 7 6 5 4 3 2 1

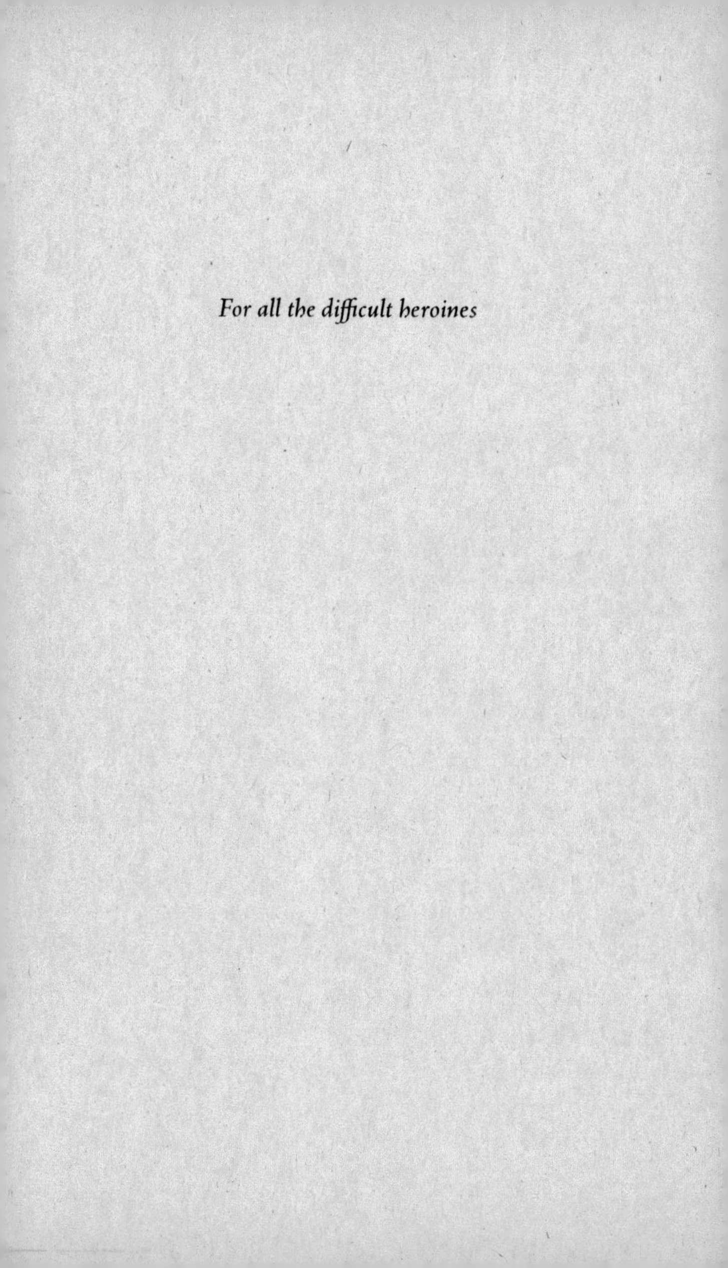

For all the difficult heroines

Acknowledgments

This book took the better part of a year that was challenging in just about every way. I'm more indebted than usual to my editor, Elle Keck, and everyone at Avon. My agent, Deirdre Knight, has as always been tremendous. Margrethe Martin not only read multiple drafts of this book but also made sure I had a constant supply of dog pictures and Danish candy. Lastly, I owe a lot to my children for taking the time to firmly and patiently explain that some villains need to die.

Chapter One

Ash knew all too well that there were two varieties of pleasure in life. The first included art, fine weather, good company, and all the rest of the world's benign delights. A man could hold these pleasures at arm's length, appreciate them with the proper detachment, and not mourn their absence overmuch. But a fellow could be ruined by overindulgence in the second category of pleasure: rich food, strong drink, high stakes gaming.

Verity Plum belonged squarely in the latter category.

For all she was one of Ash's dearest friends and one of the few constants in his life, for all she and her brother were now the closest thing to family that he had in this country, being near her was a pleasure he meted out for himself in small doses, like the bottle of French brandy he kept in his clothes press, lest he succumb to the emotional equivalent of gout.

As a very young man he had compared Verity, pen in hand and smudged spectacles balanced on the tip of her nose, to a bird diligently building a nest. Ten years later he knew it to have been the romantic delusion of a youthful idiot not to have straightaway seen the bloodlust lurking behind the spectacles; she bore more in common with a hawk picking the meat from its prey's bones than with a songbird collecting twigs and leaves.

He had arrived in town late the previous night, when the house was dark and the doors locked. He let himself in using the latchkey Mr. Plum had given him ten years ago and which he still carried on a string around his neck. Weary from the journey from Portsmouth and loath to wake the household, he left his satchel at the foot of the stairs, climbed up to the spare room, and went promptly to sleep. When he woke, a cup of coffee and a buttered roll sat on the table beside his bed, and his satchel rested on a hard-backed chair, which meant somebody at least knew he had arrived. Could be Verity, could be Nate, could be old Nan, who still came in every morning to do the cleaning. Could be a stray vagabond off the streets or one of the impecunious writers who often made their home in the garrets of the Holywell Street premises of Plum & Company, Printers and Booksellers.

Now he cast his gaze around Verity's study, taking in the cobwebs in every corner and the teetering piles of books, the grate that sat empty, the windowpane that had been cracked for over a decade. He would miss the tidy set of rooms he had shared with Roger. He would miss Roger, full stop. A sick chasm of loss threatened to open inside him. Ash's earliest memory was going to live with Roger as an apprentice engraver; before that was only a series of flickering images, fractured and haunting, scarcely seeming to belong to Ash at all. But from the point he had gone to Roger, he had a home, a name, a place to belong. He had lived with Roger for over fifteen years, first as his apprentice, then as a colleague, always as a friend. A few days earlier, when Roger was preparing to board the ship that would take him to Italy, to a climate more suited to his failing lungs, his parting words had been to advise that Ash stay with the Plums. "Yes, yes, you might well hire a quite respectable set of rooms, but you'll be talking to the shadows and naming every spider and earwig within a week. Stay with the Plums." His mentor had been pale, his voice weak from coughing, his thin gray hair whipping in the wind, so his advice, quite possibly the last words he would speak to Ash in this world, had the weight of a dying request.

"I could still come with you," Ash had said again. He had made this offer so many times it had taken on the cadence of a prayer. "It's not too late." He spoke the words into the wind, to be carried away, off the shores of this island he would never leave.

"I really can't see how you expect me to recover when I'm worried about you," Roger had replied, clasping the younger man's hands. "It's too much to ask."

"It's just seasickness," Ash replied pointlessly, because they both remembered vividly what had happened on the packet to Calais all those years ago, and then on the agonizing return journey to Dover. A storm-tossed ship was a perilous place to have a seizure.

"And I just have a summer cold," Roger had responded. And so Ash had embraced his friend one last time, watched the boat sail away, and then headed for London.

Watching Verity now, as she scribbled on a blotted and crumpled piece of paper, her pale brown hair doing unspeakable things and a vast quantity of ink on her fingers, the grief that had dogged him since Portsmouth started to thin, only to be displaced by something else entirely. She must have encountered a particularly galling turn of phrase in the manuscript she was working on, because she made a strangled sound of outrage as she scribbled it out. How many times had he seen her perform just that movement over the years? He ought to be used to how she affected him, but during the months in Bath—that last, futile effort to see if the waters might restore Roger's health—he must have forgotten how to resist her. He couldn't remember how he used to guard his heart against this sudden rush of fondness.

Without rising to his feet, he reached for an andiron and prodded the fire back to life. He still had on his gloves and coat to ward off the chill, but Verity had doubtless been toiling away in this cold room since breakfast. She occasionally made a sound of approval or a tut of frustration as she turned a page, and her pencil was forever scratching along the manuscript, but otherwise she worked in silence, perfectly still at the desk in the small room above the bookshop that she used as her office. The fire hissed, Ash idly paged through a book he had open on his lap, and Verity worked.

Finally she turned over the last page. "Guess how many times Nate used the word *liberty* in this week's *Register,*" she said without looking up from her paper, as if it hadn't been six months since they had last seen one another.

He suppressed a smile and mentally awarded her a point

in the game of feigned mutual indifference they had been playing for a decade. He didn't know which of them had started it or why, but he would hardly know how to act if they dropped the pretense.

"Four?" he asked.

"Sixteen!" She put her pen down and looked at him for the first time. There was ink on her cheekbone. "In a single article."

"How tedious of him," Ash remarked lightly. Not for love or money would Ash throw himself between the Plum siblings when they were engaged in one of their skirmishes. Three was a difficult number for friendships, and only by careful neutrality did Ash preserve their balance. "Is it any good?"

"If his goal is to get himself hanged or transported, then yes, I'd say it's quite effective. Sometimes I think he actually wants to get arrested."

Ash thought this was entirely possible. The letters he had received in Bath from friends as well as from Nate and Verity themselves suggested that the arguments between brother and sister on the subject of printing outright seditious libel were escalating even faster than the battles between radicals and the government. "He feels strongly about Pentrich," Ash said, striving for diplomacy.

Verity snorted. "He damned well does feel strongly. And so do I. But I can't see what good his swinging by a rope will do anybody. I daresay this government would be only too glad to see us all dead, then there wouldn't be anybody left to object." She took off her spectacles and rubbed her eyes, smudging ink across her cheek. "He's been saying he wants to travel north for the execution."

Ash frowned. While in Bath, with all his attention on Roger's failing health, he had followed the events in the newspaper as he might the tidings of a far-off land. In Pentrich, Derbyshire, some poor benighted fools, half-mad with hunger and deluded by the lies of a government spy, armed with nothing more than scythes and knives and a harebrained set of demands, had been convicted of high treason. Surrounded by clean white streets and well-fed gentlefolk, the stories coming from the North seemed remote, something that belonged in the past. Roger railed against tyranny until he coughed too hard to speak, while Ash listened with half an ear and reserved his anger for a God who seemed intent on leaving Ash alone in the world.

"The trouble with Nate," Ash said, "is that he's twice as clever as he needs to be."

"You wouldn't think so if you read this article," Verity countered. "He knows I can't manage the press if he goes to prison, and even less if I'm in prison as an accessory." She removed a pin from the knot of hair at the back of her head and used it to fasten a curl that had stubbornly worked its way loose, only succeeding in dislodging two more curls in the process. "At any rate, I altered some of the more incendiary phrases so at least this week's issue won't be the death of us."

She had probably also made her brother's arguments twice as cogent and therefore three times as annoying to the government, but she knew that already. "Let me have a look at it." He reached out and she placed the sheaf of papers in his hand.

Nate's bold scrawl unraveled across the page like a tangled skein of yarn, marked with slashes and arrows, then interwoven with Verity's minuscule copperplate handwriting. Charlie, the Plums' apprentice, would render a fair copy for Verity or Nate to approve before setting type, but Ash had enough practice to decipher Nate's writing without much trouble. He read a few lines and raised an eyebrow. "Mentioning the guillotine was perhaps a bridge too far." Verity had struck that line out with a stroke that nearly pierced the paper.

"You see I'm not exaggerating, then?" she demanded, her eyes bright with the prospect of an argument won.

"Mmm," he murmured, trying to sound noncommittal. But even with Verity's revisions, this article would at the very least bring the *Register* in for a level of scrutiny that would do its publishers no good. The entire country looked like a pot about to boil and Nate was all too eager to throw himself right into the hot water.

She leaned forward and he found himself looking up from the paper expectantly, his own posture mirroring hers. "Heaven help me, I missed you, Ash."

He was taken aback by this foray into earnestness but did his best to hide his surprise behind a mask of cool indifference, quickly refocusing his gaze on the paper. He wanted to tell her that she absolutely needed to stop saying that sort of thing, that he had spent years on the edge of a precipice, and it would take only the slightest breeze to tip him over completely.

But he didn't think their friendship could survive that kind of honesty: if they acknowledged the potential he felt between them, then they'd want to do something about it. Then he'd lose her. Ash had endured too many losses, and was not willing to lose either of the Plums. So he leaned back in his chair and raised an eyebrow. "Understandable," he said with a blandness that was only possible after a decade of practice. "Without me around, you'd be the worst radical on the premises."

Verity laughed, a merry gurgle that made Ash's heart almost hurt. "Speak for yourself. I'm an exceptionally good radical. Otherwise I would have let my brother print this bilge unedited even though it would be as good as turning him over to the redcoats. What I meant is that it's reassuring not to be the only one in the house who has second thoughts about giving up one's life and safety for a good cause. You heard that Mr. Hone was arrested?" William Hone, another publisher, had earlier that year spent two months in jail on charges of seditious libel. "He's being treated as a hero. And he is, but I spent the entire summer worried that Nate would be next. I suppose that's selfish, but so be it."

Ash raised an imaginary glass in a toast to the idea of not going to prison. He was not terribly keen on imprisonment himself, being fairly certain a seizure on a stone floor would not be one he would survive.

"How long has it been since the last time you lived with us?" Verity asked, tilting her head and looking at him as if she had just noticed he was there.

"Four years? It was in '13 that Roger and I took the set of rooms near Finsbury Square." They had lodged with the

Plums when first coming to London, and then occasionally returned to stay with them in between hired sets of rooms. They had changed residences often, always hoping that it was the damp of a previous lodging that had left Roger in an increasingly worrisome state of health.

"Truly, Ash, I'm glad to have you back," she said, with a frank wistfulness that made Ash's heart thud in his chest. "You've always been a stabilizing influence on Nate."

Ash tried not to be disappointed that Verity had missed him only insofar as his presence helped Nate. She had always thought first of her brother; this was nothing new, although the little worry lines that appeared around her eyes when she spoke of him definitely were.

From beyond the thin sooty window he heard the bells of St. Clement's chime for the second time since he had come in. It was time to leave. He hoisted himself to his feet and looked down at Verity. She was polishing her spectacles on the hem of her shawl; a tumble of tea-brown hair had worked its way loose to fall into her face, and that smudge of ink remained beneath her right eye. She must have sensed him looking at her, because she glanced up. Their gazes caught and lingered a moment too long. Ash promptly rose to his feet and left, closing the door behind him. If he let looks like that happen, they'd all find out exactly how fragile their arrangement was.

How one was meant to feed all these people on a couple of mutton chops Verity did not know. Supper was supposed to serve four: herself, Nate, Ash, and Charlie. But

Nate had come home with three friends he met at the pub, which would have been bad enough even if he hadn't evidently also invited Amelia Allenby, the half-grown daughter of Verity's friend. At half past seven, a carriage pulled up in front of the house and disgorged a girl in pearl earbobs and a white muslin frock, dressed as if she were going to dine with the great and good of the land, rather than pick at too few mutton chops and be an eyewitness to sedition. Amelia was seventeen and looked upon Nate with a degree of hero worship that nobody who brought three hungry radicals home to dinner deserved.

Why did it always have to be something like chops when there were unexpected guests? Six days out of seven they had stew of varying consistencies, starting out as something reasonably substantial but stretched and thinned as the week wore on, until it became a sort of watery potato soup. She supposed Nan found a bargain on mutton at the market that morning. At least there were plenty of fresh rolls from the baker. When the dish of mutton was passed around, she handed it to Ash without saying a word. He caught her eye and passed the dish to Amelia on his right without taking any meat for himself.

"Never worry, Plum," he said in a low murmur that made her remember that he was, unfortunately, a man; if she had learned anything in her quarter century in this city it was that men were more trouble than they were worth. "I have a bottle of wine and some cheese upstairs. I'll bring you some later."

"How provident of you," she said, telling herself very

firmly that she was not to lean closer to Ash. "Clearly you remember what it takes to survive in this house." The Plums had never kept a decent table, not even in Verity's mother's day, and Verity often wondered that they had any supper guests whatsoever. Not that Ash was a guest; he was, technically, a lodger, which meant he paid for this nipfarthing supper. She sighed. "But I truly can't—"

She was interrupted by raised voices from Nate's end of the table.

"They were sentenced to be hanged, drawn, and quartered. In 1817." Nate smacked his knife down with a thump that shook the table. "Of course I'm outraged. A group of men, after being convicted in a sham trial, are to have the entrails taken out of their still-living bodies. Why wouldn't I be outraged?"

"I don't think it'll come to that," said one of the hearty young men, brandishing an entire mutton chop on the end of his fork. "I don't recall hearing about Despard and his conspirators being disemboweled, although I was only a boy when that happened."

"Drawing doesn't refer to the drawing out of the entrails," said Amelia in her polished and plummy accent, as if this were normal dinner table conversation. Verity noted that the girl had not taken any meat, and appeared to be contenting herself with boiled carrots and a roll. "It refers to the drawing of the convict behind a horse. I was reading about it in a book on the Plantagenets."

"Were all those medieval chaps disemboweled just for fun, then?" the young man asked, leaning across the table towards

Amelia. "Just a bit of a flourish on the executioner's behalf, eh?" Verity had the alarming sense that the boy was attempting to flirt with Amelia. Trust one of Nate's friends to flirt by means of discussing capital punishment.

"We're eating," Verity pointed out, knowing it was hopeless. "Maybe we can save the talk of disembowelment for later."

"Or never," Ash suggested. "Never would do."

"You are missing the point," Nate said, entirely ignoring his sister and directly addressing Ash. "For them to be killed at all is barbaric. It's nothing less than murder."

"Of course it's nothing less than murder," Ash said in that deep, steady voice that he had always used to calm Nate down. "It's worse than murder, because it will go unpunished. And of course the trial was grossly wrong and unfair. We all know that. We all agree at this table." My God, they had been through this often enough in the past months. Verity opened her mouth to say as much but Ash, without looking at her, made a shooing gesture under the table which she interpreted as *Shut up, Plum*. "The only point on which we disagree is whether you're going to print a lunatic screed that gets us all arrested."

"What I wrote is the truth," Nate answered, sounding more like a child of ten than a grown man of past twenty.

"A fat lot of good the truth has ever done anyone," Verity burst out, unable to hold her tongue. "Besides, even the truth can be couched in words that don't get anyone brought before a judge."

"Wooler was acquitted!" Nate protested, referring to a

publisher who that summer had been tried for seditious libel after publishing material criticizing the House of Lords. "And I'm certain Hone will be, when he's tried later this autumn."

"And Mr. Cobbett went to America to avoid another turn in prison," she shot back, alluding to a fellow reformer who had once spent two years in prison for a pamphlet that was critical of the government. As soon as Lord Sidmouth ordered the arrest and prosecution of anyone suspected of printing sedition, Cobbett had sailed to New York.

"William Cobbett is an old man," her brother retorted.

"My father says he's done with politics," said one of the young printers, adopting a self-consciously conciliatory tone that made Verity want to crack her dinner plate over his head. "He says he'll only trade in obscenity from now on. Says people will always pay for that, paper duty or no paper duty."

"Less time in prison too," said another man. "And no chance of being done up for treason. Three years hard? Piddling stuff." Verity could not determine whether he was joking.

"Better than transportation or hanging," pointed out the first young man.

"Or disembowelment," agreed the other. They clinked their glasses together in happy salute of the manageable punishment for printing obscenities.

Verity sighed. "I'm so sorry," she told Amelia once the young men had all resumed their quarrel. "They haven't any manners at all."

"This is much more interesting than the dinners I usually attend," she said brightly. Seventeen was young enough for anything to be interesting, Verity supposed.

"I daresay your mother has kept you well clear of sedition and blasphemy. I'll have to apologize to her." Verity groaned inwardly at the prospect. It had been half a year since she and Portia Allenby had ceased being lovers. But they had been friends before, and Portia seemed determined that they would remain friends, even though every moment they spent together reminded Verity of how very ill-suited she was for affection, romance, and possibly even friendship.

Amelia furrowed her brow. "All those scientists she has on her Wednesday nights are quite blasphemous, at least if my understanding of their science and general theology are correct."

Portia Allenby had once been the mistress of a wealthy nobleman and now held a salon at which writers, scientists, and other luminaries gathered. She let her daughters have run of the house no matter what topics were being discussed. But Verity had to think that Portia might not want her eldest daughter to be at a dinner table where there was frank disparagement of the government without the benefit of decent food and wax candles. Good wine helped a great deal to make conversation seem academic rather than something that could at any moment spill out into the streets and end with pitchforks and treason trials.

"Would you ever trade in . . ." Amelia bit her lip, plainly at a loss for words. "In the sort of material the young men were talking about?"

"Lewd novels?" Verity supplied. "Explicit prints? If they were any good, perhaps." Beside her, she heard Ash's low laugh. "Well, I would," she insisted. "We don't put out many books, but I'd make an exception. My father always said that more than one bookseller made his fortune on clandestine printings of *Fanny Hill*. But I wouldn't put out another *Fanny Hill*, which I dare say a number of gentlemen have found very amusing, but it doesn't have much in it for the ladies."

Now she could feel Ash's gaze on her and it gave Verity a strange feeling to be talking about obscene literature so close to him. With so many people crowded around the small table, her shoulder nearly touched his.

"You and your brother are no different," he said, an indulgent half smile playing on his lips. "Any other person would be coming up with law-abiding ways to keep the business afloat. The two of you are fighting over which laws to break."

"If I printed that sort of thing, I'd be most careful, I assure you. Only the best filth for Plum and Company's readership."

Later, after Nate and his friends left to get soused at a gin house and Amelia had been collected by her mother's carriage, Ash and Verity sat amidst the remains of supper and the wine from Ash's room.

"Revolution is all he speaks of," she said while splitting the last roll and giving half to Ash. "And in turn all I talk about is the need for prudence, and so we go round and round. I think we've been having the same conversation since you left for Bath." The wine had gone to her head a bit. Her thoughts were muzzy and her speech was free. "I feel like a prison warden. Or a very cross nursery maid. I'm always scolding Nate or counting farthings or wondering where the last candle went." These repeated quarrels were robbing her of her affection for her brother, the bookshop, and her work. There was so little joy in it, and these days there wasn't even the thrill of working for a good cause, because she felt precious little hope for success in the face of a government bent on tyranny. She drained her glass. "With you here, though, I'm not alone." Good God, she was more than a little drunk if she was being that maudlin out loud.

Ash emptied the wine bottle into her glass. "You've never been alone. You have dozens of people in and out of this house every day—your writers, workers, customers, other booksellers. I've been back less than a day, I haven't left the house, and I've already seen almost everyone I know in this city." The firelight glinted off his dark hair and cast shadows across the strong planes of his face. She hastily looked away.

"That's not what I meant." All those people who came and went wanted or needed something from her. That was the common thread running through every relationship Verity had known, starting with her overbearing father and continuing right through to Portia Allenby. What Verity offered was never enough and now she had nothing left to give. Giving more would mean nothing remained for herself. And maybe that made her hard and unfeeling, but she'd live with that if the alternative was self-effacement.

She felt the warmth of his hand on top of hers and nearly startled in her seat. By unspoken consent, they seldom touched. They had never discussed the parameters of their friendship, but they measured out these touches as carefully as any housewife measured out the lumps in the sugar bowl. They were for special occasions, feast days, homecomings. Two, three touches a year. Any more frequent and heaven knew what would happen.

Verity knew exactly what would happen, though. Sometimes she let herself think of it, when night had fallen and she had the sheets pulled up to her chin. It was important that it never actually come to pass, because Ash was the type who would get ideas and insist on marriage. And the last thing in the world Verity needed was a husband. She had seen what marriage had done to her mother: it had worn her down, whittled her away at the edges until she had all but disappeared. Partly that was because her father had not been a particularly kind man. He had been a radical and a democrat; he had memorized passages from Mary Wollstonecraft's book. But as far as Verity could tell, the man had never once thought to apply those ideas to his own wife. It was, Verity assumed, the old adage about power corrupting: marriage gave a man too much unchecked power over his wife and children, transforming otherwise decent men into petty tyrants. Her mother had ultimately been dependent on the whims of a man who was both mercurial and self-serving, critical and harsh. Verity had fought hard to maintain a degree of control over her fate: Plum and Company was hers as much as it was Nate's, both on paper and as a matter of practical fact. The only people she relied on were those whose wages she paid. The prospect of a husband—and children, presumably—would make that independence impossible.

"Look at me," Ash said, his voice low, and Verity managed

to tear her gaze away from where their hands touched. She turned her face up to his. The candles had burnt down and the room was lit only by the fire and one weakly flickering lamp, but she could see the dusting of new beard on his jawline, the dark gleam of his eyes. She allowed herself to appreciate how very handsome he was, another practice she allowed only in the strictest moderation. His hair was nearly black and fell in haphazard waves across his forehead. His jaw was strong but his eyelashes were decadently pretty and he had a few utterly incongruous freckles scattered across his nose. There. She had noticed all those things and still was quite in her right mind.

"Plum," Ash said, and she had the fleeting impression that he was looking at her with the same tightly leashed admiration. He shook his head and let go of her hand. That ought to have been enough to restore their normal equilibrium, but she could still feel the traces of his touch on her. Later, when she was back at her desk, working by the light of a guttering candle, she caught herself wishing that Ash were with her, that his hand was on hers and his body beside hers. She had the uneasy sense that something between them had shifted out of place and she did not know how to put it back the way it belonged.

Chapter Two

After a thankless morning spent settling bills and paying wages, Verity had to face the fact that the amount left over was less than it had been the month before, or even the month before that. All the booksellers of her acquaintance had the same complaint: bread wasn't getting any cheaper and neither was coal, so people were buying fewer books. They were also buying fewer broadsides, pamphlets, tracts, ballads, and the rest of their stock in trade. *Plum's Weekly Register,* which their father had founded twenty years ago, and which Nate and Verity now published, accounted for the bulk of their profits. She had no doubt that people paid their sixpence to read Nate's impassioned tirades. If, as she had been begging him, he toned them down, they would lose readers.

She needed to come up with another way to bring in a bit of extra money, and she thought perhaps a monthly magazine for women of a class wealthy enough to afford the paper tax might be just the thing to get them through the winter, if only Verity had the faintest idea what ladies wanted to read.

She supposed she ought to know herself, although she was not precisely a lady, due to her father having been a common printer rather than an overbred drain on society. But when she considered what she wanted to read—political treatises, occasional broadsides, and too many novels than she really ought to make time for—it didn't correspond at all with the material she found in the ladies' magazines that were spread out on the desk before her. She had no use for fashion plates, because she could not afford new gowns; nor did she care for maudlin verse, improving tales, or the sort of society gossip that was punctuated with a superfluity of exclamation marks. She doubted such fare was what most women wished to read.

She was turning this puzzle over in her mind when the chatter from downstairs altered. Nate and Charlie had been laughing with the men in the workroom, but they abruptly went silent. This usually meant that a customer had come into the shop. An actual, paying customer, not one of the men Nate slipped pamphlets to without collecting the tax. But it couldn't have been a customer because a moment later she heard the light tread of expensively shod feet heading up the bare wooden stairs.

When she saw Portia Allenby standing gracefully in the doorway, Verity's first thought was that she wished she had worn something else. Not that she had anything fine to wear even if she had wanted to, but she did not know how two people were meant to converse as equals when one wore an ink-stained frock of mouse-colored wool, three years old, much mended and twice turned at the cuffs, and the other wore—she didn't quite know what Portia Allenby was wearing. The various trims and elegancies that adorned Portia's person were, to Verity, emblems of a world she found both alien and objectionable. But at the same time Verity couldn't help but see herself through the eyes of her former lover: shabby, hungry, and lacking.

Portia always looked like a small army of lady's maids had buffed and polished her to a high luster before sending her forth to grace mere mortals with her presence. Her hair was black, her skin ivory, her profile immaculate. Verity happened to know that Portia Allenby had passed her thirty-fifth birthday, but looking at her, anyone could be forgiven for having thought she was indeed her daughter Amelia's slightly older sister.

"Portia," Verity said, rising to her feet. "I haven't any tea," she blurted out. She also hadn't any other potential refreshment to offer guests. She hastily glanced around the room, as if she'd somehow notice that it was less drab and dingy than usual, as if the musty scent of books and damp would choose today to dissipate, and the windows would spontaneously shed their layers of soot and grime. This was her room, in her house, where she ran her business, and most of the time she was proud of it. Not when Portia Allenby stood there in all her splendor, though. Since they had ended their affair, they had confined their meetings to Portia's house, and now Verity remembered why.

Portia stepped forward and clasped Verity's hands before Verity could warn her to beware getting ink on her pretty gloves. At this close range, Verity could detect the perfume that always lingered close to Portia's person. Perhaps it was soap, or the fragrance of the powder that dusted Portia's face, or perhaps it came in a fine glass bottle all the way from Paris. It smelled rich and vaguely foreign, but subtle, much like Portia herself.

"Of course you don't, my dear," Portia said in her mellow, refined voice. "I'm not here to impose on you. I have the carriage waiting below, so I won't keep you from your work. I wanted to drop a word in your ear about Amelia."

Heat began to rise in Verity's cheeks. "I didn't realize Nate meant to bring his friends to supper the other night. I suppose it was rather more raucous than Amelia is accustomed to." She thought again of Amelia in her fine white muslin, listening raptly to the seditious chatter of booksellers.

"No, no. It's not that." Portia sank gracefully onto the sofa, and only then did Verity realize she was still standing. She sat abruptly in her own chair. "I have no objection to anything that Amelia hears or anyone she might meet while in your company. I quite trust your judgment. My concern is more what might happen while she's here, outside your doing."

"Pardon?"

"A raid, my dear. An arrest. That wouldn't do at all. She's nearly eighteen now, and with any luck will make her debut in the spring."

"Her debut?" Verity asked. "I hadn't realized you had such hopes for her." During the months that she had been a near-daily visitor in the Allenby household, there had been a steady stream of tutors, drawing masters, French governesses, and all the other staff essential to the raising of elegant young ladies. But Verity had thought Portia simply meant to provide her daughters with a first-rate education, not prepare them to be launched into the upper echelons of society.

"She is the daughter of a marquess. On the wrong side of the blanket, of course, but Ned acknowledged my girls as his daughters. Lord Gilbert acknowledges them as his sisters."

"And the current Lord Pembroke?"

Portia pressed her lips together. "He'll take some doing. But my point is that I don't want to jeopardize that. Pembroke is . . ." She let her voice trail decorously off.

A stuffed shirt? An unapologetic Tory? Everything that Verity had devoted her life to fighting? She couldn't help but feel the insult implicit in Portia's remarks. Of course being a guest in Verity's home would threaten Amelia's standing with the very hierarchy Verity wanted to dismantle. That was the entire point. And here Portia was asking Verity to cooperate.

"Lord Pembroke has very precise standards," Portia said, smoothing the fabric of her gown beneath her gloved hands. "I plan to ensure that Amelia adheres to those standards. Her being brought before a magistrate would quite put paid to all my hopes for her."

"All your hopes," Verity repeated. "I thought your hopes were for her to—" Verity silenced herself, suddenly aware that the very sight of her—shabbily dressed and weary—must make Portia even more eager to ensure her daughters had a different fate. She changed tack. "A debut, though. Are you sure that's what Amelia wants?" Verity had the strong impression that Amelia would prefer idling in the bookshop, arguing with Nate about the rights of man and the merits of the latest Greek translations, rather than dancing at balls and making polite chatter at tea parties.

"What she wants is immaterial. The fact of the matter is that she is a marquess's daughter. That is her birthright. Heaven knows it's her only birthright. Every shilling I saved over the years has gone towards making sure the girls had every advantage. The entire point of the salon is to persuade people to associate with us despite our background. In order to have a salon, I have to have a good house and a full staff. Why do you think I did all of that? For my own amusement? No, it was for my girls, to make sure they had the best future they possibly could." She sighed, causing the feathers on her hat to flutter sympathetically. "Marrying well is the surest way for my girls to be safe and prosperous. Their futures are not mine to throw away."

"I see," Verity said. And she did see. She couldn't blame Portia. Some quiet, traitorous part of her wished her own parents had cared half as much for her as Portia did for her daughters.

"Of course you're welcome to visit us at our house. At the salon or any time." Portia managed to make this sound like a genuine invitation, rather than a sop to Verity's pride.

"But I'll stop inviting Amelia here," Verity said.

"Thank you, my dear. And if you would do me the favor of passing that message on to your brother . . ."

"As you wish." She tried to keep the bitterness from her voice, but as soon as the words left her mouth, she knew she had failed.

"Don't be like that, Verity."

"I'm not being like anything," Verity protested. "I'm . . . all right, I'm a bit put out to hear that you want me to bar the door to your daughters. But I see your point." She let out a breath. "I just wish my brother weren't carrying on in such a way as to make this necessary."

"We have to be so careful, otherwise people are only too ready to remember who we are." While nobody quite forgot that Portia had once been the late Lord Pembroke's mistress, they had long since decided this was a point they were happy to disregard, so long as they were able to attend her salon. If one had any pretenses to sophistication, one arrived at the pragmatic conclusion that Mrs. Allenby, in her subdued but elegant attire, attended by her genteel and intelligent daughters, was no common bit of muslin. The fact that she never left the house in an ensemble costing less than a hundred guineas surely didn't hurt matters.

"I'll do whatever you need me to," Verity agreed, trying to sound as if she did not mind being forced once again into the position of telling Nate what to do. "But I'll warn you that Nate isn't terribly interested in my wishes these days." She arranged her inkwell so it covered up a blot of ink on her desk.

At this, Portia frowned, an expression of outright concern marring her usually placid countenance. "Your brother," she said, "has always flown close to the sun."

When Ash walked into the shop he found Nate tying up a parcel of books for Mrs. Allenby. He was deeply and mortifyingly aware that he would have liked Portia Allenby a good deal more if she hadn't been Verity's lover. Ash understood that he and Verity could never be together, and he accepted as the logical and reasonable conclusion that she would seek the company of other people. Indeed, he wished her well, in a theoretical sort of way. He just didn't want to know about it. It wasn't envy or even jealousy, he told himself, but one of their distant and quieter cousins; he couldn't be jealous while warding off the warmer feelings towards Verity that he was susceptible to. And he needed to not only ward off those feelings but banish them to the iciest reaches of his mind. Verity and Nate were dear to him, and he couldn't let his emotional flights of fancy compromise this makeshift family they had assembled.

As he held the door open for Mrs. Allenby, he saw that the sign over the door was peeling. It was hard to guess that the letters were supposed to spell out Plum & Co. He had the stray notion that he ought to tell Verity, but she had likely noticed months ago. Since returning from Bath, he had been struck by the change in the household: cheap cuts of meat, no fires in the bedrooms, corners that hadn't been dusted in a good while. The *Register* was now printed on a paper cheap enough to see through. Verity was saving pennies against an uncertain future. With the same sense of loss that he had while he watched Roger's ship sail away, he realized that it was not at all a sure thing that there would even be a Plum & Company a year from now.

"What miseries are you thinking of, Ash? Your face is—" Nate came out from behind the counter, arranging his own handsome face into a tragic mask.

"Economics."

"Cheerful as ever."

"You're one to talk. I read the latest *Register* and nearly walked straight into the Thames."

"That's how you're meant to feel. Then you get to the end—"

"Where you dream of the hopeful future in which Lord Sidmouth is sent to the guillotine?"

"Be fair, Ash." Nate scuffed his boot on the floor. "I don't mention the guillotine by name. I just mention that we all know how tyrants wind up sometimes."

Ash closed his eyes. "You made a pun about heads, Nathaniel." If he kept going like this, his arrest was inevitable. And if he were convicted, he would be sent away for years, maybe transported, maybe even sentenced to death like those unfortunates in Pentrich. Watching Nate flirt with arrest filled him with the same panicked dread with which he imagined Roger hundreds of miles away.

"I can't do any more prints for you," Ash said. In the past he had done at least one satire for the *Register* each month, along with his more lucrative work engraving fashion plates and frontispieces. "Prison wouldn't agree with me."

"Oh, quite right, that." He frowned apologetically, and the expression revealed lines of worry on his face.

"Are you sleeping, Nate?" Ash asked. Their rooms shared a wall, and sometimes Ash heard stirring from his friend's chamber well past midnight. Nate had never been a sound sleeper, and seemed to require only half the sleep of the average person, but now he looked haggard.

"Not much. And what sleep I get is . . . not good." Ash reached out to put a sympathetic hand on Nate's shoulder.

"I'm not going to feel bad for myself," Nate insisted. "There are bigger troubles in the world than my bad dreams."

"If you put them aside just for an evening, you might wake and feel even more equipped to fight some of those troubles," Ash said, squeezing his friend's shoulder before dropping his hand.

"It's not like that. I can't just take off my worries like an ill-fitting coat." He frowned at Ash. "Talk about something else, will you?"

"What was Mrs. Allenby doing here?" Ash tried to sound casual.

"She called on Verity for a quarter of an hour. I don't think they're resuming their . . ." He made a vague gesture that Ash decided was meant to suggest sexual congress. "If that's what you're asking."

"Ah." Ash tried not to sound relieved. "I didn't realize their . . . liaison had ended."

"And it's a damned pity, because my sister was a lot easier to deal with when she was going to bed with Portia. I don't even like the woman, filthy snob that she is. But I'd dearly like Verity to take up with almost anybody if it meant she'd stop nagging me for half a minute."

Ash bit back a smile at the reminder that Nate was more concerned with the political inclinations of his sister's lover than with her gender. A sapphic love affair with a proper revolutionary would be entirely satisfactory as far as Nate was concerned.

Ash climbed the stairs and found Verity sitting at her desk, a stack of magazines before her. It was only noon, but already her hair had escaped the confines of her coiffure, and no fewer than three ink spots adorned her face.

"Oh, there you are, Ash. Where have you been?" She gestured at the portfolio he carried.

"Southampton Street. I had to drop off the finished plates."

"Oooh," Verity said with an enthusiasm that was neither facetious nor completely sincere. "What will the ladies be wearing this winter?"

"The usual. Fur and velvet and miles of blond lace. Enough to have one longing for the guillotine along with your brother." Ash was not unaware of the tension between his two principal sources of employment—drawing political caricatures for radical pamphlets, and producing fashion plates designed to sell ridiculous fripperies at unconscionable prices to people who had more money than anybody needed, all while their fellow men starved in the street. "The good news is that waistlines will be dropping."

"Well, they could hardly go any higher. Today Portia had on a gown that shouldn't be physically possible."

"Annie," he said, referring to the dressmaker who was his principal source when drawing fashion plates, "says that now every shopgirl has hoisted her bosoms up to her armpits, the ladies will allow theirs to descend."

"What a relief," Verity said, affecting a refined accent. "One does like to breathe." Verity herself had on a simple brown woolen frock, with a plain cambric fichu tucked into the neckline. He knew she also had a black dress, equally plain and severe, because he had seen her wear it to the gravesides of both her parents. "Do you think I could write an advice column?"

Ash strove to find a diplomatic way to say *No, definitely not.* "Well, perhaps of the more bracing sort. Some people do like being flogged. Specialized interest, you know."

"I can be sympathetic," she protested.

"To people you agree with, certainly."

"Am I really that bad?"

"There's nothing bad about it. You're uncompromising. It's one of the things I like best about you. But why are you writing an advice column?"

"I've decided to start a ladies' magazine. Advice columns seem to be common, and they're among the features I could conceivably write myself, which would make it cheap to put together. A serialized novel, some theater reviews, maybe a fashion plate if you'd oblige."

"Did I hear somebody say advice columns?" asked Nate, appearing in the doorway. "Are we talking about Mrs. Merriweather?" All traces of his earlier worry were gone from his face, and he looked like the mischievous, cheerful lad he had been not so long ago. "I think I want to marry Mrs. Merriweather," he said, putting a hand over his heart and striking what he doubtless thought a romantic pose.

"I want to elect Mrs. Merriweather to Parliament," Ash mused.

"Don't tell me you both read the *Ladies Gazette*?" Verity asked.

"The *Gazette*, the *Ladies' Mercury*, the *Lady's Magazine*, all of them. But Mrs. Merriweather at the *Gazette* is the best of the lot."

"Dear Mrs. Merriweather," Ash said, as if reading aloud. "I discovered that my husband has a wife and children in Barnstaple—"

"This other wife is a very low sort—" Nate chimed in.

"Wears the cheapest muslin frocks—"

"Puts the milk in first—"

"So ought I to run off with the vicar or the canon?"

Nate burst out laughing, and when Ash glanced over at Verity, he saw that she was trying to suppress a smile but making a very poor fist of it. "I hope you're both amused with yourselves," she said shaking her head. "Utter children."

"What would you advise that letter writer?" Ash asked. "In your theoretical problem page."

"The situation you put before me is nonsense," Verity insisted.

"No it isn't," Ash and Nate answered at once.

"It's bigamy eight times out of ten," Nate added.

"The other two times are people whose servants have stolen either the silver or their employers' hearts," Ash added.

"I suppose it mainly depends on whether her husband married her or the Barnstaple woman first," Verity mused. "If the Barnstaple woman is his lawful wife, then the letter writer is well shot of him and can run off with as many clerics as she pleases. But if she's the lawful wife, she and the Barnstaple woman ought to join forces to have him sent to Australia."

"Prosecuted for bigamy and then transported, you mean?" Ash asked.

"Indeed not. I was thinking they could simply have him press-ganged or taken by pirates. Barnstaple is close enough to Cornwall, and my understanding is that piracy is still an ongoing concern in those parts."

Both men tilted their heads and regarded her. "Just out of curiosity, how often would you advise women with errant husbands to have their spouses abducted by pirates?" Nate asked.

"I'd have to look into the costs. Right now it occurs to me that one might arrange one's obnoxious brother to be taken away. Might be worth a few pounds, especially if you keep bringing strangers to eat my mutton chops."

"They weren't strangers!"

"Portia says we're not to have Amelia here anymore, because it won't do for a young lady to be an accessory before the fact."

"An accessory before what fact?" Nate asked.

"Sedition," Ash and Verity said at once with equal measures of exasperation.

"But I like Amelia," Nate said petulantly, as if referring to a favorite pet mouse. "Devilish clever girl."

"Yes, well, try to like her enough not to get her into any trouble. Oh, Ash, I have something for you. Well, it isn't for you, strictly speaking, but I think it might interest you." She began rifling through the stack of magazines and assorted papers on her desk. "Aha! Here it is."

He took the letter from her outstretched hand. It was fine linen paper, much finer than anything Ash usually encountered, the sort he had forgotten even existed. Even the sealing wax looked a cut above the usual. The writing was an even, legible, feminine hand.

"The general thrust of the letter is that a lady botanist needs someone to draw her specimens," Verity said.

At the top of the page was a family crest and a Cavendish Square address. The signature was of a Lady Caroline Talbot.

"No," Ash said. "I'm not earning my bread by drawing the hothouse flowers of some lady dilettante."

"But you'll draw the gowns they wear," Verity pointed out.

"I do those for one of your rival publishers, not for the leisured classes."

"Look, it's an opportunity to take money from the rich, without having to compromise your morals. I thought it might interest you, because, well, you're certainly not going to be doing any drawings for the *Register*." She said this so matter-of-factly, as if it hadn't pained him to realize illustrating the *Register* was no longer a risk he could take. "I just thought this would be a way for you to branch out a bit. She'll probably pay better than I do."

"She could hardly pay worse," Nate remarked from where he still stood in the doorway.

"Nathaniel," Verity said bracingly, "if you want to pay our writers and illustrators better, consider doing something that will turn a profit without getting your colleagues sent to prison. For heaven's sake."

Nate threw his hands up in surrender and left them alone.

"Is he deluded?" Verity asked. "Or is he deliberately trying to drive me mad?"

"I think he has different priorities than you," Ash said

carefully, conscious that he could not take sides between them without toppling the three-legged stool that was their friendship.

"My priorities are eating and not getting arrested."

"So are mine. But your brother is . . ." He shook his head. "Is it ludicrous to call him a genius when we both know he sometimes goes out in mismatched boots?"

That got a smile from her and he was glad of it. But it quickly dropped from her face. "He gets to be a genius, while I balance the books and haggle with tradespeople." Then she abruptly shook her head as if dislodging the thought. "I'm being silly. Now, sit down and tell me more about what to put in this advice column."

There wasn't a world where Ash could resist anything Verity asked of him, so he sat.

Chapter Three

Clutching the manuscript under her arm, Verity ran up the stairs to the top floor. Bit by bit during the two weeks since Ash returned to London, he and Nate dragged all his equipment out of the box room and set it up in the attic Ash declared to be the only place in the house with enough light to work by and enough air for him not to choke on the rosin powder he used when preparing a plate to engrave.

She paused in the open doorway, trying to make sense of the sight before her. She expected to find Ash at work, drawing with pen and ink or using the fine tools he used to produce plates for engraving. Instead, he sat on the sill of the open window, one booted foot braced on the floor, his upper body leaning out.

"Left!" he called below. "No, *your* left. The other left! Good Christ, Nate, *left*! There you go. All right, now hold it slack." He ducked back into the room. "Oh, good," he said upon seeing Verity. "Hold this, will you?" He held out one end of a cord that continued out the window.

Still unclear about what she was witnessing, she crossed the room and mutely took hold of the cord while Ash climbed onto the windowsill and hammered a nail into the top of the casement. This brought her within inches of the pair of buckskin breeches he wore. Usually he dressed in town clothes—the respectable coats and trousers of a reasonably prosperous artisan. The buckskins were entirely different. They fit close to his skin, skimming over muscled thighs and up . . . Verity jerked her head away before she could let her gaze follow the direction of her thoughts. Suddenly very conscious of the parcel she still carried under one arm, Verity felt her cheeks heat. Well-worn buckskin breeches, she decided, made it very difficult to maintain a businesslike sense of decorum.

"All right," Ash said, holding out his hand.

"What?" she asked, dazed.

"The cord, Plum."

"Right. The cord." She passed it up to him and watched as he looped it through what appeared to be an eyelet at the end of the nail.

"All clear on this end," Ash called out the window. A moment later she heard her brother's voice shout something indistinct, and Ash gave the cord a few quick tugs. She could hear a bell ringing down below.

"It's in case I have a seizure," Ash said, shutting the window. She saw that there was a hole in the casement for the cord to pass through. "The cord rings a bell in the kitchen and another in the shop."

"Oh, how clever. How long has it been since you had an episode?"

"Last year, when we all had influenza." Ash had spent a fortnight with the Plums to spare Roger the risk of infection. Verity, who had recovered first, had been the one to help Ash during his seizure, which had entailed shoving a pillow under his head and reassuring him afterward that all was well.

"That was nearly a year ago. That's very good, isn't it?"

"Indeed." He brushed some dust off his breeches. "It makes me fear that I'm due for one soon, although Nate tells me this isn't how odds work."

"I'm not sure our bodies are governed by the same principles as a pair of dice."

"I'm not sure mine works according to any logic whatsoever. But it'll happen sooner or later, and I need to figure out how to deal with it without Roger."

This was perhaps only the second time Ash had so much as said Roger's name in the past two weeks. She didn't ask whether Ash missed Roger, because of course he did. They had seldom been more than a few yards apart from one another in years. Roger had effectively been Ash's only parent, and now he was hundreds of miles away and exceedingly unlikely to return. "How long before you can expect a letter from him?"

"Two months, at the earliest." He pushed a hand through his hair and sat on the edge of his worktable. "I've already written three letters addressed to the poste restante in Italy. If—when—he arrives, he'll think I've gone clear off my head."

"He'll think nothing of the sort."

Ash smiled ruefully. "I know." He turned towards a bookcase and busied himself in arranging the mysterious jars and oddments that were the tools of his trade.

"We're happy to have you here, Nate and I," Verity said. There was something about how Ash's hand lingered over each object, which he had once shared with his mentor but was now solely his, that made her want to tell him that he wasn't truly alone. "I know you'd rather have gone with Roger, but when you wrote asking whether you could lodge with us, Nate bought a round of pints for everyone at the pub."

"And you?" He looked over his shoulder and met her eye.

"Well, I paid for the round because Nate hadn't any ready money." But he was still looking at her, as if he needed to hear more. "I would have killed the fatted calf, if I had one. You know this, Ash. I already told you."

"You don't mind that I've taken over the entire top floor of your house and drilled holes in your window casements?"

"Drill a thousand more and see if I care." She narrowed her eyes as she saw a movement along the top of the bookcase. "Ash, I don't mean to alarm you, but what on earth is that?" It appeared to be a shadow with eyes.

Ash followed her gaze. "So that's where you've gotten to, miss."

When the animal hissed in response, Verity knew precisely what it was. "I thought Nate didn't let her into the house."

"Um. Well. About that. Nate didn't let her in."

Verity raised an eyebrow. "But you did?"

Ash had the grace to look sheepish. "It was raining and she looked pitiful."

"Ash, that cat is two stone, not to mention vicious. She'll starve in here unless we're harboring a more abundant mouse population than I dare contemplate."

"She won't starve. I leave the window cracked open most of the time, and she comes and goes as she pleases. Besides, I may possibly share some of my food with her." His eyes darted to an empty dish near the window.

"Does Nate know you've suborned his cat into betraying him?"

"To be fair, I haven't quite accomplished the act yet. As you can see, she's still deciding whether I'm friend or foe." The cat hissed again, arching her back and glaring at Verity as if she had understood every word they had spoken. "Well, what's that you've brought me?" Ash gestured at the parcel she carried under her arm.

"It came in the post. Do you remember that conversation we had at dinner the night after you arrived, about the relative safety of printing obscenity compared to politics?"

"How could I forget?"

"At first I thought it was a silly idea, but in the next few months one of two things will happen. Either Nate will be more cautious about what he puts in the *Register,* which means we'll lose some income, or he'll be arrested, and we'll still be out that income." She swallowed. It was hard and unfeeling to talk about her brother's future in strictly economic terms. But she saw Ash nod. "Well, I decided that if a suitable—or unsuitable, haha—" she laughed nervously "—novel landed on my desk, I'd consider it. Well, this morning's post brought the answer to my filthiest prayers."

He was silent for a moment. "You have my attention, Plum."

"It's a perfectly competent novel along the lines of *Waverley* to which some rather more explicit material has been added." Those scenes appeared to have been appended after the fact, in a scrawled and hasty hand. Only years of practice reading Nate's chaotic penmanship had prepared Verity for this manuscript. "I thought that perhaps, if you were interested, you might agree to illustrate the first volume. If it's a success, we can consider doing the other two volumes."

He crossed his arms across his chest, which, since he wore only shirtsleeves, drew her attention to the musculature of his arms in a way she found entirely unnecessary. "I'm hardly an expert in obscenities law," he said dryly, "but it seems to me that illustrations would transform this from a slightly naughty novel to something more actionable."

"The book is really quite tasteful," she protested. "As far as these things go, at least. And we could keep the drawings vague. Suggestive," she added. "If you're not interested, I'll find somebody else. I've brought it to you so you can see for yourself." She tapped the sheaf of papers.

"If you go through with this harebrained idea, I'll do the work uncredited. I'm entirely unsuited to *durance vile*." He paused. "You might read me a passage, though."

"It's quite, ah." She had planned to leave the manuscript on his desk and flee before he read it. "I can leave it for you overnight."

He shook his head and sat on the edge of his worktable. "That won't do, Plum. If you want me to illustrate your dirty book, you can't be bashful about it."

"I wasn't—"

"Besides, I have to finish this set of sketches so I can start engraving the plates tomorrow." He gestured at the tools laid out beside him.

"Of course." She moved a stack of books off a spare chair and sat. "The premise of the novel," she said, arranging her skirts before her, "is that Perkin Warbeck has a number of amorous adventures—"

"Perkin Warbeck?" Ash repeated in tones of plain astonishment. "Perkin *Warbeck?*"

She had been similarly astonished, and had looked up from the manuscript several times to consult a book on the history of the Wars of the Roses; the tome had lingered unsold on the bookshop's shelves for so long that dust had slipped between the pages and the binding had gone brittle. That era of history was evidently not in much vogue at the moment. "How much do you remember of that affair?" Verity knew Ash's schooling had been irregular and sporadic, and ultimately had been confined to the topics Roger found of interest.

"Only that he was a pretender to the crown. Most of what I know of history comes from Shakespeare and a volume on Queen Elizabeth that Roger illustrated some years ago."

"So, in 1483, or thereabouts, Richard III probably murdered his nephews, the proper heirs to the throne. But a few years later, this boy showed up and claimed he was one of the princes, and had been spirited away to the Netherlands before Richard got a chance to murder him. In that case he would have had a better claim to the throne than Henry VII."

"Because Richard III was long dead at that point?"

"Exactly. There was intrigue and a few very poorly planned attempts at invasion, and then Henry VII captured the fellow and had him admit that he wasn't one of the princes, but rather a Dutch fellow named Perkin Warbeck. Of course, confessions extracted under pain of death aren't terribly convincing, so people do like to speculate."

"I would like to know what about that fellow screamed *write an erotic novel about me.*"

Verity snorted. "Well, in pursuit of the crown and his, um, lady love he beds various and sundry individuals before finding a lasting passion with the Earl of Warwick while imprisoned together in the Tower of London."

Ash made a choked sound. "They were both put to death for treason. It can't have been terribly lasting."

"If you have a better premise for a dirty book, please write your own," she said tartly.

"You'd better read me something, and soon, because otherwise I'm going to assume these are feverish delusions, Plum."

She paged through the manuscript until she came to the first scene with Perkin and Lady Catherine, one of the tamer passages. She cleared her throat.

It had to be the gravest flaw in Catherine's character that she was so fond of this unrepentant liar. One couldn't trust two consecutive words that came out of that pretty mouth. Surely this was something that ought to at least matter. But she hadn't even been able to feign maidenly reluctance when her father told her she was to marry this pretender to the crown. In all likelihood they were both going to wind up in the Tower, and all Catherine could think of was what would happen in the next hour. When he stepped into her chamber, the ladies who had been brushing her hair curtseyed deeply before scurrying away amidst a chorus of giggles.

"When did they marry?" Ash interrupted. "Before or after his attempted coup?"

"After his first attempted coup, he fled to Edinburgh, where the king of Scotland was so delighted to have a new way to vex Henry VII that he married Perkin—or Richard—off to his granddaughter. Or step-granddaughter. It's a bit of a muddle."

Ash's fingers tapped thoughtfully on the counterpane. "Now, are you going to read me some actual filth or am I going to know the reason why?"

Verity turned the page and skimmed ahead several paragraphs.

Then they were alone, with nothing but their lies to keep them company. He approached her wordlessly, and with one long finger lifted a strand of hair off her shoulders. On her head was a circlet of gold, a meaningless bauble that signified nothing except her father's pretenses to grandeur, but it was the echo of a coronet, and she saw the dark gleam of hunger in his eyes. Hunger for that crown, and then, as his gaze traveled from the circlet to the silken folds of her bedgown, perhaps also hunger for her. He placed a finger beneath her chin and tilted it up so she had to meet his gaze. His mouth curved into a shrewd smile, vulpine and canny. "My lady," he said. "You've been thinking of this."

"Yes, my lord," she admitted, at once ashamed and anticipatory. Then his hands were on her shoulders, heavy and hot through the rich satin Father had brought from France. He trailed a single finger down her body until it encountered the rise of her breast, circling her—

"Stop," said Ash. "That's enough."

"Don't you want to know what will happen?"

"It's entirely clear what's about to happen, Plum." His voice sounded strained.

"You didn't like it, then?"

He cleared his throat. "Whether I like it is beside the point. If the book is entirely in that vein, I can illustrate it." It wasn't, but she decided to keep that to herself for the time being. "The scene where he lifts her chin and it's menacing and tender all at once? That would make a good illustration. Candlelight reflecting off cloth of gold. Aquatint, I think." He got to his feet and began rearranging the contents of a shelf.

Knowing she was being dismissed, Verity rose to her feet. "Can I bring you anything?"

"No, but thank you, Plum."

"Shout if you change your mind," she said, and closed the door behind her.

It had done a number on his sleep, that memory of Verity reading a seduction scene, even though they had stopped before getting to the main event, as it were. But it had put sex in the room with them, a reminder of all the things he resolutely tried not to think about. Even if Verity felt the same as he did, no momentary pleasure was worth losing the only family he had. Ultimately it would end and they would be left with awkwardness and bitterness between them. He would far rather have Verity as his friend than as his former lover. Furthermore, she had made clear her intention not to marry, and Ash couldn't envision a world in which he had a protracted affair with a woman without it ending in marriage; he had long since stopped being ashamed to be illegitimate, but wasn't about to inflict that status on a child of his own.

After getting coffee and a bun, he shoved a table against the window of his attic workroom to catch the scant light that filtered through the fog and sooty glass. Then he sat, fresh paper and ink spread out before him. He thought he'd do this series of plates in aquatint in order to achieve the right depth of shadow, out of which limbs and faces could emerge. Ash doubted anybody knew what Lady Catherine Gordon and Perkin Warbeck looked like, so he let his imagination loose. As he sketched, all the while thinking of the words Verity had read, Warbeck came alive as a languidly sinister character, all long lines and sinewy grace, and his wife took shape as a strong-jawed, pert-nosed fighter whose clinging garments hardly covered the strength beneath.

Lady Catherine, Ash decided as he drew the folds of her bedgown, only made sense if she loved Warbeck. If his dim memories of history lessons were to be trusted, everyone at the York court knew Warbeck was a fraud, and Warbeck himself hardly bothered keeping up the pretense that he was a true son of Edward IV who had been thought to have died in the Tower. Nobody thought Warbeck would end his days on the throne; indeed, if that had been a real possibility, he would have found a higher-born wife than Catherine. As it was, for Catherine to have married him, she must have known she was risking her own neck. What must it have been like for her to know that her father and grandfather were willing to sacrifice her, to cast her off for no reason other than to play ducks and drakes with the English crown? Ash knew what it was to be cast aside, and wondered whether Catherine longed for some semblance of home.

He was interrupted by the sounds of a quarrel coming from downstairs. He got up and peered out the door to find Charlie, the apprentice, hovering indecisively on the landing.

"They're at it again," Charlie said. "Hammer and tongs."

"What's it this time?" Ash asked.

"He wants to go to Derby for the execution. She says she's known him since he was in nappies and she isn't such a fool as to believe that he's going to peacefully watch three people get beheaded."

Ash could very distinctly imagine Verity speaking those exact words. "What does she think he means to do?"

"Start a riot, maybe, or mix himself up in the same kind of tomfoolery that's getting Brandreth and the lot of them executed in the first place." Charlie shoved his hands in his pockets. "He has his case packed and we're meant to catch the mail coach tonight."

Ash raised his eyebrows. "You're going as well?"

"He says it'll be an education," Charlie said, his voice filled with amusement, but Ash frowned. Charlie had been the late Mr. Plum's articled apprentice. Nate was in a position of responsibility as his master; he would be doing the lad no favors by getting him mixed up with the law. Charlie had come straight from the workhouse to the Plums, and he didn't have any parents or relations to look out for him. Ash knew that it was one apprentice in ten thousand who had a master as considerate and kind as Roger had been, but he couldn't help but look on Nate's behavior and see it as an abrogation of duty.

Ash descended the stairs and found Verity and Nate in the workroom behind the bookshop that held the printing press and some other supplies. From the open jar of ink that stood on a worktable and the sheets of paper that hung from the ceiling to dry, and Ash guessed the men had cleared out to give their employers space to quarrel in relative privacy. But now the room was silent. Nate leaned against the press and Verity had her back to him, deliberately arranging a stack of freshly printed copies of the first *Ladies' Register*. It seemed, at least, that the shouting portion of the fight had subsided.

Ash cleared his throat. When Nate and Verity looked at him, he was struck by their similarity—light brown hair, pale brown eyes, and a lean, utilitarian build. But also they shared the same stubborn jaw and firm mouth. Both Plums were pigheaded to the end, as their father had been before them. This worked out perfectly well when they agreed, as they did nine times out of ten. But when they disagreed neither seemed capable of begging pardon or agreeing to differ.

He vividly remembered dozens of disputes over the years he had known them. He recalled Verity, her hair in a pair of plaits and a fresh pinafore over her frock, scolding Nate for having eaten the last of the candied apples. He remembered Nate, barely old enough to shave, hollering at Verity for having snubbed some girl he was sweet on. And then there were the supper table fights, pitched battles between Mr. Plum and his children about sugar boycotts and chimney sweeps and everything in between. Nate and Verity had fought over which coffin to bury their father in, for heaven's sake. The Plums fought the way other families played a friendly hand of whist or a round of charades. Ash had found it alarming at first; for some reason buried deep within his mind he associated raised voices with smashed crockery and crying women. But the Plums simply enjoyed a good fight, and never seemed to love one another any less for believing the other was entirely in the wrong. The late Mrs. Plum had been an exception, but it was from her that Ash learned any attempts to broker peace only spoiled their fun. Instead, he sat back and watched his friends amuse themselves, much as a spectator at a tennis match.

This time, though, he didn't know how to do that. While Verity could have been more diplomatic—tact had never been her abiding virtue—he wholeheartedly agreed with her that Nate ought to stay far away from the Pentrich executions, should avoid any situation that might tempt him to start a riot or engage in some casual treason, and under no circumstances should he embroil Charlie.

As Ash's gaze traveled between them, Verity caught his eye. He wasn't sure what she saw there—perhaps a sign that Ash was on her side—but her eyes opened wide, and then she murmured something unintelligible and left Nate and Ash alone.

"You know I don't like to intervene in your affairs," Ash said slowly, addressing Nate. "But I don't see why you have to bring Charlie."

"Come now, he wants to go," Nate said genially, as if Ash were being unreasonable. "I don't want to deny him the treat."

"He's seventeen and your apprentice. He hasn't any way to refuse you, even if he wanted to. Besides, putting him in the path of danger is a breach of your duty to him. It's not right."

"Nothing harmful about watching a hanging," said Nate. He was a terrible liar, and looked down at the toe of his boot instead of at Ash. "Some apprentices beg for a half day off to watch a hanging. They make a holiday of it."

"And they cheer and yell and buy ha'penny slices of pie while delighting in the death of people they believe to have deserved their fate. That's not what you're planning to do in Derby," Ash said.

"Charlie isn't really my apprentice anyway."

"You really want to take that line of argument? Come, Nate. If he's not your apprentice, then what is he?" The late Mr. Plum had bought Charlie from the workhouse for five pounds when the boy was twelve years old, but died before the term of Charlie's apprenticeship was complete. Upon Mr. Plum's death, Charlie probably ought to have been assigned to another master printer, but instead Nate and Verity had started to pay the lad wages. Ash believed that Charlie nevertheless regarded Nate as occupying the place of his late master, and that Nate owed the boy something for that.

"Excuse me," said Charlie, appearing in the doorway. "Don't I get a say? I want to go."

"Ha!" said Nate, triumphant.

"If I stay home, you'll have no one to keep you out of trouble," said Charlie.

"Come, now," said Nate indignantly. "That's not fair."

"Mrs. Peabody at the Rose and Crown is giving five to one odds against you coming back from Derby in one piece, so I bet in your favor. I intend to get my money. Let's go. I don't want to miss the stage coach."

"Wait for me in the street," Nate said, and the boy left them alone again. "Makes me feel like a child," he said to Ash, "when you and Verity scold me like that."

Ash privately thought Nate ought to stop acting like a spoilt child, but wasn't going to win any arguments by saying so. "Look at it from your sister's perspective. In the last few years she's lost both her parents—"

"So have I, mind you!"

"—and now she's worried about losing you."

"That's not what she said to me. She's going on about not wanting the militia rooting around in the shop."

Had the woman no sense of strategy or diplomacy whatsoever? Ash didn't doubt for a second that if Verity had clasped her brother's hands and begged him not to leave her alone, he would have agreed immediately. But Verity wouldn't admit, let alone feign, weakness. Ash decided to play her part for her. "If you get sent to prison, she'll be all alone."

"Verity?" Nate said with a huff of surprised laughter. "Like hell she will. She knows half of London."

Knowing half of London was no substitute for having people you belonged to, and few knew that better than Ash. "That's not the same as wanting to see her brother safe and well."

"First of all, I won't be well if I'm not fighting for what I know is right. Second, if Verity finds out you've been painting her as a helpless damsel, she'll eat your still-beating heart. Third, she wouldn't be alone. She'd have you."

That shouldn't have made Ash's cheeks heat. He hoped the room was too dark for Nate to see him blush. "Not the same," he repeated.

"I dare say it isn't," Nate said thoughtfully. Too thoughtfully. This was what came from knowing someone for over a decade. You saw right through one another. And even though

Nate usually had the general appearance of a man who was blessedly unconcerned with the feelings of anyone but himself, Ash supposed that over ten years some facts made their way into even Nate's thick skull.

"Don't know what you're talking about," Ash said quellingly. Nate only laughed, and swiped a copy of the *Ladies' Register* off the top of the stack and jammed it in his pocket, presumably to read during his journey north.

Verity heaped a slice of bread with quince jam, then added a wedge of ripe cheese to her plate. She sloshed some brandy into her tea and carefully carried it all upstairs, where she settled into the high-backed chair in her study. After reading a few pages of a novel she had been saving for an occasion where nothing but a new book could elevate her spirits, she heard the patter of raindrops on the window. That ought to make Nate's time on the stagecoach dreadfully uncomfortable. She couldn't make up her mind whether to feel smug or sorry, so she had another bite of bread and cheese and tucked her feet beneath her, curling into the corner of the chair.

"It'll be all right, you know."

She looked up to see Ash leaning in the doorway. He was in loose trousers and rolled-up shirtsleeves. He must have taken a break from work. "No, I don't know that. And neither do you. Here, sit down and help me eat this cheese. I took enough for the entire neighborhood."

"What I should have said is that in a week you'll know whether he's emerged unscathed from this event, at least."

He sat in the chair beside hers and helped himself to a corner of her bread and some of the cheese. "A week from now he'll be back and you'll know what you're facing. Meanwhile, I read the rest of that manuscript."

Verity nearly choked on her bread. She had been expecting another week to pass before having to speak with Ash about the book. It had been only three days since she had given him the manuscript. At the moment she was sulky and raw, and didn't have any defenses up. "Oh? How did you find it?"

"What I find is that you read me a most misleading passage."

"I found it quite tasteful," she said, not looking at him. Doubtless he had that knowing half smile. She wasn't equal to Ash's half smile at the moment.

"And so it is. Tastefully lewd, if that isn't an oxymoron."

"I feel certain it isn't. I suppose you'd rather have nothing to do with it. No worries." She tried to sound bright and unbothered. It probably would be best for her to hire another illustrator. One who didn't roll his sleeves up in such a wanton manner, for example. How she was meant to get anything done in such close proximity to forearms, she did not know.

"You suppose wrong. But I do have to warn you that I'm in no way competent to draw some of the acts described in that book, and I can't imagine where I'd find models willing to oblige me." Her cheeks heated with the thought, and it was only partly due to embarrassment. "But I did a rough sketch of the kind of illustration I have in mind." He reached into his pocket and presented her with a sheet of paper.

She steeled herself. It was attraction, nothing more. Utterly natural. Like hay fever. A minor inconvenience. Verity had long known she was susceptible to both men and women, but men usually comported themselves in such a way that quickly extinguished whatever lustful inclinations she had been harboring. There seemed little chance of Ash making things convenient for her by behaving boorishly.

She pushed her spectacles to the bridge of her nose and beheld a sketch of a man and a woman in flowing medieval robes. He was exaggeratedly sinuous and faintly mischievous; her jaw was clenched and her bare feet planted firmly on the floor, but her body canted towards the man opposite her. This, she gathered, was Perkin and Catherine. The way Ash had drawn the lady's gown, it appeared to be made of cobweb lace, clinging to the curves of her body and all but revealing the flesh beneath. But the focus of the drawing wasn't the woman's body; it was her hand, reaching towards the hip of her new husband.

She must have been silent for too long, because Ash cleared his throat and murmured, "Remember, it's only an idea."

"Ash, I've worked with you for years. I know your process. But this is very good," she said. "It's lovely. You know it's lovely. The way she's leaning towards him, and he's beckoning her with that single finger—it's a seduction, but you're barely showing it. And the, ah, bodice is . . . good." Her eyes were drawn to a ripe curve of breast, barely obscured by gossamer-fine fabric.

"I'm pleased to hear it." He took a piece of bread from the plate she still held on her lap.

She was very conscious that she was sitting so close to him that they could share a single plate, discussing private matters. "First I want to show you something." She reached beneath her chair to one of the many stacks of books that littered the room and pulled out a volume. After paging through it, she handed him the book opened to the illustration she wanted him to see. It was an image of a bare-chested woman in flagrante delicto with a man.

"Good God," Ash sputtered. "You might warn a fellow."

"Pfft. No doubt you've seen it already. It sold quite well a few years back, I understand."

"Indeed, I have seen it. I'm a bit shocked that you have, though. When in heaven's name did you start keeping dirty books in your study?"

"I started keeping dirty books in my study about ten minutes after I decided to publish dirty books. Don't think I was unaware that we carried them in the shop. Laying my hands on them was only a matter of shouting 'Oi, Nate, send up the dirty books you keep behind the counter for special customers' as I'm sure you know."

"Hmmph." He studied the print. "Is this the style you hope to emulate?" he asked in measured tones.

"No, you muttonhead. It's exactly what I don't want you to do. I hate everything about it. Look at them." She jabbed a finger at the illustration. "She's completely naked, and the only part of him we see is his . . . member." She rolled her eyes at her inability to come up with a better word. "And what good does that do anybody?"

"Ah, it appears to be doing the lady some marked good."

"No, Ash, no it does not. Look at her face. I wouldn't tolerate that vacant simper at my dinner table, much less my bedroom. Is that the expression of a woman in the throes of passion, I ask you? No, it is not. It's the face you make when you're cornered by someone you don't want to talk to, so you smile and hope he goes away. One feels sorry for the artist's bedmates."

"Does one?" he asked faintly.

"She's just bouncing up and down on that thing, and giving such a god-awful smile. Ash, I need you to draw some women who don't mind being fucked, please."

Ash made a strangled noise and when she looked at his face she saw that he was blushing. The tips of his ears were pink, which surely she shouldn't find quite so delightful.

"Even better if they actually enjoy it," she added. "I will say, this is a benefit of sapphism. It's all very straightforward. I wonder if men who seek the company of other men find matters similarly efficient and unmysterious." Her thoughts were slightly muzzy and she wondered if she had misjudged the amount of brandy she had added to her tea.

"I don't think most men have much difficulty in satisfying their passions with a bedmate of any gender."

"That," she declared, pointing at him with a crust of bread, "is an excellent point. One feels terrible for women who go to bed with men. Truly awful."

"I seem to recall you feeling otherwise a few years back when Johnny Meecham came calling."

She lobbed the crust of bread at his head and missed by a good six inches. "I was sixteen! And I certainly didn't . . ." She gestured at the book. "I understand the desire to go to bed with men, my point is that they're more trouble than they're worth, by all accounts. Oh, I beg your pardon, Ash, I'm sure your lady friends are well taken care of. Much happier than this poor girl." She frowned again at the drawing. And now she was imagining precisely what Ash might do to satisfy his bedmates, which was the last thing she ought to be thinking of. Worse still, she was enjoying it. "I do apologize. Forget I said—"

"Plum, if you think I object in the least to your perverse ruminations, you have badly misjudged me. Now," he said, rising to his feet and brushing invisible dirt from his trousers, "I'm off to draw you some well-fucked women." His ears were still pink but he seemed to have regained a degree of composure that still escaped Verity. He shot her a grin and left her alone in her study, slightly dazed, holding a hand to her heated cheek.

This would not do. They were working together and living in close quarters and she urgently needed to find a way to douse this spark before it turned into a conflagration. She had kept potential suitors and swains at a chilly distance, resolutely squashing any seed of desire she felt for any of them. Her time with Portia had been an exception, born of the misbegotten notion that an affair of the heart would be less complicated with a woman, especially a woman who had been her friend before becoming her lover. She had been wrong.

The world, Verity had always known, was filled with people who wanted things she had long since run out of: time, affection, assistance.

To take him—or anyone—as a lover was quite out of the question. There was only so much of her to go around, and she needed to keep some of that for herself or she'd disappear. That needed to be her guiding principle, her true north. She vowed to keep that in mind the next time her baser instincts threatened to get the better of her.

Chapter Four

The letter requested that Ash arrive at the peculiarly precise time of a quarter past eleven on any Tuesday or Thursday morning. Ash supposed rich people got used to ordering people about in unaccountable ways, so he didn't think much of it. When he lifted the heavy brass knocker of the house in Cavendish Square, the door was promptly opened by a liveried footman.

"I'm Ash—John Ashby, here to see Lady Caroline Talbot," Ash said, his voice echoing in the vast marble hall. "She's expecting me."

The footman murmured something and disappeared through a doorway, leaving Ash alone in a hall that could have fit the entire Holywell Street bookshop twice over and left room for a coach and four. The walls were the purest white, unblemished by any stains from soot or damp. A couple of paintings hung in gilt frames, and with a start Ash realized that one of them was quite possibly a van Dyck. Before he could make up his mind about it, his attention was drawn to the sweeping staircase that dominated one end of the hall, its banister arcing ostentatiously from the upper stories down to the pink-and-white checkerboard marble floor. It was extravagant, showy, and grossly out of proportion to the dimensions of the hall. But he couldn't quite take his eyes away from it, and not only because of its poor taste. The longer he examined it, the odder he felt.

If he had experienced any of his usual symptoms—dizziness, vagueness, that godawful headache—he might have thought he was about to have one of his episodes. When he looked at the staircase, he had the strangest sensation that the walls ought to be pale green rather than white, and that there ought to be a watercolor of the seaside instead of the possible van Dyck. He shut his eyes and filled his lungs. Perhaps this was a new symptom. It had been so long since he had an episode that he had gotten out of the habit of expecting his brain and body to inconvenience him in new and elaborate ways. Now, faced with the prospect of having a seizure alone in a strange place, he wanted nothing more than to make a hasty exit back onto the street.

Brisk footsteps interrupted his thoughts, and he opened his eyes to see a woman walking towards him. She was tall and angular, with dark hair tucked into a lace cap. "Good day. You must be Mr. Ashby." Her voice was hardly more than a whisper. "Follow me. Quickly, now." She led him through a series of corridors at a pace he had difficulty matching. "I admired the frontispiece you did for that novel, so I wrote to the book's publisher."

"Which novel?" he asked.

"The one with the wicked signor."

"A good many of them do have evil signors, ma'am," he said wryly. Was it ma'am or my lady? Or was there some other manner of addressing a woman who had Lady before her given name? Verity wouldn't know, Nate wouldn't care, and Roger was months away by letter. He tried to push away the irrational sense of abandonment that crept up on him these days whenever he thought of Roger.

"That's very true," Lady Caroline said in a small, thin voice, "but this one had a very detailed and correct heliotrope in the foreground, and I thought if you could do that, you might be able to help me. Now, oh dear, we don't have much time, so step this way, if you will."

Ash didn't know why they had these time constraints, or why the lady was scurrying like a mouse through her own home, or indeed why she was whispering. But before he could attempt to make sense of it, she opened a door and ushered Ash into a room that had to be ten degrees warmer than the rest of the house and was so packed with potted plants that he could hardly see the tiled floor.

"Oh," he breathed.

"You need not concern yourself with any of these," she said briskly, waving her hand about them. "All very common specimens."

These plants, with their peculiar leaves and brightly colored flowers, might indeed be common specimens, but if so they were common specimens of something Ash had never before seen. They had the look of faraway lands, of jungles and bazaars and places he had no hopes of seeing with his own eyes. Even the scent that permeated the room was heavy and sweet, making him forget the gray London sky, heavy with rain clouds, that loomed beyond the tall glass windows of the conservatory. There had to be a couple of coal fires blazing about somewhere to maintain this decadent warmth, but Ash couldn't see beyond the profusion of foliage.

"This, now, is what I require your assistance with." She brushed aside a fern of some sort and gestured to a small table, upon which sat a stack of papers tied loosely with a blue ribbon. "This is my herbarium," she said.

Sensing that some kind of enthusiastic response was expected, he murmured an "Ah," hoping that she would explain what precisely an herbarium was, so he wouldn't have to guess.

"You may touch it," the lady said.

Ash felt that it would be rude to refuse, so he sat on the stool that was placed before the table and untied the ribbon. On each page was a pressed plant, sometimes including everything from root to flower. They had been pressed and dried to a thinness hardly greater than that of the paper itself. Each plant was labeled in the same elegant hand as the letter Verity had received.

He carefully turned over the pages until he came to a delicate star-shaped blue flower. The flower's Latin name, which meant nothing to Ash, was written carefully. But beneath that was "Buenos Aires." The next page said Japan. He turned the page again. Damascus. Prague.

"You have traveled far, ma'am," he said, tasting the jealousy on his own tongue.

"Oh, dear me, no," she said in that brittle whisper, "I seldom leave London. I've purchased these specimens. I find out what ports a ship is meant to call at and seek out a reliable-looking junior officer to employ in pressing specimens and keeping them dry. There's quite a brisk trade in these items among collectors."

He wanted to ask whether she sold her specimens or whether such commerce was beneath the attention of a lady, but instead he turned the page again and saw that the paper was singed at the edges. So was the next sheet, and the one after that.

"That is why I require your help," she said. "There was an, ah, unfortunate accident, you see. The entire herbarium was nearly lost, so I thought I'd hire a skilled artist to make me a copy. Of course it won't be as useful as the original nor will it be worth more than a few pennies to other collectors, but it will be something. I've spent two decades doing this and I can't let it go to waste."

He looked up from the book and regarded her carefully for the first time, examining her with an illustrator's regard for detail. She was about forty, with dark hair visible beneath that fine lace cap. Her morning gown of sky blue muslin was of the first quality, and her India shawl had cost somebody a pretty penny. Her profile was what he supposed one might call patrician: straight nose, strong jaw, high cheekbones. But there were lines around her eyes, as if she were in the habit of squinting. She had the nervous twitchiness of a startled hare. And when he looked closely at her face, he had the same sensation of wrongness as when he regarded the staircase.

He shook his head and returned his attention to the herbarium. "Shall I take it with me, ma'am? I expect it would take me a fortnight."

"No!" She stepped towards him, as if she planned to snatch the book from his hands. "What I mean to say," she continued in a calmer tone, "is that it must stay with me. It must. You can perhaps visit at this hour every Tuesday and Thursday."

"I see," Ash said, even though he did not see at all. But he understood that the lady was attached to this collection of dead plants. The rich, he reminded himself, were unaccountable in their fancies and predilections. "I'm an engraver by trade. I can certainly make accurate drawings of the specimens in this book, but for the fee you mentioned in the letter, you could hire a trained botanical illustrator."

She smoothed her skirt with pale hands. "It is—I thought—if things go as planned, I might want to make a book of my specimens, in which case I would require an engraver." He didn't answer at once, mainly because he was confused about why she seemed almost embarrassed to speak these words aloud, but also because he realized that producing the engravings could keep him busy for months, if not years, and he did not know if he wanted to spend that much time in a house that left him feeling strangely seasick. But she took his silence as condemnation. "It's a silly idea, forget I said anything." Her cheeks flushed with what he took to be shame, and he knew he was not going to deny her.

"No, ma'am, you misunderstand. It's not a silly idea in the least. Indeed, I've seen similar volumes for sale at bookshops." And at quite a formidable price, no less. "I'd be only too glad to help you."

He pulled out his paper and inks and began sketching the first specimen, a fragile plant whose flowers had dried to a dusty violet but must once have been vibrantly purple. It looked like the common skullcap that grew in every park and garden, but the label indicated that it came from Shanghai. He began sketching the threadlike roots, then drew in the wispy stem. There was hardly anything holding this plant together, no substance; fifty of them in his hand would weigh no more than his pen. Rooted in the ground and nourished by water, it must have some solidity, but dried and fixed to the paper it seemed one step away from dust.

But before his pen reached the delicate flowers, Lady Caroline rose to her feet with a start. "Oh!" she said, and pulled a timepiece out of a pocket. "I heard the door. You'll need to leave." Spurred on by the urgency in the lady's voice, Ash gathered his supplies and stepped towards the door he had entered through. "No, not that way. It's too late for that. Through the garden. I can't show you the way, but you'll find the mews with no trouble. Goodbye, Mr. Ashby, I'll await your next visit."

She dropped two guineas onto the table he had been using.

"That's far too much," he protested.

"I'll pay twice as much, if you'll only leave!" If it was possible to shout without making any more noise than wind passing through bare branches, Lady Caroline Talbot was doing it.

There was no mistaking the fear in her expression, so Ash executed a brief bow, scooped up the coins, and made for the door as quickly as he could. As he reached the garden, he heard a loud male voice booming from within the house. A jealous husband, he assumed. And one whose jealousy manifested in more than disapproval. He wondered how those pages had been burnt.

The garden was bleak in its late autumn grays and browns, a heavy mist washing out whatever color lingered on the remaining leaves, but Ash suspected that if the shrubbery had been green and the rose bushes blooming, he might have had the same feeling of confused recognition that he had earlier. He brushed aside the urge to find a bench and make sense of his confusion, and instead hailed a hackney to take him to the only place that he could even pretend was his home.

Verity could not remember the last time the building had been so silent in the middle of the day. Nate had given his assistants a few days holiday while he was away, and the result was a quiet so insistent that Verity could hardly think. Even the noises from the street were muffled by the fog that settled over the city. It was hardly past noon, but she already needed a lamp to see the pages of the book that sat before her on the shop counter.

Her first thought when she saw the flutter of movement outside the shop window was surprise that she had any customers at all on so dreary a day. Then the door opened and in marched three redcoats.

"You Plum's sister or wife?" demanded the soldier who seemed to be in charge of the others.

"Sister," she answered, embarrassed to hear the fear in her voice.

"Where's he at?"

"He stepped out," Verity said. She certainly wasn't going to admit that he had gone to Derby for the Pentrich executions.

"When's he coming back?"

"I don't know. He comes and goes as he pleases." She tried to imbue her voice with sisterly irritation—not hard, under the circumstances—rather than anything they could interpret as defiance or fear. They stood too close to her, crowding her towards the back wall of the shop, and she suddenly felt a bone-deep apprehension at being alone with a group of men. "If you happen to see him you might let him know there's naught but beef tea for his supper," she added for good measure, as if Nate might stroll in the door at any moment.

One of the men showed her a piece of paper, and it took her a minute to realize it was a search warrant. She watched in helpless fury as the soldiers ransacked the shop, gritting her teeth as the few unsold copies of the first issue of the *Ladies' Register* fell to the floor and were crushed beneath booted feet. At least they hadn't had a warrant for Nate's arrest. And that, as she watched them rummage carelessly through shelves and drawers, struck her as very strange indeed. If they were looking for evidence that Plum & Company printed radical materials, they needed look no further than the latest issue of the *Register,* and they needed only sixpence to see as much, not a warrant. The back room contained nothing more than a pair of printing presses, boxes of type, jars of ink, and large rolls of paper. The redcoats tossed the room anyway. She was going to lose days of work setting things to rights.

The man who seemed to be in charge said something to the other two—Verity was too distracted by the pounding of her heart to quite understand—and they left shortly thereafter, knocking over a stack of books on their way out the door.

It could have been worse, Verity told herself, her heart still racing, her hands slick with sweat. They could have contrived to knock over a bookcase so it went through the windows. Or landed on her, for that matter. Christ, she had been alone with those men. Alone, in the half-light, on a dismal day when few people were in the street. A shiver went up her spine, but she quickly dismissed her fear. There was no time for fear. There was no time for anything except the work that lay ahead of her. There never was. She sat on the floor and began putting the books back on the shelves.

"Verity." Ash crouched beside her on the floor. She hadn't heard him come in. "Verity." He took her chin and made her look at him.

"Redcoats." She scrubbed at her face with the back of her sleeve. "I'm not crying."

"Did they hurt you?" His voice was gentle, questioning, not angry. She could imagine another man asking those words in a way that forced her to spend her dwindling supply of patience in soothing him.

"No, no. Ash, they only had a search warrant, not an arrest warrant."

"A search warrant," Ash repeated some time later, when he was helping her shelve books. She saw the moment he realized what it had taken her hours to work out. "Damnation. Has Nate been involved in something even more incendiary than the *Register*?"

"I was going to ask if you knew anything." The fact was that thus far, largely due to Verity's insistence, the *Register* hadn't strayed too far into outright sedition. That single oblique allusion to the guillotine was the furthest they had gone. But if Nate was printing pamphlets—off premises, presumably, or she would have noticed—then he could be tried for those.

Ash set his jaw. "He'd better not be." He sighed. "Here, let's be done with this," he said, gesturing to the chaos of the shop around them. "This mess will keep until tomorrow. You look like you could do with a wash and a hot meal."

She glanced down at her hands and found them covered in ink and dust. Her face had to be in much the same state. "Nan went home hours ago."

That got her a wry smile. "I can bring you hot water, Plum."

He was right, though. She did feel better after she washed, using the kettle of hot water he left outside her door. A quarter of an hour later she was sitting in bed, wrapped in a warm dressing gown, when Ash knocked at the door of her room carrying meat pie and a cup of tea.

Ash, she realized, was the sort of man who could procure pork pie at a moment's notice. A man who would make one a cup of tea without being asked, and do it without acting like it was a grand favor. He placed both cup and plate on the table beside her bed, and was half out the door before she had even managed to thank him.

"No, wait," she said. "Thank you."

"My pleasure, Plum."

"Stay? If you don't have anywhere else you need to be?" She hated asking. Asking for help was one step removed from requiring it, and in Verity's experience a woman who couldn't take care of herself was a sitting duck. Far better to practice self-sufficiency at every step.

A look passed over Ash's face, something she couldn't quite define. A sort of gentle, fond frustration. "There's nowhere I need to be," he said, making for the chair in the corner of the room. But the chair was covered with a stack of books, a cloak, and a few shifts that needed mending. He turned towards the bed and made a gesture for Verity to move over. She slid to the side, tucking her legs under the quilt and holding the plate of pork pie in her lap. The mattress dipped as Ash sat beside her, on top of the covers. She could feel the heat coming from his body, could smell the rosin and asphaltum that got under his nails while he worked and never quite came clean. When she swallowed the next mouthful of pie, she let herself sink against his side.

He put an arm around her shoulders and pulled her close

as if it were the simplest thing, as if this closeness were not unprecedented throughout the entirety of their long friendship. But her body fit against his with a familiarity that could have deceived her into believing that she could have Ash like this, that their friendship could exist between their bodies as it always had between their minds.

"When you want to talk about Nate, I'm here." His voice was low, and she felt the rumble of it against her cheek.

She burrowed into his side, hiding her face in his shirt. "I don't want to. I don't know what else there is to say."

"He's like a brother to me, and I don't want him to be hurt." He stroked her hair and she leaned into the touch. "But he isn't my brother. He's yours. While I think something has to be done to keep him safe until this blows over, it's not my place to act, at least not without your say-so."

He was doing her a favor by broaching the topic first, by acknowledging that there were things Verity could do to keep Nate out of prison. Unpleasant things, things she didn't want to think about. But nestled in the crook of Ash's arm, she thought she could almost face this problem. With his heart beating under her cheek, she felt less alone, almost like she had a partner, an ally. "He has to leave the country," she whispered. The thought had been creeping in at the edges of her consciousness for days, weeks, but saying it aloud felt like a betrayal. "But he would never agree to it."

"He might when he learns you had redcoats threatening you."

"They weren't threatening me."

"What they did to the shop was a threat. They're showing

you how easily they can do harm and how unafraid they are of any consequences." His voice was strained, his arm stiff around her. "He also might if he has enough money to set up as a printer in Boston or New York."

This was too much for Verity's nerves. She let out a high-pitched laugh. "I can hardly pay Charlie's wages, let alone such a great sum of money as it would take to set up a new establishment."

"I can help with that. I do have money saved."

"No," she said automatically. "I manage on my own."

"I know you do. But it would be my pleasure to help keep Nate safe."

She was wondering how long she had to wait before repeating her rejection of his aid, when he spoke again. "If Roger had been unable to pay for his trip to Italy, I would have helped. And you would have too, I think."

"True," she said tentatively. "But Roger was your dearest friend."

With a single finger, he tilted her chin up so she faced him. She held her breath. "Do you really need me to explain this?" He let out something between a laugh and a sigh. "Of course you do. You're important to me. You and Nate both." His words were straightforward and innocuous, but his voice was soft, his gaze intent on her. "You're dear to me, Plum."

Verity never knew what to say to expressions of fondness, beyond the absurd urge to protest. But hearing those words from Ash made her realize how much they were true for her as well. She mumbled something that she hoped he'd interpret as a return of the sentiment and then tucked her head under his chin to avoid looking him in the eye.

"Even with the money, I don't think he'd agree to go," she said. "He believes he's fighting for a worthy cause. Hell, he *is* fighting for a worthy cause."

"You could go with him. He might agree in that case."

The words hung there in the silent room. "I couldn't," she said. "And—no, Ash, I won't. My life is here." *You are here,* she wanted to say. She knew, as she formulated the thought, that Ash being in a place was reason enough for her to want to be there too. But that was terrifying, too much like letting another person dictate the terms of her life, so she pulled hard on the reins of her mind and thought about another reason she could not leave: if Verity and Nate both left, Ash would be alone. She knew him well enough to understand that his early life had been marked by a series of losses. And even if she could have asked Ash to go with them, which she would never do, because all his clients and connections were in London, he couldn't undertake an ocean voyage of three months. She shuddered at the memory of how laid up he had been after crossing the channel with Roger some years ago. Ash had suffered a seizure on board, recovered somewhat in Calais, and then suffered another seizure on the way home. "A ship is not a convenient place to have an episode, Plum," he had said with his characteristic dryness, but the haunted look in his mentor's eyes had told her of the true danger.

But it wasn't only concern for Ash that made her resist leaving. She didn't want to be parted from him. Those months he had spent in Bath had been hard enough, even though she had tried not to admit it to herself. She had missed seeing him, missed their easy conversations, but it had been more than that: when she was with him she felt warm and whole in a way she didn't otherwise. She didn't want to give that up.

She would, though. She would leave Ash, she would do whatever it took to keep Nate safe and sane, and she'd do it with the full knowledge that she was giving away even more of herself, that she was complicit in her own self-effacement.

Chapter Five

This was the third time Ash had visited the house on Cavendish Square, and while his sense of creeping familiarity in the foyer had not diminished, he had grown accustomed to it. What he found more disturbing was the hush that seemed to blanket the house in a fog of nervous silence. The servants moved on cats' feet, quick and silent. Each of his prior visits had concluded with Lady Caroline hustling him out the garden door when a man arrived home, and each time he had been relieved to be out of that house, almost gasping for air once he stepped outside.

As he worked, Lady Caroline told him about each plant he sketched. Strictly speaking, she didn't need to be there, but Ash had the sense that she didn't want to be parted from her specimens, and if carrying on a tutorial about asymmetrical flowers and other botanical rarities provided her with an excuse to keep an eye on him, Ash didn't object. He enjoyed her impromptu lectures, and once he discovered that she didn't mind interruptions, found himself asking questions.

"Sisymbrium Sophia," he said, reading the words at the bottom of the page. "What does that mean?"

"Sisymbrium is a genus in the cabbage family." Lady Caroline pronounced the word differently than Ash had.

"And Sophia means wise. I know that much. But wise cabbage?" To Ash it looked like a weed, spindly and unbeautiful, not to mention nothing like a cabbage at all. If it appeared in the gardens behind this conservatory, the gardener would surely pluck it out.

"Not cabbage, per se, but Brassica. It's a large family of herbs. Really, it's a common hedge mustard, found all over England and the continent and beyond. But it was used at some point to treat various ailments, hence Sophia." She went on at some length about lobes and leaf hairs and other characteristics, but concluded with, "But really, you could find something almost identical along any roadside."

"This didn't come from the side of any road I'm likely to travel along," Ash said. The bottom of the page bore the inscription "East Anatolia, 1812." "How did this specimen come into your hands?" She launched into a tale of a sea voyage in the Aegean, and for a moment he forgot that she had not been on this adventure. "Do you ever wish to travel?" he asked. "To collect specimens by foreign roadsides with your own hand?"

She was silent for long enough that Ash wondered if he had said something offensive. Finally she sighed. "I am not able to travel. I have duties keeping me in London."

She said the words as Persephone might speak of being trapped in the underworld for six months a year. Startled by the sorrow in her voice, he looked up. "Your husband is in Parliament, then, my lady?" He assumed that the loud, bellowing man whose return home signaled Ash's immediate need to leave was a member of the House of Lords, which would fit right in with Ash's impressions of lords and with the overall sensibility of that governmental body.

"Husband? Heavens, no, I have no husband. God save me from husbands. I have a brother and a father, and they're quite bad enough." Then, evidently realizing she had spoken too much, and before the hired help, no less, she shook her head. "I beg your pardon. Forget I spoke. My father, the duke, is an invalid and my brother is a widower. I keep house for them."

He suspected that Lady Caroline Talbot's definition of keeping house was not the same as Verity's. He doubted she put on an apron and dislodged bats from the chimney, or worried about how to feed unexpected guests on mutton chops. Arundel House—for he had gathered from the servants' chatter that such was the name of this place, and its owner none other than the Duke of Arundel—had nothing in common with the house on Holywell Street.

After several moments of no sound but the scratching of Ash's nib on the paper, Lady Caroline cleared her throat. "Are you perhaps one of the Somerset Ashbys? Any connection of the Thaddeus Ashbys of Bourton Grange?"

"No, my lady." He had been christened John Ashby at about seven years of age by the highly unimaginative rector of St. John's church in Ashby, Norfolk. He did not know what his name had been before that time or indeed whether he had any name at all.

A quarter of an hour later she cleared her throat again. "I wonder if I might have known your parents. You look familiar. Perhaps I know your mother?"

Ash gritted his teeth. He ought to have expected an aristocrat to be fixated on bloodlines. "I know nothing of my mother's people. Nor of my father's."

"You know nothing of your family?" she asked, a peculiar look in her dark eyes.

"Less than nothing," he said curtly. All Ash knew was what Roger had told him: at some point in his early childhood he was sent out to be fostered and had in due course been sent away by a succession of families who considered harboring an epileptic to be either a bad omen, a public embarrassment, or simply not worth the remnants of the funds Ash had initially been left with. Ultimately he had been sent to a charity school. His health hadn't suited him to school, however; when he was about ten or eleven he had suffered a seizure after playing at bat and ball with some other children and was ordered to be sent home. And so he would have been, if not for the fact that he had no home and nobody to claim him. One of his schoolmasters had noticed Ash's talent for drawing and arranged for Ash to be apprenticed to a friend who worked as an engraver; that engraver had been Roger.

"I see," she said. "I see." A furrow appeared between Lady Caroline's eyebrows. She opened her mouth to speak but he cut her off with a question about root systems. He did not want to talk about his illegitimacy, nor about his strange and confused childhood—his inability to remember most of it being chief among its peculiarities—with this woman in her costly dress and her enormous conservatory.

Bitterness tinged his thoughts. Ash was well aware that he had fared well compared to many unwanted and illegitimate children, and indeed better than many legitimate children who suffered from seizures. Whoever had brought him to that first foster home—presumably his mother—had at least paid for his keep, thus sparing him the orphanage or the workhouse. He remembered the condition Charlie had been in when Mr. Plum brought him from the workhouse—thin, pale, bruised, and frightened—and doubted he would have lived out a year in such a place. Ash had a vocation he enjoyed, and whatever hand of fate brought him to Roger had probably saved his life or at least his sanity; he knew well that there were people with his condition who ended their days in Bedlam. With perfect authority, Roger had declared his new charge perfectly sane and unpossessed of either devils or evil humors, and Ash had believed him. He had been lucky: he had learned a craft, he had found a tiny foothold in the world, and he shouldn't feel that every glance in a looking glass asked a question that he couldn't answer.

He worked the rest of the morning in silence, only stopping when they heard Lady Caroline's brother arrive. Ash slipped out into the garden, struck again by its eerie air of almost familiarity.

It was the evening of Portia's salon, and while Verity didn't go every month, she feared that if she didn't attend this time, only a week after the visit from the redcoats, she would look like she was in hiding. She needed to show her face to the world, prove that she was strong enough to contend with a thousand soldiers and a dozen reckless brothers. Even if by some unlikely chance the news of her shop's raid had not spread as far as Mayfair, she needed to prove it to herself. So she brushed the dust and lint from her most presentable gown, dressed her hair with more care than usual, tucked her cleanest fichu into the neckline, and fastened her mother's silver locket around her neck. Her dress was not fashionably cut but she thought the brown worsted suited her. Strictly speaking, she probably ought to wear a hat, but they always made her feel like her head was in some kind of cage, and that sensation wasn't conducive to intelligent conversation. Holding her small hand mirror at arm's length, she decided she didn't look like someone who was on the brink of financial ruin, nor a woman who was worried for her brother's life and possibly his sanity.

"You look well."

She spun to see Ash leaning in the doorway, his topcoat slung over his arm and his hat in his hand. She hastily looked away, afraid her gaze might linger tellingly on the cut of his coat, the strong lines of his jaw. Now that she knew what his arm felt like when it was wrapped around her, knew that his chest was hard beneath her cheek, she couldn't look at him without thinking about his body and how it felt against hers. "Oh," she said, putting the mirror back in the drawer of her clothes press. "Are you going out?"

"I was thinking of going to Mrs. Allenby's, if you wouldn't mind the company."

Of course she wouldn't, and it was just like Ash to realize it. She was already dreading the prospect of walking alone into Portia's house and wondering whether all the other guests had heard about her predicament. It was a stupid concern, the kind of thing that ought to occupy the mind of a girl ten years her junior, someone with no real troubles to plague her. But she drummed up a fair bit of business at Portia's salon—courting writers and readers alike—that being received there as an outcast would do her no favors.

Ash made the offer so easily and naturally that Verity was able to accept without feeling indebted to him. She was half-frantic coming up with reasons she wasn't fond of the man, grasping at any glimmer of unattractiveness on his part that might quash her burgeoning interest in him. And here he was being decent, the utter bastard.

It was a long walk to Portia's house in Bruton Street. Verity would have been content to walk the distance in silence, but Ash made a few remarks, first about the weather, then about a passing dandy's appalling waistcoat, and finally about a play he had seen. She knew he was casting lures, trying to see which conversational gambit she'd take him up on, and rather than leave him floundering she gave in. By the time they reached Bruton Street, they were engaged in a lively debate about the merits of an actor who had newly arrived on the London stage.

When Portia's butler took Ash's coat and Verity's shawl, Verity went to the cloakroom to brush some of the street dust from her hems. When she emerged, Ash was waiting for her, a glass of punch in each hand. She noticed something she hadn't been able to see in the gloom of their house or the dark of the street: Ash had shaved and tied a fresh cravat around his neck. He had taken extra care with his appearance tonight, and Verity wondered if that effort had been for her. She had made an effort as well, conscious that many people would see her and think of her brother's increasingly troublesome writings. That Ash might consider such a thing was touching, and made her resent him to the core.

She drank half the glass of punch in one go, then saw Ash regarding her quizzically, and downed the other half. She handed him the empty glass. "Walking here was thirsty work," she said inanely, and took the full glass from his hand.

When he looked at her, his gaze trailed over her body for a fragment of a moment longer than necessary. She felt a spark of want, and tried to stamp it out as if it were an ember that had alit on the hearth rug. She knew what came after one gave in to desire: the disappointment on a loved one's face, the blame and recriminations, the stilted awkwardness she had with Portia. She didn't think she could bear that with Ash.

"It's to be a poet first, and then an Egyptologist," Ash said, explaining the night's program.

"We had an Egyptologist last month," Verity said, glad they had returned to their ordinary mode of discourse.

"Ah, but this one has had a row with the last one, and Portia had to have this one give her point of view, lest there be a civil war among Egyptologists."

Ash led the way through the crowded room to the recess at the back where they usually sat. Without Nate in between them, it seemed intimate, but Verity firmly shoved those thoughts out of her head and surveyed the guests. One of the nice things about Portia's salon was that Verity could count on not being the shabbiest person in attendance. For every person of wealth and culture, there was a man whose renown was based on having calculated the orbit of some astral body that might not exist, or a woman who had translated *Beowulf* into Latin. Geniuses, Verity had come to realize, did not always take care with their appearance. Verity, in her worn-out brown frock, blended in.

Any awkwardness between them dissipated by the time the poet stood at the front of the room. Verity knew nothing about poetry. They stocked volumes of poetry in the bookshop, and occasionally included verse in the *Register*, but Verity left its selection to Nate. Did that mean she was prosaic? Perhaps her hours of balancing accounts and marketing for potatoes had sapped her of whatever it took to rise above the mundane. The prosaic and the domestic were one and the same, she suspected, and her thoughts had been so consumed with the fate of her brother and her business that there was hardly room left for anything else, not even the things she valued. When had she started to worry more about the market price of haddock than about universal suffrage? She wondered that even without the burden of a husband, she might yet wind up like her mother—crushed by duty, constantly fretting, with little existence beyond her responsibilities to others.

She wanted something for herself, damn it. She wanted to be selfish, to take and grab and do something for herself alone. If she were another woman, she might pick a posy or buy some sweetmeats. But Verity was in no mood for gentle pleasures. If she picked flowers, she'd stomp on them with the heel of her boot. Sweetmeats would taste like bile on her tongue. What she needed was a pleasure that would push back, something that was half self-indulgence and half a fight, something she had denied herself for too long.

A gentle pressure on her arm interrupted her thoughts, and she looked down to see Ash's hand on her sleeve. He still had his attention at the front of the room, but he had somehow known that she was lost in unwelcome thoughts. Or maybe he had just wanted to touch her. For the tiniest moment, she let her hand rest atop his, heard his sharp intake of breath, felt the warmth of his skin beneath hers. For the space of two heartbeats she let herself enjoy his closeness, then she stood and let it all slip away. She crossed the room to Portia so she could remind herself what lay on the other side of love.

Portia greeted Verity with the usual effusive enthusiasm and murmured commonplaces. "Darling," she breathed, pitching her voice too low to interrupt the poet who was still speaking, "I'm so pleased you came." Her brow furrowed in slight concern. "I see you don't have your brother with you."

"He's in Derby," Verity answered tersely. Then, seeing the mystification on her hostess's face, she added, "For the executions."

"Perhaps it'll do him good to see an execution," Portia

said, as if the problem was that Nate was unclear on what execution entailed.

"I'm afraid he'll think they die as martyrs."

"He'd do well to remember that martyrdom involves death."

"He's sincere in his beliefs," Verity started, in a defense of Nate that she wouldn't have believed herself capable of an hour earlier. But she was interrupted by the prickle of tears in her eyes.

"Oh, my dear," Portia said, and her sympathy was so sincere and obvious that Verity wanted to flinch. She didn't want sympathy, however well deserved, however sincerely expressed. She didn't want anything from Portia, and momentarily regretted that she had gone along with Portia's insistence that they remain friends even after their affair had run its course. Sympathy from a former lover was a bitter brew indeed. "If there's any way, any way at all, that I can be of assistance, you'll let me know, won't you?" Portia asked.

"No," Verity said too quickly. The idea of accepting help from Portia made Verity feel something like shame. Their time together had been markedly unbalanced, with Portia putting forth most of the effort. Verity had been—still was—fond of Portia, and she had been more than eager to go to bed with her, but it never quite matched Portia's sentiments towards her; by the end Verity had feared that she was cheating Portia out of a proper love affair. She winced at the idea of taking anything further from the woman. "I've got the matter in hand."

Portia rolled her eyes with an uncharacteristic inelegance.

"Good heavens, Verity. We're friends, I hope. And friends do help one another. You don't have to have to put red in your ledger every time someone comes to your aid."

Verity was rather sure that she did have to do precisely that, but wasn't about to embark on an argument. When another guest appeared at Portia's side, Verity gladly relinquished her hostess's attention and returned to Ash. She carefully avoided looking at his face, but he must not have returned the favor, because she found a clean handkerchief being pressed into her hand.

God only knew what was in Portia Allenby's punch, Ash thought as he and Verity half stumbled back to Holywell Street. The night was foggy, and even though they kept their path to streets well lit by gaslights, it was sometimes hard to see even the cobblestones beneath their feet. Ash kept close to Verity and prodded her gently with his elbow; she took the hint and rested her hand on his arm. He reminded himself that it was a meaningless gesture; they both walked arm in arm with any number of people. But he thought he detected something almost caressing in the way she let her hand drift up from his elbow. Not that he minded her touch—far from it. But it would be a very bad idea to combine spirits with half-arsed amorousness, especially since she was in a rather vulnerable and lonely state of mind and he was finding it increasingly difficult to pretend he didn't want her. With a sense of dread but also inane gratification, he realized that she had been doing the same thing; these touches were what happened when they both let their guard down for an instant. She did want him, or at least wasn't averse to the idea. Her hand slid up his arm with increased intent. Definitely not averse. He rolled his eyes at his stupidity—Verity had never been "not averse" to a damned thing in her life. She was either for it or against it. His heart stuttered at the thought.

"You mustn't do that, Plum," he choked out.

The tactful response would have been either to remain silent or to murmur something vague, the sort of apology you issued when stepping on a person's toes, but Verity had never been interested in tact. "No?" she asked, dropping her hand to her side. "Why not?" Her face tipped up towards his in plain consternation. Sometimes he forgot how small Verity actually was; she seemed larger than life, taking up so much space in his mind that it was hard to remember that the top of her head reached only an inch or two above his shoulder.

"Because it'll give me ideas," he admitted, trying to keep his tone detached.

"Ha! Ideas. You. Stuff and nonsense. If you were prone to ideas, you would have had them already. That is how ideas work." She spoke with an air of grave authority that was at odds with her slightly slurred speech.

"How do you know I haven't?" he answered, his voice laced with something like anger. Ash didn't know what got into him, what gave him the courage or foolishness to speak those words aloud. Maybe it was the punch, or the fact that they could hardly see one another through the fog and the dark. Maybe because their voices seemed muffled and remote, belonging to the night rather than to themselves, he could pretend it wasn't himself speaking, but some utter idiot who wanted to be viciously embarrassed for the rest of his life.

"As if a man could keep such a thing to himself," she said with scorn.

He could hardly argue with her without telling her far more than was good for either of them, so he steered the conversation to more anodyne topics. They made idle chatter for the remainder of the walk, the sort of go-nowhere conversation that people can share when they've been in one another's lives for nearly as long as either can remember.

"Do you think Nate will return tonight?" Verity asked as they turned onto Longacre. The execution took place a few days earlier. The Prince Regent had commuted the sentences to hanging, followed by beheading, so at least the nation was to be spared the spectacle of those young men being drawn and quartered.

"More likely tomorrow." Ash was certain Verity wouldn't know a moment's peace until her brother was safely home and she could be confident that he hadn't incited any riots during his time in the north.

By the time they got home, Verity's teeth were chattering. Last winter had been bitterly cold and it already looked like this year would be no better. It was barely November and they had already needed fires several days running. Verity said her fingers were stiff, so Ash unlocked the door and they entered the dark cold house.

"I want to see your new sketches," Verity said.

He had done two more, each of increasing explicitness.

He could have brought them to her in her bedroom, when she was snugly tucked beneath layers of quilts, warmed by a roaring fire. The previous week in that bed, her body had curled against his like a kitten, almost pliant. They could spend their time in one another's arms as easily as they could in conversation. Tonight he could show her the sketches, sit on the edge of her bed and—

"I'll lay the fire in your study," he said quickly.

"All right. But I'll lay the fire," Verity said. "You get the sketches. And if you have a bottle of wine in your room, bring that too. That'll warm us up. Otherwise we'll have to make do with the gin Nate keeps under the counter in the shop."

When he entered the study, a bottle of wine under one arm and his drawings in his hand, Verity already had the fire crackling. He paused in the doorway for a moment to admire her as she knelt before the hearth. Her dress was thin and worn and decidedly out of fashion, if it ever had precisely been in fashion in the first place, which very plain garments seldom were. Her figure wasn't statuesque, like Portia Allenby, or elegantly wispy like the women in the fashion plates he drew. She was, however, perfect. When he saw her, he felt something like relief, as if the sight of her had quenched a thirst he hardly knew he had.

He had known for what seemed like forever that his feelings for Verity Plum were on the knife's edge between friendship and something infinitely more perilous, and he had done a damned lot of work keeping them there. But watching her lay the fire with deft and competent hands, he realized that in working so hard not to let his warmer feelings for her tip over into lust, he had let in a tide of other feelings that weren't so easy to tame. She was necessary to him, and he thought he might be necessary to her. They knew one another so damned well it was almost intrusively intimate. How did two people negotiate attraction when their lives were already entangled? He was certain the only answer was to avoid the matter entirely, and equally certain this was a solution that wouldn't last forever.

Verity turned towards him when he uncorked the bottle. Her gaze flicked up and down his body before darting hastily away. She produced two glasses from a desk drawer, but instead of sitting behind her desk, she sat beside him on the sofa.

"Are you going to show me your pictures?" she asked after he filled both glasses with wine.

"Or we could wait until we're less, ah, foxed."

She made a rude noise and held out her hand with a grabbing gesture. He handed her the first sketch and studied her face as she examined it. Lit only by flickering firelight, she was made of nothing but uncompromising hard lines softened only by shadow. He found he was holding his breath.

In the illustration she was examining, Catherine straddled her husband's lap, and he had his head lowered to her bosom. Because of the arrangement of her dressing gown and the angle of perspective, the only exposed part of her body was a single breast. Without the benefit of a model, he had spent an afternoon in the British Museum examining a Renaissance Madonna to ensure sure he got that breast right.

"Ah," she said.

"It's only an—"

"It's perfect. Although I don't think they wore top boots in 1480."

"I decided that if I put Perkin Warbeck in doublet and hose he'd look like a stage jester." He had regarded the fifteenth-century portraits at the museum in some dismay, not sure how such outlandish garments could be rendered either suitably erotic or in line with his own aesthetic. "Consider it poetic license. But I can change it if you prefer."

"No, it's quite, ah, appealing." She tucked her feet beneath her in a way that brought her markedly closer to him, but her gaze remained on the drawing. "I love how his hand is on her waist. You can see the marks each finger is making on her skin, through the dressing gown. Will that be apparent after the engraving?"

"Certainly it will. All the detail you see will render perfectly." As if he didn't know his craft. Roger had taught him well, and he wished he could see his former master's face when he learned Ash was using his skills to such an end.

"Very well, Ash." She elbowed him gently in the side. "I didn't mean to besmirch your talents."

God, she was close now. Too close and not nearly close enough. He took hold of her arm before she could pull it away. "I told you—" he said from between gritted teeth.

"I beg your pardon," she said, sitting up straight. "I'm quite forgetting myself this evening."

"No, for heaven's sake, that's not what I meant." It had been exactly what he meant, but Verity close to him was better than Verity far away, no matter what havoc it wreaked with his mind. So he put his arm around her waist and pulled her close so they were sitting shoulder to shoulder.

"Here's the other one," he said, producing the second sketch. This one depicted Catherine leaning against a wall, one leg wrapped around Perkin's waist. Their robes were a tangle of light and shadow, doing more to emphasize their undress rather than to obscure it. The focus of the picture was one of Perkin's arms, braced against the wall. But as he looked at it, he couldn't help but notice that he had drawn Catherine to resemble Verity. It was all there, in the jaw and the wild hair. He hadn't meant to—not precisely—but any woman he drew turned into Verity. He'd have to alter the sketch before doing the etching.

Verity took the paper from his hand and held it at arm's length. She fumbled in her pocket and came up with a pair of spectacles that she slipped crookedly onto her nose. "Hmm," she said, and shifted her gaze to his face. For a moment he thought she might suspect the truth, that she might see in the drawing what she saw in the looking glass. He became very conscious of the arm that was still wrapped around her.

"All right then," he said, striving for a normal tone, as if he weren't thinking only of all the places their bodies touched. "I'll carry on doing illustrations for the rest of the volume. A total of four, is that right?"

She nodded. "Four for each volume," she said, yawning and settling her head against his shoulder. "What I like about the book, and about your drawings, is that they both seem to be enjoying each other. I don't know what it's like to be with a man, but it can't be so fundamentally different than being with a woman, which I quite enjoyed. Have you ever thought about how funny it is that people go to bed with people of a different gender?"

Ash blinked. "I do believe most people's preferences run that way," he said, amused.

"Do you? I rather thought everybody was like me." She raised a hand to her mouth to cover a yawn.

"Which is to say . . ." he prompted, unsure of what she meant.

"Desirous of all manner of people. Like Perkin Warbeck," she said without a hint of irony, and he realized that for Verity, this novel had supplanted any history she had previously read on the topic. Perkin Warbeck was now the lover of the doomed Earl of Warwick, and there was no going back.

"You thought it a baffling coincidence that most people confined their amorous activities to one gender?" Ash tried to keep a straight face.

"Not a coincidence, but a constraint put on them by the law and fear of judgment. Which is quite understandable, of course." She frowned, as if items were slotting into place in her mind. "But if you're saying it's more of an inborn preference, then I feel quite silly."

"Not silly." He kissed the top of her head. A terrible idea, but he had the sense that he'd fling himself headfirst towards any bad idea that brought him closer to Verity. He sat up straight and tried to clear his head. "By the way, I've been meaning to ask you who the author is. I didn't recognize the handwriting or the style." The love scenes, which had clearly been added after the body of the text was complete, were written in a messier penmanship, but that could have to do with the haste of the insertion rather than an indication that two separate authors were at work.

"I don't know. She didn't give a name or an address, but requested that I direct correspondence to the Fox and Hound in Leicester Square."

Ash's stomach clenched in fear. "Let me understand," he said, trying to sound calm. "When this book goes to press, no matter how clandestinely you mean to advertise it, there is at least one stranger who knows that you're the publisher."

"True, but it's in her best interest to keep mum, otherwise she could be in hot water."

"No," Ash said patiently, "she will not be. Because you don't know who she is. This is unwise, Verity." She looked up sharply at his use of her first name.

"I've already paid her, and now I can't afford not to go to press with the book."

"Just like your brother," he said. "I don't know why my two closest friends need to play fast and loose with their safety like this. I've come to expect as much from Nate, but I hoped you knew better." The thought of losing them the way he had lost everyone else made his blood chill and he couldn't stand the thought of it for one moment longer. He rose to his feet, needing to get out of this room. "Good night, Plum." He made his way towards the door and glanced at her over his shoulder. "I trust you're sober enough to make it up the stairs on your own?"

She nodded but said nothing, only looking up at him

with wide eyes. In the shadows, he could see an expression of confused hurt on her face. That wouldn't do.

"Oh, damn it, Plum. Come here." But even as he spoke, he was already crossing the room, going to her, taking her hand, pulling her to her feet. He couldn't say that he had a plan. He knew only that he couldn't part from her with anything like coldness or resentment between them. He squeezed her hands. "I just . . . I can't lose you, Plum."

He must have said the wrong words, or the right ones, because she was on her toes, her lips brushing over his, her hands on his shoulders. His hands somehow found the small of her back, the nape of her neck. Ash tried to act like a man who had some semblance of sangfroid, rather than one who was being offered a ladle of water after crossing an endless desert. Or maybe he was being offered a lit fuse, an unexploded mortar shell, a disaster waiting to happen. One or the other. His mind was too consumed with the feel of Verity's mouth moving against his to figure it out. She tasted of wine and smelled of hair soap and ink, and her lips were soft and searching.

Her kisses changed from exploratory assays into something downright purposeful as she licked along his bottom lip. He clamped his hands onto her hips, feeling the sharpness of her hipbone and the softness beyond. She was kissing him in earnest now, kissing him as comprehensively and unyieldingly as she did everything else in life. She steered him towards the sofa and pushed him down. He went willingly—was there a word that meant more than *willingly*? He did not know and his mind wasn't forming thoughts now anyway—and she straddled his lap.

They fit together as if this were not their first kiss but their hundredth, their thousandth, as if they had been doing this all along. As if they were gears from the same clock, coming together finally, finally. As if this was what they were meant to do. This was what he had wanted for years, what he had dreaded too. This was it, the end of their precarious balancing act, the beginning of his losing her.

He moved a hand to her cheek and pulled back. "Wait."

"Why?" she asked, her eyes unfocused.

"I need a moment to get my bearings."

She smiled, a lazy twist of one side of her mouth. "You're on my sofa, between my thighs."

She was wrong. He was in a new world, an uncharted sea where Verity Plum said that sort of thing to him. "I can't. We know how this will end, and I can't stand the thought of it."

Eyes narrowed, she got to her feet and glared down at him. She wasn't angry, just vexed and working herself up to a lather; this was a look he knew well. He had the wonderful feeling that she was about to dress him down and explain why he was being an idiot. He'd agree, and then they'd ruin everything that mattered to him. He would know with every kiss and every caress that he was one step closer to losing her, one step closer to being utterly adrift in the world.

Chapter Six

They were interrupted by the sound of the front door swinging open.

"Good God," came Nate's voice, nearly a shout. "What the devil happened in this shop?"

Ash watched the relief wash over Verity's face at the realization that her brother had returned safely. He got to his feet and squeezed her hand. "And why the hell is that cat in the house?" Nate shouted.

"I'll go with you," he said. "But hold still." Her hair had come loose when he had touched her. "Hold still." He lifted the errant lock and tried to coax it in the general direction of the rest of Verity's coiffure, fastening it with a hairpin that he fished out of his pocket. "There," he said, surveying his handiwork. She no longer looked like he had been pawing at her, at least. Her cheeks flushed, as if she knew the direction of his thoughts, and she looked hastily away.

Nate and Charlie were in the shop, a single satchel on the

floor between them. Charlie looked merely tired while Nate had the look of a man who hadn't slept in days.

"What happened here?" Nate asked, gesturing at the shelves Ash and Verity had spent several mornings setting to rights.

"The redcoats tossed the place and we put everything back as best as we could," Verity said tersely.

Charlie groaned and buried his face in his hands, but Nate seemed unsurprised. "Well, I suppose it was bound to happen. Sorry it was when I wasn't here to help, Verity."

Ash watched Verity. She opened her mouth and snapped it shut.

"I'm going to find something to eat," Charlie cut in. "We can quarrel in the kitchen as well as we can in the shop."

They settled around the plain deal table that had been in the kitchen since long before Ash first set foot in the place. Charlie ducked into the larder, emerging with his arms full of bread, cheese, and apples. He placed half the food in front of Nate. "Eat."

From his seat beside Verity, Ash could see her twist the fabric of her skirt in her hands. "I think you've got to go to America," she blurted out.

"Not happening," Nate said, breaking a piece of bread into crumbs. "We're close to a victory. You should have seen them. It wasn't your ordinary hanging. The crowd wasn't for it. There was no cheering after the hangman showed Brandreth's head to the crowd. People aren't going to take this sitting down."

"Eat that piece of bread, will you," Charlie muttered. "Maybe you'll think straight with some food in you."

"The government can't keep executing everyone who rises up," Nate protested.

"Like hell they can't," Verity responded, at the same moment Ash said, "Would you wager your life on that?"

Nate glared at all of them.

"I just don't want you to die," Verity said, the words coming out quick, running together, as if she were ashamed. "You're my brother and I don't want you to die."

Good Christ, she really was ashamed. Ash didn't think he had ever seen that look on Verity's face before. Ashamed to be asking for something? He wasn't certain. Under the table, he took her hand, running his thumbs over her knuckles. She squeezed back, then took a deep breath.

"I've been thinking all week," she said. "There's a ship leaving for New York next week. I have enough saved for your passage. And Ash has enough saved to set you up as a jobbing printer, if you'd like. Or you could write. It's up to you."

"Like hell it is. What if I don't agree?" Nate shot back. "Would you have me kidnapped by pirates like you advised your letter writer to do to her bigamous husband?"

A silence stretched out. "Then I'll go to America on my own."

"What?" the three men asked at once.

"I'll use the money I've saved and book my own passage to America," Verity said, her gaze skittering away from Ash's, her cheeks reddening, and Ash wondered if she had come up with this scheme to ensure that Ash not be left alone—no matter what, one of the Plums would remain in England.

"And what will you do there?" Nate demanded.

"Not watch you go to prison."

Ash was holding his breath and thought Charlie was too.

"I don't believe you," Nate said.

"Do you really want to call my bluff?"

"Damn it, Verity. This isn't fair play."

"The *Queen of Arabia* sails from Liverpool. If you leave tomorrow on the stagecoach, you can get there with time to spare."

"Tomorrow," Nate repeated. "This is madness."

"You need to be gone before the redcoats come back with an arrest warrant," she said. "Either you get on the ship or I do."

Nate threw his hands up and stalked out of the shop.

"Two passages?" Charlie asked, eyes narrowed.

"One is yours, if you want it," Verity said. "I don't want you to get caught up in whatever trouble is coming Nate's way. And I don't want to send Nate alone. He needs someone to look after him, and I know that isn't what you signed on for—"

"Bollocks. You and Nate have always treated me as family, and I reckon family usually try to stop one another from getting killed by redcoats or beaten senseless by a mob."

"Yes, but we Plums treat our family terribly." Her voice was heavy with weariness.

"Maybe so, but I don't have anyone to compare you to, do I? Besides, you and Nate don't treat one another badly. You just quarrel like Athens and Sparta. If you didn't care about him, you wouldn't be doing this."

Verity looked away, as if embarrassed. "Will you go, then?" she asked. "To America?"

"All right," Charlie said with a shrug. "I don't like the idea of him rattling around America on his own, forgetting to sleep and eat."

"Thank you, Charlie." She stood and rounded the table, holding her arms out as if to embrace him. She stopped short; Verity wasn't in the habit of embracing people. Charlie, seeing her halt, rolled his eyes.

"You'll be bored off your head without us, you know," he said, rising to his feet and wrapping his arms around her without hesitation. Charlie was a full head taller than Verity now, as tall as Nate, nearly as tall as Ash.

"I will," she admitted. "I've spent so long caring for Nate, I don't know how I'll abide on my own."

"Me neither," Charlie said, not letting Verity go. "Maybe that's why I'm going with him."

Ash sensed that he was intruding, that he ought to leave them alone to say their farewells, to make whatever arrangements needed to be made. "I'm going to follow Nate," Ash said, squeezing Verity's arm on the way out the door.

Ash found Nate at the public house in the next street, sitting at a table in the corner. It was late and most of the tables were empty, chairs upturned on the tables, the barman already sweeping the floors. When Nate saw Ash approach he kicked a chair out for Ash to sit in. It was what he always did, half invitation and half presumption that Ash would sit with Nate as a matter of course. Ash had always been grateful for the casual, proprietary nature of Nate's friendship. As vague and selfish as Nate could be, Ash never doubted that they were friends. Ash felt a pang at the thought that in two days Nate would be at sea, not to return for years.

"My sister has a pistol to my head," Nate said before Ash had even sat. "I know when I'm being strong-armed, and I don't like it."

Ash wasn't going to argue about tactics. "You and Verity are my family," he said. If it were true for Charlie, it was true for Ash himself, and the words shouldn't feel like a lie on his tongue. He had thought of the Plums as a family for years, now, but had never put voice to the thought. "You're my family," he repeated, "so I'm not going to let you be put in prison. And, Nate, I don't think I can watch your sister suffer the way she has this past month."

Nate's eyebrows shot up. "Oh, it's like that, is it?"

Ash opened his mouth to deny it or to feign ignorance, but there was nothing to gain from hiding the truth, and he didn't feel ashamed of it anyway. He leaned back in his chair. "For me, it is," he admitted. "And it has been for a while."

Nate scowled at him. "So, if I don't go, then she's going to martyr herself by leaving you behind. Either I go, or I've ruined the happiness of the two people I care most about."

Ash sucked in a breath. "Don't—that's not—I wouldn't have told you if I thought you'd take it as forcing your hand."

"You were already forcing my hand. Don't think I missed that bit about how you're footing the bill for this madness."

"The two of you are my closest friends," Ash said.

Nate regarded him for a long moment, and Ash wondered what the other man saw in his face. "Be careful with my sister, Ash."

"I'm never anything other than careful with Verity."

"I meant take care to protect yourself. I don't know if Verity knows how to be careful with other people's hearts."

Ash frowned. "You're cross with her, that's understandable."

"Things ended badly between her and that Allenby woman. She's not warm, my sister."

"I've seen things end badly between you and half a dozen people, but I'd never call you cold."

"What I'm trying to say is that you aren't like that. The whole time I've known you, you've never taken up with anyone." Ash watched in grim mortification as Nate's eyes widened in realization. "Because you've been holding out for Verity. That's right, isn't it?"

"I'm not going to deny that I've always held your sister in the highest regard—" He closed his eyes and winced. "Yes. You're right. I've never wanted anyone but her."

"Do you think my sister will marry you?" Nate asked skeptically.

"We both know she doesn't want a husband."

"Can't blame her." Nate frowned, and Ash knew he was thinking of his mother.

"But I—" Ash shook his head. The truth was that he would marry Verity in a heartbeat, had known so for years. But that wasn't what she wanted, and at the moment Ash couldn't envision what a compromise would look like. "Look.

It's very early days yet. I haven't broached the topic and, ah, please don't either."

"When she's through with you, where will that leave you? I'll be in Boston—or is it New York?—wherever that ship leaves me, Roger will be in Italy, and Verity will keep you at arm's length. Damn it, Ash. Now you have me feeling sorry for you rather than myself." He waved over the barman for a pair of pints.

"I think you're wrong," Ash said. "I'm not going to ask your sister for anything she doesn't want to give." Still, Nate's words sat uneasily with him. He had seen the strain it cost her to maintain her friendship with Mrs. Allenby and did not want to ask her to do the same for him. Thus far, he could dismiss everything that happened as the result of wine and anxiety. A one off, a bit of silly fumbling about. It wasn't too late to go back. Ash knew how he felt about her, but Verity did not. They could revert to being friends.

Nate regarded him flatly. "For your sake, I hope you're right, mate."

It shouldn't be this easy to exile a man to the other side of the world, Verity thought as she tightened the buttons on Nate's coats and made sure his linens were in good repair and neatly packed. She had never been any good at mending, her stitches tending to meander while her thread wound itself into a succession of knots, but she felt that she ought to have to do some kind of work to send Nate on his way. So far, it had been too easy. It made her think the past years of her life were an illusion of stability—a flick of a pen and a few well-chosen words and her life went up like a puff of dust.

Nate staggered in while she sat in the shop, a half-mended shirt discarded on the counter before her, her arms full of books she meant to tuck into his trunk. "Are you only coming home now?" His clothes were rumpled, his jaw unshaven, and he smelled faintly of wine. It was ten in the morning.

"I had to make my farewells," he said. As he approached the counter she saw lines of fatigue and sleeplessness on his face. "And some business to wrap up. I owed Johnny Burkett five bob for a job he did for me."

"A job he did for you?" Verity echoed, eyes narrowing. Burkett ran a rival printshop a few doors down. "Why would you need to hire a printer?"

Nate had the grace to blush. "He printed a pamphlet for me. My name wasn't on it, but even so." He scuffed the toe of his boot. "Ash was quite insistent about that. Said he'd throw my presses into the river with his own hands if I printed anything even the least reasonable Tory magistrate could construe as sedition while you lived under this roof."

"I daresay those pamphlets were what the redcoats were after." She sighed. "I suppose that solves one mystery, at least."

"Since when does that cat come indoors?" he asked, gesturing with his chin towards the top of a bookcase.

"That's Ash's doing. He started leaving a dish out for her and now she follows him around when he's home. Otherwise she stares at me like she's ready to gouge my eyes out. A charming cat, can't imagine why we didn't bring her in sooner."

Nate reached up and made a soothing noise. The cat hissed. "Leave it to Ash to spend a fortnight courting the meanest cat in London." He looked at her, his eyes lit up with amusement, his mouth round with surprise. "He has a type."

She felt her cheeks heat and turned away so he wouldn't notice. "I can't imagine what you're talking about," she said, evening out a row of books.

"Miss Verity," Nan called from the street door, "where should I put the post?" Verity was about to tell her to put it on the desk upstairs, as usual, when she looked up and saw that instead of the usual three or four letters, Nan held a bulging mail sack.

Nate took the bag out of the older woman's hands and half an hour later they had the letters sorted on the counter. There were the usual handful of letters from writers and requests for subscriptions, but the largest stack consisted of correspondence addressed to the *Ladies' Register*, either requesting advice or taking issue with the advice she had dispensed. She knew she ought to remind Nate to go upstairs and see that his trunk contained everything he meant to pack, but it was good to share space with her brother without a quarrel looming on the horizon.

"'Dear sir or madam.' Ooh," Nate said, wincing, "that's never a good start, is it. 'I'm writing with a heavy heart and a sense of the direst disappointment that a publication intended for the consumption of the fairer sex would expose ladies to such vile—'" Nate looked up. "He goes on like that for three entire paragraphs. What the devil did you publish, Verity? A treatise on venereal disease?" Nate hoisted himself onto the counter and picked up another letter at random.

"It was the problem page," Verity said. She had manufactured a letter from a woman who discovered that her husband was bigamous. It was more or less verbatim what Nate and Ash invented in her office a few weeks earlier.

Nate opened his eyes wide. "I read that aloud to the other passengers on the stagecoach. Come to think, some of them might have thought it a bit beyond the pale to actually advise that the wives pool their funds and have the fellow knocked on the head and sent to foreign parts."

"I think it was a very measured response," Verity sniffed, feigning affront. Nate threw his head back and laughed. Verity wished they could wind back the clock to a time when the sight of her brother merry and carefree was nothing extraordinary.

"Are all the letters like this?" Nate asked, gesturing to the contents of the mail bag.

"About half are in favor of having the bigamist sent to the colonies and praise my pragmatism in advising the lady so. The other half are less enthusiastic."

"What would the dissenters have advised your fictional lady?"

"They're of several minds. Either the lady ought to go to the magistrate—"

"Excellent advice if she wants to be made a public spectacle and laughingstock," Nate said.

"Precisely. But you'd be shocked at the number of men who believe that the law is a perfectly operating organ."

"No, Verity, I would not," he said dryly. "You may have noticed that I've been slightly agitated about the prevalence of that belief."

Verity laughed despite herself. She missed this Nate, the brother who made her laugh, who saw eye to eye with her on nearly all topics. "A few other correspondents suggested that the lady herself was at fault for marrying someone whose antecedents were unknown to her people. And a few writers suggested that having the husband press-ganged and sent to parts unknown was insufficient punishment, and that sailors could be bribed to have him thrown overboard."

Nate raised his eyebrows. "I suppose I ought to be glad that I'm only to be sent to New York with a substantial bank draught."

"Nate," she said with a sigh.

"It's all right, Verity, I was trying to make a joke of it."

"I know you think I forced your hand."

"You did force my hand, damn you. And I think you're being overcautious. But I'm going along with your plan because you're my sister. Even though I think you're wrong. I mean, you are wrong, which time will tell, and when I come back I'm going to have a good gloat about it. I plan to be thoroughly sickening, let me tell you. But meanwhile I'm willing to go because that's what you need." There was something about the way he spoke the words that made her think he was repeating lines someone had spoken to him, and she sensed Ash's hand at work.

"It's not what I need," she protested. "It's what's good for you."

"Why is it so hard for you to admit that you need something? What's the worst that could happen?"

The fact that he even had to ask just went to show how two people reared under the same roof could have radically different lives. Verity had to stand on her own two feet, had long ago learned that there was nobody to go to for help. But there was no use trying to explain, not now. "If you make me cry I really will have you thrown overboard."

"In any event," Nate said, chucking her on the shoulder, "I'd say your first issue was a success."

"I have half a bag of letters requesting advice," Verity said, still stunned. "Where am I supposed to come up with actual wisdom for these poor unfortunates?"

"Piffle," Nate said. "You'll do fine. You always do. Frightfully competent and all that. I'm only sorry I'll hear about it secondhand." He slid off the counter and made for the door leading upstairs.

"It's only for the time being." She pulled at his sleeve, drawing him into an embrace. "I hope one day . . ." She didn't know how to finish that sentence in a way that wouldn't bring tears to her eyes, and she was determined not to cry. "Here," she said instead, pointing to the stack of books she had put aside for him. "Take whatever else you want. I haven't tied up your trunk yet, and I left room for a good dozen books."

Within the hour, Nate and Ash reappeared downstairs carrying the trunk between them.

"The hackney's waiting," Charlie said from the door.

Ash embraced Nate, then shook hands with Charlie and gave him a letter that Verity knew to be a draught on his bank.

"I see you handing that to Charlie," Nate said as he slapped his hat onto his head. "It's a damned insult, is what it is," he said, but he was laughing. "Farewell, Verity," he said, pulling her into a tight hug.

"Be safe," she said. "Take care of him," she said to Charlie, over Nate's shoulder.

And then they were gone, leaving Verity and Ash alone in the quiet of the shop. She reached for his hand, maybe because she wanted to prove to herself that she wasn't alone, that despite having dismantled her own life and his as well, they still had one another. He squeezed her hand and then drew her close. She tucked her head under his chin, breathing in the scent of hard soap, ink, and copper that he always carried with him. His arms were tight around her, his pulse fast under her ear. His cravat was loose, the skin of his throat bare and exposed.

"Ash," she said, tilting her head up. She wanted comfort, reassurance, a chance to lose herself in whatever he had to offer.

"Verity," he said, his voice strangled. "I think I ought to go upstairs." But he didn't let her go.

"I'll go with you," she said, pressing up onto her toes, speaking the words into the stubbly skin under his jaw.

He groaned. "I can't. We can't."

She pulled back and regarded him in confusion. It had been only yesterday that they had been in one another's arms. What could possibly have changed in less than a day?

Then she saw the tightness around his eyes. His mouth was flat, his dark eyes flinty. He likely thought she was a monster for manipulating Nate the way she had. Hell, she might agree with him.

"I see," she said, stepping away. The absence of his touch felt like a layer of her skin had just been flayed off.

"No, Verity, it's just that we got carried away last night. It's not a good idea." Of course it wasn't a good idea, she wanted to yell. What kind of fool would think it was a good idea to entrust one's heart to a cold, unfeeling creature such as she? "We're good friends and we work well together," he continued, infuriatingly calm. "I don't want to jeopardize that."

"You don't want to jeopardize our working together," she repeated. And he hadn't even called her Plum. It was a slap in the face in addition to a rejection.

He made as if he wanted to step close to her, then checked the movement. She bade him good night and heard the soft, final click of the door upstairs as Ash closed it.

Chapter Seven

Later, Ash realized the entire course of his life would have unspooled quite differently if he had gone to Arundel House in a more complaisant mood. As it was, he was on the edge of fury, mainly directed inward at himself because he seemed as good a target as any. He had spent a night tossing and turning, woken by fragmented dreams—a staircase, a ship, but always alone. The loss of Roger and Nate had awakened some pitiful, childish part of himself, a voice that told him he would always be abandoned, always sent away. It wasn't true, he knew this. It was the story his childish mind had invented to make sense of events that held no reason, but it had taken root in his mind like an oft-repeated fable, and it had shaped his life. The loss of both Roger and Nate, and in such a short span of time, felt like the workings of a vengeful fate.

The safest course of action was to hew closely to the rules of friendship he and Verity had tacitly established: no touching, no lingering glances, no giving voice to feelings better left ignored. They could continue on that path indefinitely. It might not be what either of them wanted in this moment, but in the long run it would be best.

He remembered Verity's face as he turned her away, baffled and hurt. If he were a different man he could have brought her to bed. Instead he had spent the night cold and alone, his sleep interrupted by dreams of fear and loss.

By God, he didn't want to live like that. He wanted to take a risk, to prove to himself that his existence didn't need to be small and self-contained. He thought of how Verity had touched him and looked at him. It seemed to him the height of madness to meekly love someone from afar when you actually lived under the same roof. He wanted to mean something to somebody. But he couldn't without risking ending up with nothing and nobody at all.

So it was that he all but stormed into the conservatory, more than ready to lose himself in the intricacies of foliage and Lady Caroline's tales of far-off lands that neither of them would ever set eyes on. Lady Caroline turned to greet him, took one look at his face, and dropped a potted orchid.

Before Ash could stoop to pick up the remnants of the plant from the mess of clay shards and soil, two servants materialized seemingly out of thin air, one with a dust basin and broom and the other carrying a clay pot. So it was that he had no excuse to avoid the look of barely contained fright on the lady's face as he greeted her. "Are you quite all right, ma'am?" he asked as soon as the servants left. "If I can be of any assistance, you need only ask."

She remained silent, giving him only a quick shake of

her head. But as he sat down to work, he felt her eyes on him, curious and searching. He sensed that she was working herself up to speech.

"Are you quite certain," she asked after several moments of silence, "that you aren't distantly connected to the Talbots? When you walked into the room you looked so much like my brother."

Frustrated, Ash put down his pen. He was too unpracticed in the art of self-deception to deny the possibility that he was indeed the natural child of a Talbot servant and her master. He was certainly somebody's natural child, and when he looked at Lady Caroline, he saw the same cleft chin and strong nose that he saw in his own reflection. When he considered the eerie familiarity of this house, he thought it possible that he might have lived in it for some time before being sent to his succession of foster homes. While it would be unusual for a servant to rear her own child in her employer's home, perhaps one extra child would go unnoticed in a household as large as this one. But his blood family had ceased to matter to him the moment they had cast him off. He felt it was only right to pay as little regard for his antecedents as they had paid him.

"My lady, if you say I look like I have Talbot blood in my veins, then I have no doubt you're entirely in the right. If you have a relative you suspect of siring bastards, then I daresay he's my father." He realized too late that he had spoken too coarsely. "I apologize for my language, but not for the sentiment."

"Indeed, there is nothing to apologize for. Talbots are no

strangers to vice. However, the fact that you are alive and in good health suggests that you were well provided for in your early years. That doesn't sound in the least like something a man of my family would do. A Talbot man would be much more likely to leave one of his by-blows to die of exposure on a hillside. I suppose I ought to apologize for suggesting that you might be a Talbot, after having spoken so badly of them."

"My lady, you are yourself a Talbot and I don't see any evidence of evildoing on your part. I doubt you would leave a child to die of exposure." It was meant as a jest, but the lady's face drained of color.

"Indeed. I would not let a child die," she said in a faint voice.

Ash worried he had said something to recall a bad experience to the lady's mind, and scrambled to find a way to make it right. But before he could come up with a suitable response, she stepped towards him.

"Do you have scar on your forearm, Mr. Ashby? It would be your left arm, halfway between the wrist and elbow." She reached out to him, as if she meant to check for herself, but then arrested the motion. Ash was already on his feet, stepping back from the woman's hand as if it were a viper. "I beg your pardon," she said, blushing fiercely. "That was terribly inappropriate of me."

But as he looked at her outstretched hand, he saw a ring of bruises around her wrist, of the sort he imagined might be caused by a large hand gripping her. "I find it hard to believe that you would wish to have another Talbot man in proximity to you," he said, trying to make his voice gentle. "They do not seem to do you much good."

"They don't do anyone any good whatsoever," she said, tucking her hands behind her back when she saw that Ash had observed her discolored wrists. "I mitigate the harm as well as I can, which sometimes isn't very well at all." She spoke these last words with something like grief, her gaze not moving from his face.

"You'll understand that even if I am the natural child of some connection of yours, I don't especially wish to dwell on it, nor do I wish to make the acquaintance of people who threw me away."

"Thrown away. You misunderstand—" Lady Caroline went pale. "I beg your pardon. I just thought—family is good to have."

It wasn't until he was halfway home that Ash realized she might have been talking about her own wish for family—family that didn't leave bruises on her arms or cause her to hide within her own home. If he were a different sort of person he might have been able to negotiate some kind of relationship with this family that could be his. He might be able to provide some comfort to this woman who, despite her fine clothes and grand house, seemed more alone than Ash.

Verity was inspecting the proofs for the November issue of the *Ladies' Register* when a woman entered the shop. She had a black velvet cloak pulled over her head and a fur muff covering her hands. At a glance, Verity could tell that this was not the sort of customer they usually got. But then the girl flung off her hood. It was Amelia Allenby, looking vaguely dismayed to see Verity.

"Oh!" Amelia said, standing in the shop door. "You never work behind the counter."

"Well, what with Nate being—" Verity clapped a hand to her forehead. "Oh, Amelia, I ought to have sent word."

The girl looked stricken. "Is he in prison?"

"No, God no." Verity explained Nate's departure and watched the girl's open countenance progress from surprise to relief to, finally, what seemed to be mild consternation.

"Your brother certainly doesn't make things easy," Amelia said.

This was such an understatement that Verity couldn't hold back a laugh. "You don't know the half of it," she said. But why did Amelia speak as if she were personally aggrieved by Nate's behavior? In fact, what was Amelia even doing here in the first place? "I thought you weren't supposed to come here," she pointed out.

"That was to keep me away from Nate. If he isn't here, then it hardly matters."

Verity folded her arms across her chest. "But you came to see him."

"Trifling details," Amelia said breezily. "Oh, is that the second issue of the *Ladies' Register* you have there? We've dearly been looking forward to it."

Verity's eyes narrowed. Could it be that Amelia had arrived for some kind of assignation with Nate? Or Charlie, even? "Amelia, are you and Nate—"

"Stop, you sound like Mama. She thinks I have a *tendre* for your brother. She'll be over the moon to discover he's at a safe distance from me."

"You wouldn't be the first person who did," she said carefully.

"I'm exceptionally fond of your brother, and of you and Mr. Ashby. You're all so clever and quick-witted and I enjoy your company very much. And your brother is handsome, no question. But Mama thinks that means I want to elope with him. You know Mama, she thinks every young lady will drift helplessly towards an amorous misadventure if given half a chance."

"Well," Verity said, striving for delicacy, "that may be due to the fact that this is precisely what she did at your age." Portia had been very young indeed when she met Amelia's father.

"Truly, though, I don't even want to kiss Nate or anybody else. I just like to look at him and listen to him. It's envy, not romance."

"Envy?" Verity repeated, gazing pointedly at Amelia's velvet cloak.

"Imagine being able to do exactly as you please. I know that sounds childish, when there might well have been dire consequences for him, which is why he's on a ship at the moment. But he's a man, and, well, not a gentleman. He doesn't need to stand on ceremony. Whereas I feel like a prize pony. Every word I say and every step I take is judged, sometimes right in front of my face. I do feel bad for Mama. She has such a poor horse to show."

"Oh, Amelia." Not for the first time, Verity wondered if Portia had been thinking quite clearly in bringing up her girls the way she had. Amelia had all the burdens of gentility with none of the security and none of the status. Verity could at least fend for herself. She did not think she could stand a single day in Amelia's shoes, being judged and found wanting by people with money and titles—the very group she held responsible for most of what ailed the nation. Well, Verity could endure a day, but that day would end with her throwing her drink in somebody's face and then going back to her normal life. Because Verity had work; she could take care of herself. Amelia's future was dependent on the approval of people she did not respect or care for.

"In any event," Amelia went on, waving an airy hand. "I'll miss your brother terribly and I'll likely convince myself he's my lost love the next time I'm feeling dramatic, but I have to agree with you that he can't go on like this, risking arrest and throwing your lives into chaos. I'll pretend to be devastated so Mama thinks my life is more interesting than it really is, and so she'll have the satisfaction of thinking a crisis has been averted."

"Does she even know you're here?"

"No. The coachman is pretending not to notice that I'm at a bookshop instead of the milliner, and my maid is quite charmingly bribable. I only meant to duck in." Her brow furrowed. "But if Nate isn't here, I'm faced with a problem," she murmured.

"Are you? Are you quite certain this wasn't mean to be a, ah, rendezvous, Amelia?"

"Oh, never mind!" Amelia assured her with patently false brightness. "Here," she said, dropping sixpence on the counter. "I'll take a copy of the *Ladies' Register.* We laughed so hard when we read the last issue that Lizzie was nearly sick and Mama had tears coming down her face."

Verity had been partly responsible for hundreds of issues of the *Register,* but the *Ladies' Register* was the first publication she had managed entirely on her own and she felt proud beyond all measure. "It's only the proofs, not a proper copy," Verity protested, but Amelia insisted it did not matter, and shoved the stack of papers into her muff, which seemed to already contain quite a collection of other papers.

"Send Mr. Ashby my regards!" Amelia called, already whisking out the door before Verity could ask why she had really come.

The weather obliged in providing a melancholy backdrop that perfectly suited Verity's mood. The sky was a dirty shade of gray and there was a layer of fog seeping into the cracks between buildings and leeching the city of all its color. As she looked out the shop window, her view was a study in gray and brown. Verity adjusted her shawl around her shoulders.

She heard the door to the back room open and out of the corner of her eye saw a person approach. Without turning her head she knew that it was Ash. It wasn't any particular scent of his or a way he moved, just the way his body seemed to fit beside hers even without touching.

"Brought you some tea," he said, putting a cup down on the counter.

"Thank you," she said. "I suppose you don't despise me enough to make me go without tea."

"Despise you?"

"Despise, detest, resent, revile. Take your pick."

"Plum," he said in a voice that somehow managed to make itself heard over the noise, "are you suffering from some kind of affliction?" He was facing her now, but she didn't return his gaze, instead keeping her attention on the fog outside the shop window.

"Maybe that's the explanation for my wickedness," she said. "An affliction. Let's go with that."

"Your—What maggots have got into your brain to make you think I despise you?"

"You've been avoiding me all week, ever since Nate left. You plainly disapprove."

"I don't disapprove of a single thing you've ever done in your life, Plum." He shook his head, as if perplexed. "I don't think I could." There was something dark and needy in his voice that made her look directly at him. The strong planes of his face were even starker in the flickering candlelight, and his dark eyes gleamed with intent. "If you hadn't persuaded Nate to go in the way you did, I don't think I would have known a moment's peace. Damn it, Plum, I miss your brother. I think England is a better place with him on its shores. But there was no way I was going to stand idly by while he threw his life away and yours into the bargain."

"Then why haven't you talked to me?" Her voice sounded

small and weak and she hated it. "I've been all alone for days now." This was so close to asking—begging, even—for help, for reassurance, that she felt small and weak even speaking the words. She needed to hear it, though, needed proof that she was not the only one in over her head. She couldn't make herself speak the words aloud, so she squeezed his arm, willing him to answer the question she could not ask.

She heard his breath catch. "You know perfectly well," he said, as if he had heard her thoughts. But he must have seen the uncertainty in her expression. In a voice that was nearly a growl, he said, "I see you do not." The next thing she knew he had bolted the shop door and slipped his arm into hers, not a gentlemanly offer of support so much as a means of more or less dragging her from the room. "This way. We're not having this conversation for an audience." He led her out of the shop and up to her study. Ash kicked the door shut behind them and they were alone in the dark, his mouth on hers, his body caging her against the wall. The room was cold and the wall was damp against her back, but he was a wall of heat in front of her, around her, everywhere she needed him to be. And his mouth—he was kissing her as if he were running out of time, as if there were a very serious kiss shortage and reasonable people had to set about stockpiling. She contemplated rucking up her skirts and seeing what they could do against the closed door, fully dressed.

He paused only enough to speak. "You matter more to me than anything in the world and you fucking know it. And it won't do us a penny's worth of good. It simply won't do."

But he spoke the words against her mouth, his lips moving against her own.

She kissed him again, then pulled away just enough to speak. "You're wrong. I've known you for ages and you've never been as wrong as you are now." Another kiss, and this time she nipped at his lower lip. He groaned.

All that mattered was the taste of tea on his lips, the pressure of his hands on her waist, the way their bodies and their lives fit together and made her forget everything else. She wrapped a leg around his waist at the same time he got his hands under her bottom and lifted her, pressing the hard length of his arousal against her, kissing her with a rhythm that suggested something more than kisses.

"Please," she said, not sure what she was asking for. "Ash."

He groaned and pulled away, the cold air rushing in between them. "We can't. I can't." He let out a bitter laugh that she didn't understand. "I certainly can't."

"If you're worried about my virtue I assure that's not of the least concern. I don't expect—"

"I don't give a damn about your virtue. I can't explain, Verity," he said with a mix of frustration and sorrow, and left her alone in the cold dark room.

Chapter Eight

The door to Ash's studio was closed, so Verity took a deep breath and straightened her back before knocking. For the two days since their last encounter, they had been behaving towards one another with exaggerated cordiality, carefully preserving a respectable distance between their bodies and hewing to only the most harmless conversational topics. If this was what a couple of kisses did to a friendship, then Verity was staunchly opposed to kissing. Or she would at least act like she was. Because however delightful those moments in Ash's arms had been, nothing was worth having her friendship with Ash reduced to mere civility.

Only when she heard footsteps approaching the door did she think to adjust her skirts or check her hair, and a quick glance at the former and pat of the latter confirmed that she was all askew, but there was nothing to do about it now. And besides, she was not here to seduce Ash with her elegance. The thought of it made her smile—if Ash required elegance, he would not have kissed her in the first place.

The door opened, and Ash stood there in shirtsleeves. Before he could open his mouth to say something blandly polite, Verity blurted out, "I thought you might like to go to the chophouse. I finished the last of the bread at breakfast and forgot to buy more so it's the chophouse or a slow starvation, your choice." She paused to take a breath. "My treat."

Ash blinked. "The chophouse it is, then. Let me get on a clean shirt." He gestured to a few ink stains on the white linen.

"Oh don't. I'm probably covered with ink myself. In fact, you ought to do something about your hair. Make it messier." She pulled at the strand that had come loose from its pin. "That way we match."

Ash gave her the sort of laugh that was really just a smile and an exhale. She felt her cheeks heat. Forced awkward friendliness was even worse than forced awkward civility and Verity wanted to run back down the stairs and hide in her study. "I'm covered in cat hair," he said. "If that helps."

"That'll have to do," she said with the air of making a great concession. "I'm impressed that you've used your manly wiles to get the cat to come close enough to leave hair on you."

"I haven't. She just likes to sit on all my furniture when I'm out. When I'm in, she perches on the bookcase and stares at me." Sure enough, there was the cat, staring at them from atop the bookcase with an expression of concentrated malevolence. "I think she's making up her mind whether to murder me or let me pet her. My strategy is to pretend that I haven't noticed that she's there. I think she's a bit depressed about finding my rooms more comfortable than the street this autumn and consoles herself by acting like we're enemies."

"A sound plan."

"All right," he said, and slipped into his coat. "Chophouse or oyster room?"

"Ooh, oysters."

Ash shrugged into his coat while Verity attempted to wrangle her hair into a pin. "No matter how many pins I use in the morning, it's all over my shoulders by the afternoon. I could use five hundred pins with quite the same result. I think my hair simply opposes order. It's anarchical."

"It's not all your hair," Ash said, digging through his pockets. "Just that one strand. It's the Jacobin wing." He held out a hairpin.

"When did you start carrying those in your pocket?" she asked, recalling that this was not the first time he had produced a timely hairpin.

A very faint blush darkened Ash's cheekbones and Verity felt her lips curl upward in response. "I find them all over the house," he said. "You ought to consider what conditions you're subjecting your hairpins to if they'd rather plummet to their death than work for you. Here," he said, lifting a loose tendril of hair. "You expect your pins to do the work of subjugating the masses. It's oppression. Your hair clearly wants to be free."

"I think you've lost track of which party is the oppressed working class—the pins or my hair."

"Both, Plum," he said, and leaned close to pin the loose strand of hair in place. "There. That'll do."

She expected him to step back, but he stayed where he was, one hand still on the side of her head, his expression grave but wanting. This, she realized, was not about her. Whatever had stopped him from kissing her again had nothing to do with the strength of his feelings for her. He wanted to, body and soul. And he knew she wanted the same. But he was holding back, for whatever reason, and she needed to respect that. She needed to let him know that she was his friend, kisses or no. For God's sake, he had lost two-thirds of his closest friends in the past month alone; the least she could do was assure him that he wasn't going to lose her, no matter what.

"Come, Ash," she said, stepping back and flashing him as bright a smile as she could. "Say good-night to your surly cat and let's go out to supper."

"Can't do that," Ash stage-whispered. "Then she'll know we've noticed she's there."

"Silly me."

The oyster room was crowded with people having supper before heading to the theater, so Ash and Verity had to make do with a small table in a dark corner.

"Do you think Nate could have written it?" she asked without preamble, trusting Ash to know she referred to the Perkin Warbeck book. "There are parts where the handwriting is terribly like his. And since he left, my letters to the writer have gone unanswered."

"Ordinarily I'd say your brother is capable of anything, but perhaps not writing a three-volume novel that more or less upholds hereditary rule. All bad handwriting has a way of looking the same. However . . ." He tapped his fingers on the white linen table cloth. "He may have written the explicit scenes. I ought to have recognized his writing myself."

"Why wouldn't he have just told me?"

"Presumably because you would have insisted on knowing who wrote the rest of the book. And say what you will about Nate, but he's not one to spill another person's secrets."

She held up her glass of wine and he tapped his against it in a silent salute to Nate.

After they had eaten and there was nothing left on the table but dishes of empty oyster shells, and the main room had more or less cleared out except for a handful of men and some women Verity supposed were prostitutes or courtesans, Ash cleared his throat. "Lady Caroline Talbot thinks I'm her brother's natural son. She hasn't said it in so many words, but she's hinted strongly."

"Is this some odd fancy of hers?" she asked hopefully, because from the look on Ash's face he did not think being related to his lady botanist would be a good thing.

"No," he said, with a grim shake of his head. "I'm afraid not. I keep thinking I ought to be glad to have blood family. To know where I came from. But I'm really not."

She slid her hand across the table and took his. "You don't need to be."

"I wish I had never gone there. I feel like fate or God took away Roger and Nate and instead gave me these awful people. Well, she's not awful. But that house." He visibly shuddered.

"You don't need to go back. It doesn't matter that you might be related to them. In fact, that's all the more reason to wash your hands of them, since they hardly did right by you."

"But that's just it. She didn't cast me off. She's hardly ten years older than us. And—" He picked up his wineglass, saw that it was empty, and grimaced. Verity shoved her still-full glass across the table at him and he promptly downed it. "Her brother—my father?—hurts her. I saw the bruises. And her father is either an invalid or a recluse. Plum, there's an actual duke lurking in the attics while his son rampages about. I don't think she has any family that isn't demonstrably horrible. And I don't have any family at all, so it seems I ought to at least try to be her family."

She squeezed his hand hard. "You do have a family. And, look, Ash, you aren't getting rid of me. I don't have any lung conditions and I'm not in any danger of needing to flee the country to avoid criminal charges. You're stuck with me. Understand?" He nodded but she squeezed his hand harder and lowered her voice. "It doesn't matter if we don't go to bed together. That's a minor detail." That was a lie, but she'd make it the truth if it was what Ash needed. "You're my friend and I'm yours and that's how it's going to be, no matter what."

He looked relieved, and she wondered how badly she had managed their friendship if he could have cause to doubt it. But he squeezed her hand back.

Feeling thoroughly farcical, Ash pulled the brim of his hat lower over his forehead. He arrived early at Cavendish Square and positioned himself behind a tree in the park across the street. If Lady Caroline timed Ash's visits to coincide with the absence of her brother—Lord Montagu, Ash had learned—then it stood to reason that one might catch a glimpse of the man leaving the front door of Arundel House sometime after ten. He didn't have to wait long. At half past ten the door was flung open by a footman and out came a tall man in a many-caped greatcoat. Even from Ash's vantage point of several yards away, he could see that Lord Montagu had the same straight nose and firm jaw as his sister, the same dark hair, the same eyebrows that cut like slashes across the face.

This, Ash thought grimly, was how he would look in a few decades. There was no denying the family resemblance. It had been one thing to see his features echoed in the face of a woman and to understand that there was probably some family connection between them. But recognizing those same features on a man, a man of approximately his own size and build no less, he could no longer ignore the significance of the connection. This man, who was presently shouting at his coachman, this man who left bruises on the wrists of his sister, was perhaps his own father. It was not a welcome thought. Ash far preferred to imagine that he had no family at all.

After the carriage was out of sight, Ash crossed the street and knocked on the door as usual. The footman, who a moment before had been pale and trembling, was now all calm efficiency as he sought his mistress.

"I saw Lord Montagu," he said after Lady Caroline had presented him with today's specimen.

"Did he come see you?" the lady asked, leaning forward urgently.

"I—no, why would he do that?" Ash responded in confusion. "I watched him leave from across the street." He was not going to admit that he had been hiding behind a tree like a character in a pantomime.

"I see." She sagged in relief. "Don't do that again. I beg of you. He mustn't catch sight of you. Please don't arrive before a quarter past eleven. In fact, perhaps you shouldn't come around at all. It was foolish of me to even consider it after realizing . . ." Her voice trailed off.

"Does he resent the time you spend on your plants and your studies so very much?" he asked, trying to make sense of Lady Caroline's distress. "Or is it that he wouldn't want you to spend time with a man?"

"Oh, both of those things, certainly. But also—" She shook her head. "I can't explain. He's used to getting his own way, and when he doesn't, he is quick to assign blame elsewhere. He blamed his wife for a good many things, and after she died, he found it convenient to transfer that blame to me."

She spoke with a cool, neutral tone, but her hands shook as she turned over the pages of the herbarium. The purple half-moons that were always beneath her eyes seemed darker than they had the previous week. She looked up and caught his eye. He wasn't certain what she saw there, but when she spoke it was in a tone of resolve. "Mr. Ashby, do you have a scar on your left forearm? You didn't answer me last week."

Ash sighed. Lady Caroline spent her days in obvious terror of her brother and literally tiptoeing around her father; it was only natural for her to wish she had a family member who did not make her quake with fear. She might be looking for stray family members, but Ash was not. He had surrounded himself with exactly who he pleased, and had created a sort of secondhand family. He did not want or need any connection with the people who had abandoned him. "I agree that there's a family resemblance," he said as gently as he could. "It seems likely that I'm an illegitimate relation of yours. But I don't seek to profit from the connection, I assure you." He let his gaze stray meaningfully to her wrists, where beneath the lace of her sleeves, traces of the bruises her brother left still lingered. "And I know it isn't my place to say so, but Lord Montagu would perhaps retaliate against you if he knew you had sought out a baseborn relation. I would hate to be the cause of any harm to you."

Something about this must have been dreadfully amusing, because she let out a burst of stunned laughter. "No, no, you quite misunderstand. Scar or no scar, Mr. Ashby?"

Ash tried to ignore her, tried to ignore the spot on his arm that seemed to pulse with awareness. He dipped his pen in the inkwell and drew a faint line on the page, but the ink blotted, marring the paper. There would be no drawing today, he already knew that. And he would not return to this house, to this woman whose life was so fraught that she sought ghosts from the past. He glanced at the delicate cup-like flowers of the specimen he would never get a chance to draw. *Primula auricula*, Lady Caroline's feathered handwriting neatly stated; this specimen had traveled from high in the Apennines. He would miss coming here, miss hearing tales of flowers that bloomed in lands he would never visit.

"Fine," Ash said, laying down his pen. He might as well get this over with, figure out how he was connected to this lot. Then Lady Caroline would perhaps have some peace of mind, and he could walk away with a clear conscience. "Before I give you an answer, I want to know who you believe me to be." His mind snagged on that. He knew who he was and where he belonged, and nothing this woman could say would alter that. He cleared his throat. "Or, rather, who you believe has a scar on his left forearm. I think you could tell me that in the spirit of fairness."

"Fair," she repeated with a little laugh. "Would that fairness entered into the question of who belonged to this family." She passed a hand over her eyes. "My eldest brother died over twenty years ago. He left a son. That child suffered a fall when he was four years old, severely breaking his arm. I believe it is called an open fracture, and there is no question but that it would have left a scar. The last time I saw the child was only hours after his injury."

Ash did his best to brush off a memory of unguents and plasters, an arm burning hot as an oven. "What was that child's name?"

"James."

Ash let out a breath he hadn't realized he had been holding. He had half expected to hear a name that tugged at his memory the way the stairs, this garden, and Lady Caroline's face all persisted in doing. "I have never been called James."

Lady Caroline raised her eyebrows, but didn't ask precisely

what other names Ash had been known by, which was fortunate because Ash couldn't have told her. He suspected he had repeatedly been removed from homes immediately after a seizure, when his memory was shot through with holes, with the result that the people at his next lodging called him whatever they pleased. The only reason John Ashby stuck was that it was under this name that he was sent to school.

"Neither was he," Lady Caroline said. "We called him—"

"Don't." He didn't want to know. He didn't want to risk finding out that all along he had a true name, a true identity that had been thrown away as surely as he had been.

"Do you have the scar, Mr. Ashby?" she whispered. "I quite understand if you'd prefer not to have anything to do with this family. Truly, I sympathize. But my father is very old and infirm, and he doted on y—on his grandson, and—"

"Please," he said, holding his hand up to stop her from going on. Ash's head was spinning and he didn't know how to make sense of half her words. A duke doting on a bastard grandchild? A child who had been reared in the duke's own household for the first years of his life?

"You don't know what this means," she insisted.

"It means there's yet another bastard sired by a profligate nobleman." It was a story that repeated itself every day across all the continents of the world. "And that he was cast aside to make his way in a world that treats bastards unkindly. I did well for myself despite your family's treatment of me, and I don't wish to be claimed now."

"Oh, no," Lady Caroline said, shaking her head. "You quite misunderstand."

"I think I understand perfectly well," he said, trying to mask his impatience.

"My brother married your mother."

Ash blinked. "I'm sorry—"

"Your mother was Lady Eleanor Carstairs, the youngest daughter of the Earl of Staffordshire," she added, as if this would clear things up. "She died when you were an infant. Your father died shortly thereafter."

Ash gripped the edges of the table. "You're telling me that I was legitimate?" Nothing, nothing at all, of the early part of his life, what little he knew of it, made sense if he were legitimate. If he hadn't been a cast-off baseborn child, then he didn't know who he was. And then, all at once, the rest of the lady's words slotted into place. "If my father was your eldest brother, that makes me . . ." Before the words had quite left his mouth, the swirling mass of confusion in his mind coalesced into something that took an appalling shape. "No, certainly not." He rose to his feet and stepped back from her, his chair squeaking loudly against the conservatory floor. "I'm not getting caught up in this. I'm going home, and I won't return here." He was halfway to the garden door. His pen and ink remained on the table and he wasn't going back to get them. He took another step. "If anyone ever asks, I'll deny this entire conversation."

"Understandable. But before you do that, you perhaps will consider that you are the only thing standing between my brother and a dukedom. With that title will come a good deal of power and money and I know to a certainty that he'll use both to do harm."

His hand was on the door; all he had to do was push it open and walk through. But even as he felt the cool brass of the handle he knew he couldn't. Lady Caroline was asking for his help. Help only he could provide. And Ash—whoever he was—wasn't someone who could turn down a request for aid. He turned around, still leaning against the closed door.

"How came I to be sent away?" There were likely a dozen other questions he ought to be asking but that was all he could think of: why had he been sent away that first time, the abandonment that set in motion all the subsequent abandonments. The patchwork of memories that came before Roger, the constant disorientation, the sense of recovering from each seizure in a new and foreign place—none of that made sense if he had been the legitimate heir to a dukedom.

"That was entirely my doing, I'm afraid." He stared at her. "You told me once that you didn't think I would leave a child to die. After your father—my elder brother—died, you were all that stood between my other brother and a title. You survived the fall down the stairs but I was afraid you wouldn't survive the next attempt. I had no choice but to send you away."

"Attempt," Ash repeated, not wanting her words to mean what he thought they might.

"Attempt on your life. I saw him push you down the stairs with my own eyes."

Ash sat back down and buried his face in his hands. His first thought was to go home and tell Verity that his life had taken a turn that was ripped from one of the gothic novels she occasionally published—a lost heir, a wicked uncle, a dying duke. It struck him that this would likely be the last conversation he would have with Verity—Verity Plum, confirmed radical, would not rub shoulders with the heir to a dukedom. And whatever life was like for a duke, or a duke-in-waiting, or whatever he was, it likely did not entail illustrating dirty books and living in a ramshackle house in Holywell Street. He was going to lose Verity no matter what. He was going to lose everything that made him who he was.

"I planned to bring you back," she continued, "once I was of age or married to someone with enough power to help me. But I had underestimated how easy it is for a child to slip through the cracks. There was simply no trace of you when I went to look. I am terribly sorry, and there is nothing I can say or do to make that right. In my defense I was sixteen, and perhaps not as clever as I thought I was. It remains the greatest regret of my life."

He didn't know if it was his imagination or the whisper of a memory, but he thought he could picture a younger Lady Caroline, equally worried, but bolder, less timid. She couldn't have been more than fifteen. If this entire business seemed the scheme of a fanciful child, perhaps that was because it had been. "If you are correct, then it seems that you saved my life, ma'am. I thank you."

"Piffle. I made a poor fist of the entire operation," she said, as if referring to bungling the repotting of an orchid, and not foiling her brother's murder plot. He supposed that, living the life she led, murderous brothers and potted orchids featured equally.

"Will your brother not revenge himself upon you when he finds out that you mean to unseat him?"

She let out a nervous breath of laughter. "He tried to murder a child of four years old. Come now, Mr. Ashby. Or, Lord Montagu, I ought to say." His stomach turned at hearing her brother's title applied to him. "You know well that he'll try to harm me one way or the other. I only ask if you'll help me stop him from doing more harm."

Ash had the sense of his old, self-constructed family crumbling away, leaving him only with those who had cast him out to begin with.

"I have one condition," he said. "I need time. A month." A month wouldn't be enough, not nearly enough, to get used to the idea that he might be the person Lady Caroline thought he was, to assimilate all that meant. And it wouldn't be enough time to bid farewell to the life he thought was his own. But he could spend that month living without the fear of losing more people, because that—if Lady Caroline was correct—was now all but a certainty. He would lose Verity, he would lose his work and his life. He could spend a month living as a man with nothing to lose.

Chapter Nine

Verity looked up from cutting a new nib to find Ash leaning against the doorway to her office, feigning nonchalance. That was his tell. Verity hadn't lost a single hand of cards to him since discovering that Ash's only way of dissembling was to feign absolute indifference to things that he considered greatly important.

"I brought you something," he said when she beckoned him to enter. He placed a few items on her desk and sat in his usual chair, crossing his legs languidly. If Verity hadn't known better, she'd have thought he was bored, come to dismiss a tiresome errand.

"A bottle of wine and a stack of explicit illustrations," she said, surveying Ash's offerings. "Two of my favorite things. And"—she peered inside a paper-wrapped parcel he placed on her desk—" a wedge of cheddar. Three of my favorite things, then. Thank you. To what do I owe these earthly delights?"

"It's a celebration. I saw you've sold out of the *Ladies' Register* again."

She grinned. The second issue had been easier to compile than the first—a few letters requesting advice, a theater review, and a scary story. The third issue could be devoted almost entirely to answering correspondence, and she was looking forward to it with something like relish. "Will you join me, or am I meant to celebrate in solitude?"

He tsked. "Be serious, Plum. There's far too much cheese for you to eat on your own."

"How little you know me," she said mournfully. This was a seduction. She was being seduced with cheese and lewd drawings and she could not be happier about it. From the top drawer of her desk she removed a corkscrew and a knife and passed the latter to Ash so he could pare the cheese while she opened the wine.

"I noticed you're answering the letters under your own name." Ash slid a piece of cheese to her as she took a pull from the bottle and handed it to him.

"I figured Verity Plum already sounds enough like someone's nom de plume, so might as well take advantage of it." For the first issue, she had answered the letters anonymously. For the second, she hadn't bothered. "The truth is that I never put my name on the *Register*. First because it was Nate and my father's, and later because I didn't want to go to prison. And it never felt necessary. Everyone knows I ran the *Register* from the week my father died." She supposed she might sound arrogant, but it was the simple truth, and to Ash she could own it. Even with Nate in the middle of the Atlantic Ocean, she was having surprisingly little difficulty managing the business on her own. "But with the *Ladies' Register*, it's mine and I want to put my name all over it."

"You should be proud."

"I am." For a moment there was no sound but the distant murmur from the street below. Nan had left, the shop was closed, and the men in the print room had finished for the day. Ash and Verity were alone in the house. She took the bottle from his hand and drank, feeling his gaze on her. When she put the bottle down he was still looking at her, not bothering to conceal it. She looked back. He raised an eyebrow. She gave him what she knew to be an especially feral smile.

"Plum," he said. Not warningly, but with intent.

"My cards are on the table, Ash. Every last one of them. You can play yours however you like and there's no losing."

Ash's mouth went dry. She was making this easy for him, he knew that, but the sight of her, wine bottle in hand, mouth quirked up in half a smile, was more than he could face with equanimity. But if he let her see how invested he was in this—hell, if he let himself see it, if for even half a minute he acknowledged to himself how badly he wanted this, and how horrible everything was going to be when it was over—then he didn't know how he was meant to go on.

He didn't know whether he was acting on false pretenses. If he were heir to a dukedom—and he was filled with an odd sense of mortification at the thought, as if he had done something shameful and was waiting for his disgrace to become public knowledge—then he owed that information to a woman he planned to . . . court. But this was no common courtship: Verity didn't want a husband. Maybe, though. Maybe she would change her mind. Maybe she could see a way forward with him even though he wasn't who she thought, wasn't even who *he* had thought. Maybe after seeing how good they could be together, she'd agree to be with him anyway. She was his best, his closest, his dearest friend. Maybe she could accept him despite everything. And when he thought of the child who had been sent from place to place, without a name or a home or even a sense of who he was, he wanted to believe more than anything that she would.

So he raised one finger and beckoned her over, praying to any gods that might be watching that she'd understand all of what he couldn't say, understand that he was hanging on by the fingernails.

She pushed out of her chair and stood before him, one hand on her hip and an oddly serious expression on her face. He swallowed.

"Is this to be a lecture?" he asked, looking up at her. The last bits of his composure were in tattered shreds and he could hear the urgency in his own voice. "Teach me, Plum."

She settled in his lap, the soft curve of her breasts so close to his face, the scent of her soap and books and just *Verity* filling his senses. "I'm trying to decide what to do."

"Ah." She loosened his cravat, her fingers deft and sure against his throat. "For the record, Plum, I can't see that

I'd object to anything you might choose. I'm feeling—" he groaned as she settled further into his lap, pressing against him "—very amenable." She rocked into him, as if to show him that she knew exactly how amenable he was, and, really, at this proximity there could be no mistaking the matter. He bit back a groan and she made a soft shushing sound. She took hold of his cravat and gave it a tug, not hard enough to actually pull him near, but quite hard enough to make his prick take an avid interest in the proceedings. Then, still holding him fast, she leaned forward and brushed her lips against his as if it were the merest trifle, as if it weren't the single most important event to have happened in months, years, of his life.

He realized that he was going to have to perform some kind of conversion, as if from a foreign currency, where kisses had an entirely different value to Verity than they did to him. It was fine, he told himself. He had a month to wind up his affairs, to do what it took to bid farewell to his old life; he had thirty days to engrave a handful of plates and to get his fill of Verity. The other night in the oyster room she had told him that this—his hands on her, her lips on his, the way their bodies felt pressed together—was something she could take or leave. And that was for the best—it meant that when their month was up, she'd be unharmed. But it was proof that she had a totally different relationship to these things than he did. His main goal at the moment was to avoid dismaying her or embarrassing himself with undue displays of fervor. She needed him to provide a pleasant distraction or to chase away her cares and burdens; he needed her as a plant needed sunlight. Nothing was wrong with that disparity. What mattered was that he never let her know.

She nipped his lower lip and he thought he might faint.

"Wait," he breathed. "Slow."

She gentled her kisses and then pulled away. "Is this all right?"

He moved his hips so she could feel his hardness, biting the inside of his cheek to keep some semblance of calm. "More than all right." He slid his hands around her shoulder blades and started working open the buttons of her gown. She made a soft sound of satisfaction at the contact of his fingers on her back. He could not begin to understand how to get her out of her frock, so instead he rucked up the hem, seeking skin that way. She responded by hauling him close by the collar and giving him a punishing kiss. He had never allowed himself to imagine what this would be like, but when the thought crept unawares into his mind, it had never taken this form—Verity on top of him, manhandling him, having her way with him.

As he ran his hand up her leg, past the top of her stocking and over the soft skin of her thigh, his hand encountered nothing but bare skin. His hand progressed unimpeded up her leg until he was cupping her backside in one palm. "Plum," he managed. "I hate to be to the bearer of bad news, but your drawers seem to have gone missing."

She stopped kissing long enough to lean back and wrinkle her nose. "I don't wear drawers. Mother always said they were common."

Ash tried to assimilate the knowledge that Verity had

been wearing nothing under her shift for the past ten years, during each and every one of their meals and conversations. He was going to need to consider this in considerable detail in private, but for now he tried to look as if he had only a scholarly interest in her underpinnings. "Is that so? I'd have thought in that case you'd have worn a dozen pairs. All at once. Embroidered with *liberté, égalité—*"

She shut him up with a kiss. "You cannot mean to jest," she murmured into the skin of his jaw. "Are you always this unserious when you have your hand up a woman's petticoats?"

"One hundred percent of the time, Plum," he said in absolute honesty.

"Now I'm going to ask every woman I know about her drawers," she said, kissing the sensitive skin just under his jaw. He thought he might black out. "I will be known far and wide for my scholarly interest in drawers."

He gave her backside a firm pinch to silence her. She must have liked that because she took hold of his shoulders and pushed him firmly against the back of the chair, her hands greedily running over his arms and chest. He slid his hand between her legs, feeling the slick heat of her. She sighed and pushed against his palm, riding his hand. The entirety of his universe shrank to the place where he touched her, the rhythm of her hips, the sounds she made. "You'd better show me how you pleasure yourself," he said, trying for the tone one uses when buffing one's fingernails on one's lapels and instead landing on something like a dying man's prayer.

She leaned back and gazed at him, somehow managing

to look both dazed and arch. "What, *you're* not going to do it for me?"

"I fancy watching *you*. Indulge me, Plum."

"Well, then." She hitched her skirt up. Shameless. He loved her—he let himself form that thought and hold it for a full heartbeat before sending it away. He watched, enraptured, as she made little circles with one finger. He didn't know why he expected that she'd touch inside herself, but she didn't.

He tore his gaze away from where her fingers stroked between her legs and grinned at her. She met his eyes. "Well, you asked," she said.

"Perfect," he managed. "You're perfect, Verity." Her skin was glistening with wetness, though, and he needed to touch her. He slid his hand beside hers, not interfering with what she was doing, just stroking the folds of skin and damp curls beneath his fingertips.

"Yes," she said, guiding his fingers to her entrance. When he slid two fingers inside, she started rocking into his palm, and he thought he might come on the spot. All he could think of was how her slick heat would feel around his cock. He wanted desperately to unfasten his trousers, take himself in hand, do anything to ease the pressure. But he knew that if he did that, it would put paid to any hopes he had of watching Verity climax, and he wanted to see that very badly. He watched his fingers disappear inside her again and again, felt her clench around him, rising and falling on his hand as if she were riding him. Their fingers tangled and their hands bumped into one another, and it ought to have been clumsy and awkward but it was perfect.

"Plum," he said from between gritted teeth, "this is the best thing I've seen in my life." She clenched around his fingers. "Thought I ought to let you know."

With the hand that wasn't busy stroking herself, she cupped his head and gave him a hungry kiss.

"Oh," she murmured, pulling away. Her body went as taut as a bowstring and then she came apart in his arms, contracting around his fingers, soft moans on her lips.

"Christ, Plum, you utter fucking genius." He had no idea why that of all things was the praise that came to him, but it was true, and it was probably a minor miracle that he said anything intelligible at all, his entire mind being occupied with the alarming state of his cock.

Her eyes were shut, her lips parted, and she collapsed onto his shoulder. He slid his fingers out of her—they had been inside Verity's body, what a world—and wiped them on his trousers.

"Let me touch you," she said.

"Please," he managed. There ensued a flurry of tussling and hand swatting over who got to unfasten Ash's trousers. Verity prevailed.

"I've always wanted to see how these things worked," she mused as she wrapped her hand around him.

"I'm happy to oblige," he said "I'm afraid you'd better be a quick study, because you've got about three strokes before the lesson concludes."

She gave a happy, throaty laugh and gave him a slow stroke. "I want to put it in my mouth."

If she kept talking like that, he wasn't even going to last three strokes, so he pulled her close, thrusting into her fist, imagining it was the tight heat inside her. He kissed her for a moment, a disorganized tangle of tongues and teeth. "I'm going to—"

"Wait, I want to see." She sat back and watched him, and as the pleasure took over his body, all he could see was Verity watching him, her hand on his cock, her lip between her teeth, his entire heart under the sole of her shoe, if that was what she chose.

He took a few ragged breaths and gave her the handkerchief from his trouser pocket. After she made use of it he half expected her to sit at her desk and get to work now that they had concluded their business. But she collapsed on top of him, soft and sleepy. He let himself run his fingers through her disordered hair. When she nestled her face into his neck, he kissed her forehead. *Thirty days,* he thought. *We can have this for thirty days.*

"You smell good," she murmured. "You feel good too. This is the best idea we've ever had."

He hoped she wasn't wrong.

Chapter Ten

Ash woke with a gasp, his heart pounding and his sheets soaked in sweat. He had dreamed again of Arundel House, of sweeping stairs and marble floors. Of falling. It was an old dream, one that sometimes visited him nightly and other times waited years to reappear. But now he knew the setting to be Arundel House, and he knew the fall to have been the accident that injured his arm. Not an accident, he reminded himself, but his uncle's attempt to murder him. Unless, of course, Lady Caroline was mistaken. It could be an odd series of coincidences, surely.

"Ash?" Verity stood in the door to his room. "I knocked but there was no answer."

He probably hadn't heard her over the sound of his heart thudding and the blood rushing in his ears. "Bad dream," he said.

"You called out. I thought you might have had a seizure." She wore only a night rail, not even having bothered to reach for a dressing gown before rushing to his door.

"Just a nightmare." He wished he could tell her the truth, but she was the last person he could talk to because she was the most affected by his future. If he were to be a duke—utterly ludicrous—then any future with Verity would either make her a duke's mistress or a duchess, and as much as he wanted to believe that she'd want to be with him no matter his title or status, he did not think she would jump at either option. That left them with this month, and he wasn't going to ruin it for her—for them—by burdening her with truths she'd find out eventually.

"You can go back to sleep," he said.

"You're shivering." She sat on the edge of the bed and pressed a cool hand to his forehead. "You're freezing cold, Ash."

"My sheets are sweaty," he admitted.

"Come to bed with me. It's warm." At his hesitation, she squeezed his hand. "Just sleeping, Ash. Otherwise I'll help you change your sheets."

He went with her. When she got under her quilt, he stripped out of his nightshirt and climbed into bed beside her. The next time he woke was when Verity's forearm landed on his face. He opened his eyes. The woman took up a full three-quarters of her bed, leaving Ash with a sliver of mattress and a scrap of quilt. He was marveling over the mathematical precision with which her not-particularly-large body was arranged to occupy the lion's share of a not-particularly-small bed, when he heard a hiss. It was pitch black, but following the direction of the sound he found a pair of glittering eyes staring at him from on top of Verity's clothes press.

"It's too early to be laughing," Verity mumbled, pressing her face into the pillow and somehow pushing him even further off the bed. "Save your levity for business hours."

He pushed a lock of her hair out of his mouth. "The cat thinks you're attacking me. Which, to be fair, is not an unreasonable interpretation of the facts."

She opened an eye. "Slander." But she wriggled backward on the bed and made room for Ash to have a less precarious relationship with the mattress. "How did she even get in here? The door is shut."

"She probably just walked in when we did. She's an enterprising kitty."

"Or possibly a demon." The cat hissed again as Verity rolled on top of Ash, causing him to dissolve into another bout of laughter. Verity was warm and soft on top of him, and he could feel her smile against the side of his neck. This was real, he thought. This was his life. Arundel House was only the backdrop for his nightmares, vague and dreamlike and unreal. Verity's fingers slid down his shoulders, past his elbows, across the scar that bisected his forearm. He grabbed her hands and rolled her over, kissing her, as if that would make this moment solidify into reality, displacing old scars.

Ash knocked on the front door of Arundel house at precisely a quarter past eleven the following morning. It was Wednesday—not one of his usual days for visiting, but he watched the house until he saw Lady Caroline's brother leave. Ash didn't know why he went back—he hadn't intended to return until the month was through. But when he and Verity had finally gotten out of bed, he decided that there was nothing for it but to lie. He would tell Lady Caroline that he did not have a scar, that he was not the nephew she had known. Surely there was some other way for her to be safe, to protect her father and servants from her brother. Ash didn't need to be a part of it. Lady Caroline's ghastly brother could keep his title.

The footman showed him not to the conservatory, but to a small upstairs parlor.

"Mr.—Lord—I'm afraid I don't know what to call you." Lady Caroline wore a gown he had not seen before. He had come to realize that she had a pale blue frock she wore on Tuesdays and a pale rose for Thursdays; he suspected she had seven morning gowns which she cycled through each week and gathered he had now seen Wednesday's frock. He recognized each as coming directly from a fashion plate, right down to the sleeve pattern, the number of flounces, and the quantity and quality of trim. At first he had thought her fanatically devoted to fashion, but now he guessed that she had simply commissioned the first seven morning gowns in the dressmaker's book. He wondered if she did the same with afternoon gowns and evening gowns. It depressed him in a way he found acutely annoying; here he was prepared to be hard-nosed and deceitful and she had the nerve to make a fifty guinea lilac frock look sad. He reminded himself that whatever trials she faced had nothing to do with him, nothing at all.

"Please continue to call me Mr. Ashby." His voice was

tight and cold and he saw the disappointment in her face. "Or Ash," he added. "My friends call me Ash."

"I daresay you haven't come to work?" she asked. She poured tea into a cup that hadn't been there a moment ago, and he recalled that the servants in this house were experts in making themselves invisible in order to escape the anger of a tyrannical master. He forcibly reminded himself that the fate of the servants was not his responsibility either.

He had intended to remain standing, his hat in his hand. This was not a social call. But Lady Caroline looked so forlorn—no. He hardened his heart. "I've come to tell you that I won't go through with it. Surely it would be for the best if we let sleeping dogs lie," he continued. "Leave this house. You must have friends, relations, somewhere safe to go."

"I ought to give up my home and leave my servants and my invalid father to the whims of my brother? I think not. I have a duty to them."

The word *duty* brought him up short. If she had a duty, then didn't he as well? If he had been born to power and wealth, didn't he have a duty to take up that mantle of authority and use it wisely? Wasn't that the very least of what he believed? Beneath his sleeve, he could almost feel his scar as a living thing. He sat on the sofa across from Lady Caroline.

The lady, perhaps assessing her advantage, pressed on. "My brother is cruel and vindictive. Being a duke would only widen the field of people he could be cruel and vindictive towards. I watched him drive one wife to an early grave once it became clear she couldn't produce an heir, and as a duke he'd have his pick of debutantes. I won't watch him ruin another life. No, it's quite out of the question. If you don't want to cooperate, I'll take matters into my own hands, but I'd much rather solve this problem through honesty rather than crime."

Had this woman—his aunt—just confessed an intention to murder his uncle? Ash could not believe that this was the substance of the life he was being asked to lead.

He could still lie. He could insist that Lady Caroline was mad or mistaken, could pretend that he had memories that disagreed with the history she had laid out. Then he could go back to Holywell Street—to Verity, to his work, to his real life—and pretend none of this had happened. If he were a different man entirely he might even be able to go through with it. But here he was given a chance to do actual good in the world. He had always been acutely aware that he owed his profession, maybe even his life, to the kindness Roger had shown a total stranger. Now Ash could prevent his uncle from doing further harm; he could help his aunt get out from under her brother's thumb. He didn't think he could live with himself if he failed to help.

"What kind of proof do you have?" he asked. Perhaps it was a moot point; perhaps there would be nothing but an old scar and a woman's memories. Surely that wasn't enough. But that seemed too much to hope: Lady Caroline kept detailed records regarding her specimens and various horticultural experiments. She would not attempt to claim that a common engraver was next in line to a dukedom without ample evidence.

"The diaries are in the safekeeping of my solicitor."

"Diaries, ma'am?" His heart sank.

"The diaries in which I detailed the events that led up to your father's death and your departure from this house. I also have a letter from my lady's maid who took you to her sister in Norfolk."

"You planned this out," he said.

"Of course I planned it out," she said, frowning. "Did you think I discarded my own nephew like I might a cracked tea pot? Passing him off to the firstcomer?" Ash's expression must have betrayed his feelings, because she frowned. "I see that is precisely what you think. Well, I did plan it, but very badly indeed, because when I went to find you, there was no trace of you or of my money."

"Your money?" he repeated.

"You didn't think my brother financed this scheme, did you? I saved my pin money for over two years, starting as soon as your father was sent to the asylum and I became concerned that you would be sent away as well."

"My father?" He needed to stop repeating everything she said, but he was quite incapable of forming sentences of his own. "Asylum?"

"I forget how little you know. Your father was an epileptic. He was sent to an institution by my father and younger brother to avoid the shame and scandal of a Duke of Arundel who was beset by seizures. He died within a twelvemonth of being sent to that place, which I suppose was their intention in the first place."

"I have seizures," Ash said. "I'm epileptic." Of all the new information Ash was having thrown at him, the picture of his father as a victim of the aristocracy rather than a base and negligent villain was perhaps the most difficult to accept, and he thought that if he spent overlong thinking about dying alone in a lunatic asylum he might—damn it, he might feel something for this father he had never had, this aunt who had grieved her brother's death by forming a plan to rescue his son.

Lady Caroline took his hand. "I know, my dear. You started having seizures when you were very young indeed. I saw the way my brother looked at you, and worried that you'd be dispatched in the same way your father had been. But instead he pushed you down the stairs."

"And then what happened?"

"I let him believe you died after the fall. We borrowed the body of a boy of similar age who had died in St. Giles. In the middle of the night, while that poor unfortunate child's body was being laid out, I bundled you into a carriage and sent you to my maid's sister's house in Norfolk. I ought to have waited until your arm was set, but time was of the essence, and I had to bring you to a place where my brother and father couldn't find you. I often wondered if your arm had healed."

"It healed," Ash managed. "There's only a small scar." Her eyes went wide, and he realized this was the first time he had acknowledged that he did have the scar, and that he was the nephew she had once known. With a sigh, he shrugged out of his coat and proceeded to roll up his sleeve. There was no going back now. "A month," he said. "I still need a month."

"But you'll do it," she said. "You'll go through with it."

"I don't see that I have a choice," he said.

She pressed her lips together. "We always have a choice."

"Not if I want to be the man I know myself to be."

Almost immediately after Ash kissed her temple and left her alone in her study with a cup of tea and some buttered bread, Verity was visited by the harrowing realization that by doing what she had done with Ash, she had thrown herself headlong into disaster. She had hoped for an hour of shared pleasure, the satisfaction of wanting something and getting it. What she got instead was the devastating knowledge that she craved more of the same, and only from Ash.

With Portia—and she was conscious that it did neither Portia nor Ash any favors by comparing the two—they had been friends and taken their friendship into bed when they discovered a mutual attraction. Verity had seen no disadvantage to having a friendship that included both affection and physical release. It had been simple and straightforward on Verity's end, less so on Portia's. When Portia had expressed a desire—a need, even—for something lasting and meaningful, Verity had fled as if from a house on fire. The idea of another human being with expectations of her had been enough to make her close down, to become what Portia, in a fit of anger, called cold.

She had thought that with Ash it would be different because he had never asked her for a single thing. Even if she could believe that Ash would continue not to want things she couldn't give, it would be Verity herself who wanted more. She could already feel the demand welling up inside her—she wanted all of Ash, and she wanted him in a way she couldn't even identify. She wanted him in bed, she wanted his friendship. When she woke in his arms, she had felt some chilly part of her melt. Or maybe she had never had a core of ice to begin with. Maybe she was warm and alive and it was only Ash who let her feel safe enough to realize it. It would have been so easy, frighteningly easy, to delude herself into thinking nothing mattered outside the cocoon that contained the two of them.

Instead she went to Portia's house. It would be a bracing reminder that love affairs did not last forever, and that she needed to guard herself against the certainty that she would need to navigate a similar course with Ash. Portia's house, however, was in a state of mild chaos in preparation for that evening's salon. The slightly harried butler ushered Verity into the morning room where Amelia sat with a stack of papers on a desk before her and a pair of spectacles on the top of her head.

"Mama's in the green parlor having strong words with the wine merchant," Amelia whispered. "He tried to pass off corked Bordeaux and I don't think he'll make that mistake again."

"No, I dare say he'll find that he wants to take up an entirely new trade after your mother's through with him. Perhaps retire to the country."

"Oh, that reminds me." Amelia wrinkled her nose. "Mama somehow got an invitation to the Featherstones' for a shooting party, so we're meant to decamp to Hampshire next week."

"You sound less than pleased."

"You have no idea how exhausting it is to talk to people."

"You make perfectly lovely conversation."

"I can talk about electricity and Ovid and sugar boycotts as well as anyone, but nobody at the Featherstones' house party will wish to discuss any of those things. Or perhaps they will, but if I dare to say a word about, say, the Thames tunnel or explosive gases, they'll take it as proof that I've been badly brought up. Whereas if I sit quietly that'll also be proof of my low origins. So I must confine my conversation to the weather, lesser society gossip, and some of the more bland aspects of the theater." She recited this list as if she had heard it many times. "And the constant scrutiny is . . ." She shuddered. "I don't know how Mama bears it. I wish I could stay with you instead."

"Really?" Verity had always thought Nate was the reason Amelia enjoyed spending time at their house.

"Do you want to know what's droll? My mother has gone to all this trouble to make sure I don't make a bad marriage, but the truth is that I swear I'd marry the first interesting man to make an offer if it got me a bit of freedom. I told you the truth when I said I wasn't in love with your brother, but I'd have married him in half a heartbeat. When we were—" She broke off, glancing at her papers, then at Verity, before composing herself. "When we were discussing a topic of mutual interest—and no, that is not a euphemism, Verity—I thought it would be the easiest thing in the world to take all this fragile respectability that Mama is so set on protecting, and just cast it to the ground and never have to worry about it again."

Verity sympathized. In Amelia's shoes she might well have acted on that impulse. But she felt obligated to argue the responsible point of view. "If you make a bad marriage, you'll be thoroughly impoverished."

"We're thoroughly impoverished now. I'd worry about winding up a governess, except that no good family would want me as a governess." Amelia straightened some of the papers before her. "Mama's belief that she can find me a wealthy husband is the only silly idea she's had in two decades."

"Give your mother some credit," Verity said, but she felt a surge of anxiety for her friends.

She left before Portia had done with the wine merchant so she decided to walk in the direction of Cavendish Square. Arundel House was minutes from Portia's, and Ash had mentioned needing to pay a call on Lady Caroline Talbot. Verity thought that she might be able to catch up with him and they could either walk home together or share a hackney.

He had explained the necessity of leaving through the garden gate, so Verity found the mews that ran behind the house and waited, leaning against the wall of what had to be the carriage house. She took a book out of her pocket and started to read, but found her attention diverted by the sheer amount of foot traffic passing before her. This lane couldn't possibly access more than three, possibly four, houses, which meant this small army of servants, tradespeople, carters, and coachmen were all in the service of at most four households. Her house in Holywell Street had always been a busy place, with customers and workers and friends coming and going at all hours, but it had nothing on the mews behind Arundel House. There were men with spades, boys leading pony carts, three girls beating a rug, a washerwoman carrying a bucket, and deliveries of ale, fish, apples, and coal. And that was merely what she saw glancing up between sentences. Eventually she gave up and tucked the book in her pocket.

A few people glanced at her, some curious, some suspicious. She wondered how they could tell she didn't belong—she wasn't dressed much differently than any upper servant—and then realized it was because she stood still. Remaining idle was the most conspicuous thing she could have done in this place. She tried to calculate, in pounds sterling, what it must cost to employ this many people. But before she got far, the garden gate swung open.

Ash looked frankly terrible. His face was a sickly gray and his mouth was pressed into a flat line. As she watched, he leaned against the wall opposite her, his hands covering his eyes. She went to him.

"Ash?" She touched his arm lightly.

He dropped his hand and stared at her, as if struggling to recognize her in this unfamiliar setting. "What are you doing here?"

"I was in the neighborhood. Are you well? Do you need a carriage? A glass of water?"

"I'm not going to have a seizure." He looked at her, bleaker than she had ever seen him. "I don't want to go back there," he said, tipping his head towards Arundel House.

"Then don't. There will be other jobs."

"It's not that. It's the, ah, family connection." His voice was low enough so they couldn't be overheard by anyone walking past. "Apparently the men in my family are vicious bastards." He swallowed, and Verity had the sense he was weighing his words. "And Lady Caroline could use an ally. So I need to help her."

Verity didn't know how Lady Caroline Talbot, the daughter of a duke, could possibly need the help of an illustrator she happened to be related to. But then she remembered Ash's nightmare. Whatever was going on, it weighed heavily on him. Verity had always had an abundance of connections, both blood and otherwise. She couldn't imagine what it must be like to discover blood ties at the age of twenty-six.

"Do you want to tell me about it?" she asked.

"God no."

"Come here, then," she said, and drew him into her arms.

He sank against her, wrapping his own arms tightly around her. She felt his heart hammering against her chest, his pulse fast and unsettled against her cheek. But he held her tight and stroked the hair that had come loose at the nape of her neck.

"People will see," he murmured, but didn't slacken his grip.

"Let them."

They stayed that way another minute or five or ten until finally he pulled away, his hands still firm and sure on Verity's arms. "Do you know what I'd like?" he asked. "Hot food and about half a bottle of claret."

"Sounds like you need somebody to drink the other half."

He bent to press a kiss on her forehead. "Thank you, Plum."

"I like claret. It's no sacrifice." His lips were still warm on her skin.

"That's not what I mean." He pulled away and looped his arm through hers. "At some point I'm going to have to deal with this soberly, but perhaps not today."

"Intoxication it is, then. Lead the way, my friend."

Chapter Eleven

By mutual consent they proceeded to Hinton's, an eating house that was a mere five minutes' walk from Cavendish Square. It was only just past noon and the establishment was far from empty, but the clamor and bustle of other patrons would provide almost as great a sense of privacy as if they had been alone. In due time they were ensconced in the upstairs saloon with dishes of roast fowl and potatoes before them, making good headway into a bottle of wine.

Ash leaned back loosely in his chair, glass of wine in one hand. The shadow of a beard was visible on his jaw and Verity wanted to crawl into his lap and rub her cheek against his face like a demented cat. "Would you like to hear a tale of high society?" he asked too casually. This, she gathered, was how he was going to ease into telling her about what was bothering him.

"I think I'd like to hear anything you have a mind to say," she answered equally lightly.

He sat forward in his chair and beckoned her to do the

same. "Lady Caroline says my uncle murdered his wife because she failed to get him an heir," he whispered, then sat back again. "Tell me that isn't a plot you've read ten times in books put out by rival publishers."

Verity deliberately avoided asking about Ash's use of the word *uncle*. He was plainly coming sideways at acknowledging the family connection; if he wanted to talk about murder rather than the precise nature of his relationship to the Talbots, she'd oblige. "Be fair, Ash, I've put out about three books with that plot myself. But do you think she's entirely in her right mind?"

"Yes, damn me, I do. I think she means to murder him unless she comes up with a better plan."

Verity took a sip of her wine and regarded her friend. He wasn't even pretending not to care mightily about this. There wasn't even a shadow of feigned nonchalance or studied indifference about him. "Then, based on what you've said, I'd lend her a spade."

He let out a shaky breath. "Is that what you'd advise her to do if she wrote to the *Ladies' Register*? Get a friend to help bury the body?"

Verity paused, chewing a mouthful of roast potato. "No. I'd tell her to pack a valise, sew her jewels into the hem of a gown, and leave before the brother could take revenge on her."

"That's more or less what I suggested. She says that knowing what she does, she can't let him marry again. Exposing him is out of the question. He'll be a duke in a matter of weeks, according to the old man's doctors. Whereas she's an eccentric spinster. We know which of them will be believed."

"In a novel, he would fall down a convenient flight of stairs."

Ash went pale. She put down her fork and reached for his hand; it was cold and clammy. "Ash, whatever is the matter? Something is plainly very wrong indeed and I'm quite worried about you. If you want to talk about it, you know I'll listen."

"I can't, Verity." He turned his hand so his palm was against hers, holding her hand tight. His fingers were strong and callused, and she remembered the feel of them against her body the previous night. "I can't." His voice was a low, scratchy rumble, even quieter than the near whisper in which they had conducted the earlier part of their conversation. "I'll tell you what I want. I want to pretend the past two hours haven't happened. I want to go home with you and take you to bed. I want anything you'll give me and want to give you anything you need. That's what I want."

Her cheeks felt hot and her heart was pounding. "I want that too. Wanted it for a while, if I'm honest. Don't know how I've held out so long. Last night was only a start."

He rubbed his thumb along the soft inside of her wrist. "God help me, Plum, but I don't know how to do this. I know how to be with you at a chophouse and, if last night is any indication"—his cheeks flushed—"I think I know how to be with you in my arms, but I don't know how to bridge the gap. Is there supposed to be a difference in our manner towards one another? Am I behaving horribly by discussing murder when I ought to be complimenting your fine eyes?"

"I'd think you had suffered a mental decline if you started

mooning over me." She had long suspected that compliments and grand declarations were attempts to chisel away at a woman's resistance, although she also suspected that this was fairly cynical even by her standards. In either case, she felt vaguely sick at the idea of Ash attempting to woo her, perhaps because there was only one way a successful wooing could end, and that was marriage, and out of the question. "Besides, you can't imagine that I have any better answers than you do. I think we're muddling through quite all right on our own." She slid her foot under the table to touch the side of his boot.

He swirled the contents of his wineglass. "Well, you could hardly be more ignorant than I am. After all, you had your friendship with Mrs. Allenby."

"Yes, but—" She peered quizzically at him, and then, when his meaning hit home, raised her eyebrows. "Are you saying—are you saying that you've never had a lover?"

He drank from his glass and put it back on the table before nodding. "That's right, Plum."

"I assumed you were discreet. You used to go out with my brother, and I've never been under the impression that he spends his nights in quiet contemplation. Why not, though? You're very handsome. Desperately so. I assure you I've found your looks terribly distracting, quite inconvenient. You'd have your pick of girls." She was babbling, and only the sound of his laughter stopped her mouth from running.

"I have no intention of bringing a bastard into the world." His words might have been harsh but for the gentleness of his tone. "We have a duty to children, and that duty is hard to fulfill when a child has no name and no people."

"You're aware there are things a couple can do that don't involve any chance of pregnancy? If not, I can't imagine what you thought was happening in that plate you engraved for chapter five."

"I'm aware, Plum," he said dryly. "In the event that imagination failed me, you know that for a couple shillings I can see whatever I want. I've asked around, and learned that there are places that specialize in couples who enjoy being watched."

"I did not know that," she said, imagining Ash calmly sketching various manners of fornication. "You teach me the loveliest things, Ash. Do let me know if you intend to visit such a place for any of the illustrations in the final volume of the novel, and I'll be sure to reimburse you. Meanwhile, I'm finding myself very eager to get home." She didn't know if this was some unique perversion on her part, but knowing that he hadn't been with anyone else made her desire take on the sharp edge of urgency.

"You're leering at me, Plum."

She leered more emphatically. "Wait until you see what I do to you when we get home."

They took a hackney, mutually agreeing that the faster they got to Holywell Street, the better. As soon as the carriage door shut, Ash tugged Verity onto his lap and kissed her. That was something, being hauled about as if she weighed no more than a house cat. Before last night, she hadn't quite realized how strong Ash was, his arms ropy with lean muscle, his chest broad and hard. She traced the lines of his biceps beneath his coat, wishing the hackney would hurry so she could get their clothes off and appreciate him properly. But evidently every carriage, pony cart, and other conveyance in the entirety of London was en route between Marylebone and the Strand, because the hackney proceeded at a mere crawl.

"Damn it," she said into the scratchy stubble on his neck. "We should have walked."

"Then I couldn't have done this." He cupped her breast through her gown, running his thumb across her already-firm nipple. She groaned. "You like that?" he asked.

"More," she begged, clasping her own hand over his, feeling him feel her. She needed his skin, and there weren't many ways to make that happen in a hackney, so she unbuttoned his cuff, stowing the stud in her pocket. She brought his newly bare wrist to her hand, kissing the underside of it, then biting where she had kissed. He made a strangled sound, so she pushed up his coat sleeve as much as she could, the shirtsleeve following, and kissed a path up the tender inside of his forearm. Her lips found a scar that she had seen before when he worked with his sleeves rolled up. When she licked along the length of it, he flinched away from her touch. She realized she had—for the third or fourth time that day—accidentally dredged up something unpleasant. She wasn't used to conversation with Ash being so riddled with traps. Whatever was happening with the Talbots, it was cutting up Ash's peace of mind in a serious way. She put his sleeves back in order. And because she didn't want his mind to linger on whatever was troubling him, she kissed him again. He met her mouth halfway, his lips soft and pliant.

"Verity, make me a promise," Ash said, leaning back against the seat, his eyes still shut. "What date is it?"

"The twenty-sixth of November."

"A month from now—Boxing Day, easy to remember—remind yourself that I adore you, Plum. Remind yourself that I've never been as honest with you as I was today."

He spoke as if he were under a death sentence. "Are you quite certain you're all—"

"Don't ask if I'm all right. You won't like the answer."

She gripped his shoulders. "I'm truly worried now, Ash. Have you been to a doctor and received bad news?"

"Oh God, no, Verity, nothing like that."

She kissed him, relief and concern and frustration mingling together into desperate contact.

Ash left the hackney driver with a random assortment of coinage, probably triple the fare, but he was not wasting a single second counting out pennies when he could be with Verity.

The shopman tried to get Verity's attention when she went inside, but she made a vague excuse—pressing engagement, so sorry—and all but ran up the stairs. Ash could hardly chase her without the shopman and the men in the workroom all knowing what they were about, so he made a show of hanging his coat on a peg and his key on the hook before following her upstairs at a more leisurely pace.

He found her in her bedroom flinging her boots aside. Leaning in the doorway, he admired the sight.

"You could help a girl out," she said, and he didn't need a second invitation. Standing behind her, he unfastened the buttons at the back of her gown, kissing each piece of skin he exposed. She leaned back into him, which hardly gave him room to work, but that was all right because he knew how to pretend to be a man who wasn't in a hurry. God help him, nothing could have prepared him for the way Verity almost melted under his touch. She wanted his hands on her body as much as he did; and now she was reaching behind her, trying to touch him as well, and he did not think he could ever get used to the idea that this was something they both wanted, something they both got to have.

When she raised her arms, he pulled the dress over her head and threw it onto the chair where she seemed to fling all her clothes. Because of course she didn't stow things neatly in a clothes press; her room was a jumble of ribbons and bootlaces and haphazard stacks of books. He skimmed his hands up the softness of her belly to her breasts, each a perfect palmful through her shift and stays.

He tried to silence the voice that told him it was temporary at best, a lie at worst, and no matter what would last a mere month. The fact that she probably wouldn't so much as breathe the same air as him if she knew the truth was something he needed to set aside for the moment, as one would carefully push away a wasp's nest.

"What on earth are you thinking of?" Verity pivoted in his arms and regarded him with hazy eyes.

"Wasps. And primogeniture."

"Am I that uninteresting?" she asked with feigned outrage, gripping his cravat and pulling him close with an attempt at menace that he was surprised to find both erotic and endearing. His heart was so full of her that he knew it would be his undoing when they parted.

He took a steadying breath, trying to master himself, trying to focus on this moment, their bodies together, her in his arms. "I'm sorry to break it to you, Plum, but I'm exceedingly bored." He rocked his pelvis into her belly so she could properly appreciate just how interested he truly was. At the fleeting contact with her softness and warmth, he had to bite back a groan.

"What a pity," she said, tugging off his cravat and swiftly divesting him of coat and waistcoat, then steering him towards the bed and pushing him down by the shoulders. "We'll have to see what we can do about that." His shirt hit the floor as she shimmied out of her stays and straddled his lap. Now she was in her shift, the peaks of her breasts veiled only by thin linen.

"Still bored," he said and he saw her purse her lips to keep from smiling. Surely this game was both perverse and bizarre but it amused Verity, got his cock hard, and let him think about something other than the condition of his heart.

She leaned forward, bringing her breasts to within an inch of his face, but not moving closer. He tried to give them what he considered a disinterested appraisal, rather than burying his face in between them, which was what he wanted to do. "Hmm," he said with an arched brow. She shifted on her knees, bringing the peaks of her breasts to his lips. He leaned forward.

"Tut," she chided. She pulled away, covering her breasts with her hands. "I don't want to bore you with my tiresome breasts."

"I share your concern," he managed, "but I'm fairly certain it's your shift that's the problem. Perhaps we ought to dispense with it."

Biting back a smile, she reached for the hem, as if she had been waiting for his request, but then paused when she reached the top of her thighs.

"Plum, I wish you could see yourself." Her hair was a riot, her lips swollen, her gaze wanton, as if she wanted to devour him. He swallowed.

"Like what?" she asked, rucking the hem of the shift another inch so he could see the shadow between her legs.

"Like I'd better do exactly what you tell me," he said, trying not to sound too hopeful on that point.

She unfastened his trousers. "What are we going to do about this?" She grinned wolfishly at him and grasped his cock, giving it a long, slow stroke. "We can do more of what we did last night. We don't need to—"

"I want to. Please. Anything. Everything. We can be careful."

She pulled off her shift without further ado. Ash fastened his mouth over one dark pink nipple, her other breast in his hand. She let out a sound that was half relief, half entreaty, so he kept going, kissing and stroking. Her hands were everywhere—his hair, his shoulders, his jaw.

Then he slid his hand up her thigh and stroked her already-wet folds the way she had touched herself the last time she was in his arms. He went back to kissing her breasts while she rocked against his palm. She went still, her body rigid, one of her hands painfully tight in his hair and the other touching the wrist of the hand that was between her legs.

"Ash," she said, her inner muscles tightening around his fingers as he continued to stroke her, slower and more soothingly.

"Yes, sweetheart." Damn it, he hadn't meant to say that, but it was too late to recover.

Her mouth was against his ear, so close he could feel the movement of her lips. "I need your clothing off and I need it now. I want you inside me."

He lifted his hips only enough to kick off his trousers. "Plum," he choked out as she ran her hands over his shoulders and biceps with a look in her eyes he could only describe as hungry, "I'm beginning to think you like the look of me." He knew he was looking at her the same way, desperate and needy. They had both spent years burying and ignoring the current of desire that existed between them, and now that it was out in the open he was stunned by the force of it.

He grabbed her backside and pulled her closer, bringing the warmth and wetness between her legs to brush against the head of his cock. He clamped his hands on her hips and kissed the corner of her grin. Above him, against him, ready to take him into her body, she looked like some kind of goddess. She was always beautiful, but at this moment he worshiped the ground beneath her feet.

As the head of his cock brushed her entrance, he hissed, bucking his hips slightly, chasing after more of that sensation she had teased him with. As she lowered onto him, surrounding him and drawing him in, he kept his eyes locked on her face. She hadn't done this specific act before either, and he wanted to see every reaction writ on her face. But then she sank lower and he closed his eyes with a groan.

She was tight and hot around him, but the real miracle was that it was her, his Verity, and they were joined. He was inside her, she was around him, and their hearts were pounding against one another. Her hair had come unpinned and fell in soft waves that he buried his face in, her breasts were soft and warm against his chest. She circled her hips and the resulting surge of pleasure had his fingers clasping vise-like on her arse. "So good," he groaned.

She pulled back and he saw that her mouth was parted, her eyes shut. As he watched, she opened her eyes and brought a hand to where their bodies were joined, tracing the base of his cock and then dragging moisture up over her folds in a slow glide. "Look at you," she said. "Inside me. Just like that."

"I want to watch you come with me buried inside you," he said. "Just . . . please."

"Is that what you want?" she asked, circling her hips a bit.

It was all he wanted. He was not certain he had ever wanted anything more, or even at all. The world of uncertain futures and lies of omission fell away, leaving only this. Warmth and softness. Her arms around his neck, her mouth on his, together.

He dropped his hand to touch her entrance the way she had, feeling the way her body made room for him, welcomed him, drew him in. Then he touched her the way he had before, small and gentle circles that made her gasp and moan as she slid up and down his cock. He was perilously close to climax but he forced it away.

As she came, she gripped his shoulders so tightly it was almost like she was holding him down, and that thought sent him rushing to the edge. "Now, Verity," he gritted out. She lifted off him and took him in her hand, stroking and stroking as his orgasm washed over him. He came on her belly and in her hand, and she looked at him with a combination of unabashed triumph and sleepy content, as if she were exceptionally proud of herself and knew she had done something very clever indeed.

"What are you laughing about?" she asked in mock severity.

"Only that I adore you, Plum. With my entire heart, and I wish I knew what to do about it."

Chapter Twelve

It seemed deeply unfair that they now had to get dressed and proceed with the rest of the day when the sensible thing would be to never again stir from under the quilt. Ash seemed to be much of the same mind, his hands lazily drifting up and down Verity's back as she lay with her face in the pillow.

"Why did you make an exception for me?" Verity asked.

"Hmm?" he murmured.

"You said you hadn't had a lover because you wanted to avoid a child."

His hand momentarily stilled. "That wasn't the only reason. Besides, with you, it's different. Everything with you is different, Plum. Daft of you not to have figured that out."

She supposed that the reason it was different was that he thought she'd have to marry him if she got with child. That was about the last thing she wanted to think about when she was sated and happy. The idea seemed to take what they had—sweet and easy and good—and shove it into a shape that was familiar and wrong.

"None of that," he said, as if reading her thoughts, and wrapped his arm around her. She gladly nestled against his shoulder, wanting the warmth and solidity of his body to chase away her thoughts. He smelled good, too, his usual scent of ink and soap overlaid with sex. But now dread of the future crept into her mind and she was reminded of all the reasons why she and Ash hadn't done this years ago. "Stop thinking," he said into her hair. "Go to sleep."

"It's not even five o'clock," she protested. "The shopman tried to speak to me earlier. I have to see what he wants. And I need to make sure that the boys have the *Ladies' Register* typeset." And there were a dozen other small matters she had to attend to. She really could not spend all afternoon in bed, not even with Ash.

"All right," he said, sitting up and groping for his trousers. "I'll check on the boys, you talk to the shopman?"

"No, that's kind of you, but it's my responsibility."

"And you discharge all your responsibilities admirably, even though without Nate here I have no idea how you're managing it. I'm offering to help—which, I'll remind you, is not unprecedented—and it's not because I'm trying to get you back into bed as fast as I can. Not that I'd object if you felt so inclined." He sketched a polite little bow, which would have made her smile even if he hadn't been in the process of pulling on his trousers.

"It's just—" She shook her head. She didn't know how to make him understand. Her job was hers. She was proud that she ran the business on her own, that the men in the shop treated her little differently than they had treated her father and Nate, and she took pride in being a fair employer. But mainly she was so used to shouldering every burden on her own, that she feared accepting help would make her burdens feel heavier once the help was gone.

"How about I go fetch us some supper and then undo whatever mischief the cat wrought in my studio this morning," he suggested.

"Yes, thank you," she said, relieved, and they went down the stairs together.

Downstairs, though, it was not the shopman but Nan who stood in the shop waiting for her. "The lads said you'd want to see this," said the older woman, handing Verity a newspaper.

Verity scanned the small type on the first page. Ash, looking over her shoulder, must have seen it first, because she heard his sharply indrawn breath.

Hone, the radical publisher who had been arrested for seditious libel, had been found not guilty. Nate needn't have left after all. Verity had strong-armed her brother into going thousands of miles away for nothing. He had done it only for her, and now she bore the burden of her mistake. Every time she saw his empty chair at the table, she would be reminded of what happened when loved ones made sacrifices on her behalf—creeping knowledge of a debt that couldn't be repaid, a burden that wouldn't be lifted.

"I'm happy for Mr. Hone, of course," she managed. "And pleased to see the courts have yielded a just result." That was true. Of course it was. She did not wish innocent men to be punished in order to justify her concern; that was madness. But she was not thinking entirely clearly.

"Naturally," Ash said. "But it was still prudent for Nate to go, especially since now Sidmouth will find other ways of cracking down on radicals."

Verity dismissed this kindness with a wave of her hand. She was a shrew and a harpy and utterly incapable of the basic give-and-take of human relationships. She had bungled things with Portia, with her brother, and would soon do so with Ash.

She checked on the men in the workroom, answered her mail, tended the fire in her study, and only then did she notice a stack of papers on the small table by the window. She picked one up and saw that they were the first prints of the engravings Ash had made for *A Princely Pretense*. There was Perkin Warbeck beckoning to his bride, there was the pale and drawn Earl of Warwick awkward but laughing in his lover's arms. Here were all the scenes, exactly as they would appear in the finished novel. And they were beautiful, each image a delicate arrangement of light and shadow. These were no crude woodcut images of naked women that a man could buy for tuppence. She felt a surge of fondness and admiration for Ash for having created this beauty, for having drawn these characters as people—there were no coy innocents here, but no villains either. He saw the best in people who the rest of the world dismissed, and Verity knew that included herself. He was good and kind, and he deserved better than her, but she was far too selfish to give him up now.

It was not ideal timing.

When Ash's arm started to twitch, he just managed to

pull the bell cord, so that was something. That it was Verity who appeared in the door of his workroom was regrettable; in a last moment of mad vanity before losing consciousness, he wished it had been Nan. But when he came to he had a pillow under his head and no obvious injuries. Verity assured him that it had been only a minute since he had lost consciousness. She didn't fuss over him, thank God; she had, after all, seen this happen a handful of times and the fact that they had gone to bed together the previous night shouldn't change anything.

"Nan will bring up tea in bit," she said, smoothing a piece of hair off his forehead.

His limbs felt heavy and unreliable, and it would be several minutes before he could hold a teacup, longer still before his skull felt like it contained a proper brain rather than bits of eggshell and cobweb rattling around. He couldn't even make a guess as to what month it was and only Verity's presence gave him the clue he needed to remember where he was.

As a child, he had often woken terrified, bruised, utterly disoriented. Facts like his name and the names of people around him hovered frustratingly out of reach, and sometimes he would remain in that state of confusion for days, would be brought to a new house and new people and be called by a new name before the fog lifted. Each episode was like being reborn. Staring at the slanted ceiling of his workroom, he thought it was no wonder Lady Caroline hadn't been able to find him. He had hardly been able to find himself. He hadn't been abandoned so much as lost. He had thought he had found himself here, a name and a place and a life of his own, but he was going to be lost again.

His eyes started to prickle with tears, easy emotion being another effect of his seizure.

"Don't worry, I'm not going to sit here staring at you," Verity said, getting to her feet. "I'll sit over here by the window pretending that your cat isn't planning my death, and you enjoy yourself on the floor over there."

He made a sound that was the ghost of a laugh. Sure enough, the cat was perched on the edge of his worktable, shifting her baleful gaze between Ash and Verity.

"She probably thinks you've poisoned me," he croaked.

"She's onto me," Verity intoned.

He tentatively dragged himself up onto his elbows. To his surprise, the cat leaped off the table and came to his side. She made a sound that he hadn't heard before.

"Is that cat purring?" Verity asked, looking up from one of Ash's art books.

Ash held his hand out and the cat rubbed her whiskers against it. "Well, I'll be damned," he said. "Do you think she knows I've been unwell?"

"I daresay demons in feline form are typically quite intelligent."

"The lady is slandering you," Ash told the cat. This was evidently quite enough affection for one day, because she retreated to the top of the bookcase. Ash pushed himself up into a sitting position. His muscles felt both tense and unreliable. "Everyone agrees that being liked by animals is a sign of excellent character," he observed complacently. "I notice I'm the only person in the room of excellent character."

Verity snorted and went back to her book. By the time Nan arrived with the tea tray, he had hoisted himself into a chair and felt like an approximation of his usual self. He was still a bit shaken, as he always was, and there was the vague sense of trauma that came with his body and his time being abruptly stolen away from him. Tomorrow he would wake with odd bruises and a headache. But for now he drank his tea, he watched Verity slather fresh butter on a slab of bread, and it was fine, as fine as these things ever were.

They spent the rest of the afternoon together, Ash reading and dozing and Verity writing, while occasionally running downstairs to help in the shop or talk to the men in the workshop. He had a glimpse of what a life with her might look like, working side by side, each independent but turning to one another for comfort, warmth, companionship. He could see how everything, from his seizures to his cat, would fit into this life. Except for how it couldn't happen, would never happen, and would all be revealed to be a lie.

Chapter Thirteen

Waking to the sound of church bells and the pleasant weight of one of Ash's arms across her body, Verity knew a moment of undiluted happiness. If this sort of complacency was what happened after a few days of shared pleasure, foolish laughter, and the dreamlike prospect of building a life together, then it was no wonder people made such bad choices when they were in love.

She rolled to face him. The half of his face that wasn't pressed into his pillow was obscured by hair that had fallen onto his forehead. She loved this Ash, with his disheveled hair and stubbly jaw. Well, she loved all versions of Ash. She was dangerously fond of him, and had been for as long as she could remember. It had been safer when she had known how to ignore how she felt about him and pretend not to know how he felt about her. But time in his arms had razed her defenses, leaving her with nothing to do but capitulate.

He opened an eye and she watched as he registered where he was and who he was with. A lazy smile spread across his handsome face. "Morning, Verity," he said. "Do you think there's any goose left?" Yesterday he had come home from the market with a goose over his shoulder, asked Nan to show him how to cook it, and then sent her home.

He had called Verity by her Christian name several times now, almost as if by accident, as if that was how he thought of her, and she could not decide how she felt about it. Once he had even called her sweetheart, but it had sounded like a slip of the tongue rather than an endearment. She was decidedly not the type of woman anybody referred to as sweetheart.

"Not a chance," she said. "I sent each of the men home with some." The shop was closed for Sunday and they would have the house to themselves for a full day. Verity did not intend to get out of bed more than strictly necessary.

The sun shone brightly through the window of Ash's room, or at least as brightly as it got in London at the beginning of December, so she could see his face clearly as he rolled on top of her, his weight a pleasant heaviness pressing her into the mattress.

"One of the things I like most about you," he said, speaking the words into her neck, "is your capacity for forethought." He nipped her collarbone and then pressed a kiss over the place he had bitten. She slid her hands down his shoulders and back, feeling his muscles work as he settled over her, then she spread her legs invitingly and watched his face as he thrust inside her. He looked like he was holding himself back. He almost always did. Ash had a stronger set of defensive walls than she did. And that was fine. She didn't want to be inside anyone's walls. Defenses were good. They kept people safe. But she suspected it was more than that, that whatever had been bothering him about his newfound relations was preventing him from being entirely free with himself. She smoothed a hand down his back again, felt his muscles tense and shift as he groaned with the pleasure of burying himself inside her, still somehow holding himself in check.

She wrapped her legs around him, taking him deep and savoring the stretch and fullness of him inside her. "Look at me," she said.

"As if I could look anywhere else," he said, propping himself up on a forearm and taking her chin in his other hand.

"Do you see my expression?" she asked, trying hard to keep a straight face. "Would you say it's similar to the engraving of that woman in—" He shut her up with a kiss that turned clumsy because both of them were laughing, and the odd seriousness of a few moments earlier dissolved into silliness.

"How about this?" She assumed a vapid smile.

He responded by thrusting hard into her and she arched up against him.

"Swear to God, Plum," he said afterward, when they lay sated in the tangled sheets. "If I weren't so hungry you couldn't make me leave this bed."

"I think I could stay hungry for a few more hours," she said. "But this bed has a sad lack of tea."

The room was cold when they weren't in one another's arms, so she washed and dressed hastily. When she went to the kitchen, she found Ash there, a kettle already on the fire and a crumpet toasting at the end of a fork. She greeted him by wrapping her arms around him, pressing her chest to his back.

"Did you miss me?" he asked, turning his head just enough to meet her mouth for a kiss.

It had been ten minutes since they were in bed together, but the truth was that she had indeed missed him. She wanted more nights like last night, more mornings like this one. And maybe she could have that. Maybe they could come to some sort of arrangement; maybe Ash could content himself with what Verity had to offer, and wouldn't ask for more.

They ate buttered crumpets and drank sweet tea while sharing the kind of glances that hinted at what they'd be doing after breakfast. But before Verity finished her last bite, there was a knock at the door.

"That's the shop door," Ash said, puzzled. It was Sunday, which meant it couldn't be a customer. Verity put down her cup of tea and shook out her skirts before heading to the door, Ash right behind her. When she unbolted the door, Verity saw a tall woman in a dark velvet cloak and the sort of bonnet that cast her face in shadows. Behind her, Ash sucked in a breath.

"I beg your pardon," the stranger said to Verity, and the words sounded like a genuine apology. "I'm here to see . . ." She looked over Verity's shoulder.

"Lady Caroline, this is Miss Plum," Ash said in a voice that sounded like it came from very far away. "Verity, this is my . . . aunt." He was standing right beside her, but he didn't touch her arm, didn't even bump against her with his shoulder, and instead of his warmth she felt only the cold air from the street.

"I do beg your pardon," Lady Caroline repeated, her gaze wavering between the two of them. "Oh dear."

"Please come in," Verity said. "It's bitterly cold." They hadn't laid a fire anywhere but Ash's bedchamber and the kitchen, but the shop was warmer than the street.

"No, no," Lady Caroline protested. "I don't mean to come in. I only wanted to see if—if Mr. Ashby is safe. And I see that he is, so I'll be on my way." The light shifted, revealing that the redness on one side of the lady's face was not the flush of embarrassment but rather a fresh bruise. Verity stifled a gasp.

"My lady," Ash said gravely. "I cannot let you leave unless I know you have someplace safe to go." There was a quality to Ash's voice that Verity hadn't expected to hear, a note of affection and warmth that she hadn't expected Ash to feel towards this strange woman, and which was at odds with the formality of his language.

"My brother left for the country this morning, so there is no immediate danger. I feared that he might have visited you on his way out of town. But I see he has not, so I will be on my way."

"My lady. Aunt." He laid his hand on her sleeve. "Visit your solicitor. I beg of you."

Verity watched as the two of them stared at one another. Ash's jaw clenched and his aunt looked up at him in confusion. "But, the terms of our arrangement," Lady Caroline said incomprehensibly. "Your month is not up."

"This has to be stopped, and now. Send me the time and direction and I'll go with you to the solicitor." He looked miserable. Verity did not know what they were talking about, but it certainly wasn't a mere visit to a family solicitor. Something was happening that was beyond her comprehension, something that made Ash look more morose than she had ever seen him. He must have sensed her gaze on him, because he met her eyes and frowned. "I wish it could be otherwise," he said, and she didn't know whether he was speaking to her or to himself.

Lady Caroline left, and Verity and Ash stood two paces apart on the shop floor, he regarding her with a look so bleak that she knew they were both about to get their hearts broken.

"I've been lying to you," Ash said. He ought to have rehearsed what he'd say to Verity, how he'd explain both the truth and why he waited to tell her. But every time the thought bubbled to the surface of his mind, he refused to think about it. He thought he'd have more time, even as he knew that no amount of time in the world would have made this easier.

"Ash," she said gently. "Just tell me what's going on."

He wished she wouldn't be gentle. She was going to be furious with him and he didn't think he could stand to see her affection transform into anger right before his eyes. "I told you that Lady Caroline believed me to be her brother's son. That much is true. But my parents were married at the time of my birth. And my father was the Duke of Arundel's oldest son."

She went absolutely still before his eyes. He wasn't even certain she was breathing; she certainly wasn't blinking. "Does she have evidence?"

"Yes, unfortunately."

"This is what you were talking about when you said your uncle had to be stopped. You weren't talking about murdering him, but disinheriting him."

"My aunt believes any future wife of his will be in danger. I'm more worried that he'll murder my aunt." Verity stared at him. "I know she's almost a stranger, but I've grown fond of her. I don't know if it's because of some inherited sympathy for one another, but for whatever reason I can't stand to let this man harm her."

"You don't need to explain to me why you don't want to stand idly by while innocent women are killed," Verity said slowly. "I think I know you well enough to understand that."

"But you see what this will mean for me," he said. "For us."

She hadn't. He could see the dismay fall across her face like a veil as she understood. "Quite," she said at length. "How long have you known, Ash?"

"I only found out a week ago."

"The day you kissed me," she said wistfully. "That was the first thing you did after finding out, Ash?"

"Being with you was the one thing I wanted, the one thing I wouldn't be able to do . . . after."

"Bollocks, you couldn't." There it was, that flash of anger he had been waiting for. "Utter bollocks."

"I know I ought to have said something, but I wanted this month so damned badly and I thought you did too. I thought . . ." He had harbored the shadow of a hope that somehow none of it would matter to her, that they would find a way. But that hope had started out flimsy and feeble, nothing he could really convince himself of. Now, standing in front of her, truth out in the open, he knew it for the lie it had always been.

"You think I wouldn't have wanted to be with you if I knew the truth?" Her fists were balled at her sides.

Oh God, she was going to make him spell it out. "There's no future between us. You wouldn't marry anyone, let alone a duke. Don't even pretend to tell me you'd consent to that."

"Of course I wouldn't. But there's a middle ground between marriage and just fucking off out of my life forever, Ash. Christ, give me a little bit of credit, will you?"

"What would that middle ground look like? I visit you here, on my way to my seat in the House of Lords? Everyone you know refers to you as the Duke of Arundel's mistress? You fall pregnant and I—no, Verity. No, there isn't a middle ground."

"There's friendship, Ash. There's everything we've been to one another for more than ten years. If you think I'd throw that away and disclaim you just because your parents happened to be married and one of them titled, then you don't know me at all."

"A pox on friendship. I'm in love with you, you stubborn ass, and I don't know how to undo that!"

"Nobody is asking you to, you thick-headed idiot!"

It was entirely plain that she was not hearing him. "I ought to go before we have a row."

She threw her hands up in a gesture of frustration that he had seen her use dozens of times when exasperated during a quarrel with Nate. "Bit late for that! By all means go. You were planning on leaving for good, after all." She shook her head and went upstairs, and he resisted the urge to go after her, to try and make things right. This couldn't be made right.

An hour later he stood at the front door of Arundel House.

Chapter Fourteen

"Dear Miss Plum, I have these five years been married to a man most would account a most excellent husband. He is neither cruel nor miserly. However, after reading a treatise written by a learned gentleman, he has become a proponent of free love, which he claims is what the Creator must have intended in a perfect a state of nature. He says he wishes to lie with other women, and I am free to do as he does, but I do not wish to dally with other men. It seems I have no say in this and I know not what to do."

"Dear Miss Plum, My wife has lost two stone and I no longer like the look of her bosoms, please advise."

In response, Verity wrote a four-page tirade on the merits of spinsterhood, the urgent need to reform divorce law, and the benefits that would devolve to all by banning men from the public sphere. She feared this would not be a suitable answer to either correspondent, nor to their spouses, but she found it moderately cathartic.

She supposed that she ought to be grateful for having work to distract her, but she felt singularly ill-equipped to answer these letters. In fact she could not imagine anyone less suited to advising people on their families, friendships, and attachments than she, who had in the span of a month lost the two people who mattered most to her. The house echoed with an emptiness that felt like failure, a mirror of her own cold heart. When she went to the shop, Nate's absence was an almost palpable loss.

Ash's absence, though, was vague and inchoate; she felt his loss not in any particular room but in her entire being. There was nowhere she could go to be rid of the thought of him. He was a part of her, but now he was gone; it was as simple as that. Hard work ought to be the best medicine for this ache, but work was yet another place from which Ash was absent. She did not want to sit at her desk knowing he would never walk into the room. She worked anyway, though, and after a week the sharp sting of loss had mellowed to the dull nagging pain of an old injury.

Ash had neither called on her nor written since he had left the previous week. Based on what she read in the papers, he had been very busy indeed: three days after he left, the newspapers reported that a man purporting to be the Duke of Arundel's legitimate grandson had brought a suit against his grandfather and uncle for the income of properties associated with the entail and the will of a Talbot ancestor. This, Verity gathered, was the solicitor's strategy for ensuring that

Ash's identity was settled before the present duke's imminent death.

Portia called on Verity after the first piece about Ash appeared in the papers. Verity told Nan to send her away: she was in no state for either curiosity or sympathy. The following day's post brought a letter from Portia; Verity, in a fit of self-pity and feeling entirely unequal to the basic requirements of friendship, threw it into the fire unread. When, a few days later, Portia called once again, Nan put her foot down. The older woman would not send such a fine lady away, and in such foul weather too.

"She can stay in her carriage. I'm sure she has a warm brick at her feet," Verity said sulkily.

"She was just standing there, her poor bonnet ruined and her cloak soaked straight through. I had to let her in."

Verity glanced out the window and saw nothing but an expanse of gray. "And now she's dripping onto my shop floor, I suppose." She sighed. "Send her up."

Nan nodded. "I'll have tea and cakes sent up as well."

From the moment Verity informed Nan that Mr. Ashby would be seeking lodgings elsewhere, an assortment of cakes and biscuits had begun appearing at all hours. "Broken hearts are best mended with a sweet tooth," Nan had said, despite Verity insisting that she did not have a broken heart and that this was not even a proper maxim anyway. She ate the sweets nonetheless, and they didn't make anything worse, at least. Cake had never made anything worse.

"I don't want to talk about it," Verity said when Portia, sodden and blue lipped, walked into the room.

"Of course you don't," Portia said from between chattering teeth. "Did you think I came for gossip? What do you take me for? I came to see if you wanted company." She peeled off her wet cloak and frowned at her sodden bonnet.

Verity stood in silence for a moment, regarding the woman who was her only friend this side of the Atlantic. "You'd better sit by the fire. I'm behaving churlishly but I warn you I have no intention of stopping."

"Of course you don't. When are you going to see him again?" Portia extended one ruined slipper towards the fire.

Verity let out a bitter laugh. "When? Never, if he has his way."

"Nonsense." Portia turned sharply towards Verity. "You can't toss someone from your life after being in one another's pockets for ten years."

"Tell that to Ash. He has all manner of high-minded ideas about not sullying my honor with an improper connection."

"What about a proper connection? I will admit that I don't expect it to do me any harm to have my close friend become a duchess, so I'm hardly unbiased."

"You can't be serious. You're mad if you think I'd agree to anything of the sort. I'm perfectly content in this house, eating cakes and publishing magazines and dirty books about Perkin Warbeck. I do honest work that I'm very good at. Being a duchess does not sound in the least interesting, even if it weren't against all of my principles."

"Perkin Warbeck?" Portia asked, her features almost comically distorted by consternation. "Is he all the rage these days? First Amelia, now you, after having gone a good thirty-five years without ever hearing anyone speak his name aloud."

"All I know is that I like him more than anyone else in my life at the moment." Then Verity realized what Portia had just told her. "Do you mean to say Amelia has developed an interest in Perkin Warbeck?" Verity schooled her face into a semblance of mild curiosity.

"All summer and well into the autumn she was knee deep in books about the man. I think she meant to write a biography. I tell you, I despair of the girl."

"He must be a very fashionable topic," Verity said faintly. Any other time she might be gratified at possibly identifying her anonymous author, but today she had other concerns. "I do beg your pardon, Portia. I'm taking out all my frustration on you because I haven't anyone else to be surly to."

"That's why I came, you absurd creature. Well, not for you to be rude to me, but because I'm well aware that Ash is your closest friend, and that you're without support at a time when you need it. Did you think I stood about in the rain for my own amusement?"

Verity shifted, uncomfortable with the idea that Portia had gone out of her way. "You must know it's going to cause a great deal of scandal. I wouldn't have thought you'd want your name caught up in scandal so close to Amelia's debut."

"This is an emergency." Portia spoke with such gravity that Verity was momentarily taken aback. When Verity failed to respond, Portia frowned. "I'm not keeping a balance sheet, you know. I'm not writing *stood about in rain, jeopardized Amelia's debut* in red ink under your name. There's no tally of your debts. There aren't any debts at all. You don't owe me."

"I know—"

"I don't think you do. People help those they care about. That's a good thing. That's why you sent Nate away."

"That's not what he believes. He only went to humor me. And it turned out he needn't—"

"Precisely," Portia said brightly, as if congratulating a pupil. "You did it for one another. Accepting help doesn't make you weak."

"I don't need a remedial course in friendship, Portia."

Portia gave her a look that plainly said that she thought this was precisely what Verity needed. "Friends ease one another's burdens. We get all tangled together, and sometimes you don't know whether you're helping a friend for their own good or for yourself because it's all the same in the end. You can't separate it out neatly."

But Verity had to separate it out. She had to know that she stood on her own two feet, that she was ultimately her own mistress.

"Come now," Portia went on. "You've been going to bed with him, no? Surely you know that sooner or later he would have insisted on marrying you."

"I don't think he would have. He knows my stance on that topic. He was around when . . ." She gestured around the room, the house, the walls that held memories of exactly what it looked like when a woman's identity dwindled into nothingness.

"Do you think that falling in love with you is part of his sinister plan to subjugate you?"

"No, of course not, but marriage—"

"We're not talking about marriage, but about friendship. Marriage can be just one form that friendship takes."

"It's the shape of a shackle," Verity protested.

Portia broke into a laugh. "Good lord, you're just like your brother. So dramatic."

Verity blushed. "I know that not all marriages are terrible. But it can make otherwise decent men into tyrants." She thought of Ash's offer to help in the shop, thought of his endless offers of tea and cheese, and had to admit it was hard to see the seeds of despotism there.

"If the best you can say about Ash is that he's decent, and if you think he secretly has the soul of a tyrant, then I can't imagine why we're having this conversation in the first place. Surely you can see that, which is why you love him."

"Tell me, Portia," Verity said a moment later, "is there any chance that Ash's suit will fail?"

When Portia hesitated, Verity knew a mad flutter of hope. Her antipathy towards marriage would be a moot point. They might at least have a way forward if Ash were not the duke's legal heir. She could be friends and lovers with someone who was not the next in line to a dukedom. With a duke she could have nothing.

Portia frowned sympathetically and Verity wanted to fling her teacup across the room. "An exceptionally slim one. Apparently, Lady Caroline's diaries are rather specific and the solicitor has been very busy collecting statements. There's almost enough evidence to establish Ash's progress from Arundel House in London to a foster family in Wisbech to a village called Ashby to a school in King's Lynn."

"This is all circumstantial," insisted Verity, still clinging to that idiotic scrap of hope. "And surely the duke's surviving son has many allies in positions of power."

"True." Portia's frown deepened. "Powerful men with titles and money don't often turn on one of their own. They close ranks."

Verity shuddered at the thought of Ash becoming one of those men.

Portia sighed and continued. "But Ash's father was one of their own, too, and a gross injustice was done to him. He's still fondly remembered by many."

After Portia left, Verity returned to her desk and retrieved the tirade on divorce law and the perfidy of men, balled it up, and threw it into the fire. Then she answered both questions as honestly as she could. She did not know, she wrote, how affection was meant to endure all life's vicissitudes. The person to whom one bound one's life at twenty could not be, in any meaningful sense, the same person at forty. The best one could hope for was that each person might alter and grow in ways that fit together, and for any changes falling outside those parameters to be met with reason and charity. Love, marriage, friendship, indeed any tie that bound people together, was a constant exchange of promises, of sacrifices freely made, of favors one didn't need to ask for. Each of these was an opportunity for failure, and it was a wonder so many marriages worked out as well as they did, but an even greater wonder that anyone, especially women, chose to marry at all. The explanation, she wrote, had to be that people possessed either a delusional degree of optimism or a flinty determination to pay any price for even the bare chance that their union might be one of the successful ones. Or, perhaps, it was a combination of the two, because there might not be a difference between hope and stubbornness.

It was an utterly unsatisfying answer, both to write and probably for those who had mailed her their questions. But it was the best answer she could give them, and it might also be the best answer she could give herself.

Ash's hands itched for his pen and ink, but they were still in the attics of Verity's house, and besides, there was no time for drawing, even less for engraving. He had hastily packed a single change of clothes and his shaving kit before leaving for Arundel House, and it quickly became apparent that he needn't have even packed so much. Three consecutive afternoons were spent with tailors and haberdashers, being measured and outfitted for a life he did not particularly want. With every morning that he woke in his absurdly soft bed, he felt less like he had ever known a life before Arundel House. In saying goodbye to people, Ash had gotten good at leaving behind parts of himself. Holywell Street, engraving, Nate, Verity—they all belonged to an Ash who was gone. Within a week, he thought they belonged to an Ash who might never have been real in the first place.

The staff at Arundel House had always been efficiently

cordial to him, but there was a shift in their manners, a shift that measured the difference between how a good servant treated a visiting tradesman and how he treated the heir to a dukedom—the heir to a dukedom who would disinherit his cruel master, no less. There was a degree of deference in the footman's speed and the maid's bobbed curtsey that set him on edge. He felt that he was being corrupted from the outside in.

He had half expected Verity to write him a hastily scrawled note, perhaps, or to simply send over his engraving supplies. But the days came and went and there was no word from her. He had been excised from her life as comprehensively as he had been cast out of the Talbot family twenty years ago. He knew this wasn't fair; he knew that he had been the one who had left her. And now he also knew that he hadn't been cast out by the Talbots after all. But he spent so many years believing it to be true that he couldn't help but think that it was his fate to lose everyone he cared for. Verity had become the latest in a series of people he had loved and lost, and from Ash's new home in Arundel House her loss felt as inevitable as those that had preceded it.

Instead of Verity, he met with a bewildering stream of visitors. There were lawyers and peers and a man he later discovered was the Duke of Wellington's private secretary. After them, there came the women: dowagers and countesses and the patronesses of Almack's. All seemed preposterously glad to have met him. He wondered if he could get rid of them by behaving very rudely, and thereby get his old life back, then remembered there was no old life to return to.

"Is your brother such a notorious villain that people will welcome any comer to replace him?" he peevishly asked his aunt after a dinner attended by a particularly sycophantic set of aristocrats.

She blinked rapidly, which he learned was how she responded to any question she could not answer with rigorous correctness. "Well, he is a villain, but not precisely notorious. He doesn't matter, though. People know we will prevail, so they court your favor."

Ash snorted derisively, even as his aunt's *we* warmed a chilly corner of his heart. "Why are they so certain? It still seems like moonshine to me."

She gave him a gentle smile. "It really isn't, though."

"Bol—" He cleared his throat. "Balderdash. If this all goes pear-shaped, I supposed I'll be locked up in a lunatic asylum as my father was." He settled gloomily into a corner of the stiff drawing room sofa and downed a glass of whisky.

The following morning an elderly woman was presented to him as Lady Staffordshire. He had a vague sense that he ought to recall this name, but he had met and heard of so many people this past week, he simply could not keep track. She was plump and short, with pure white hair. "Oh my," she breathed, clasping his hand. "The very image of his father. You weren't exaggerating, Caro."

"This is your grandmother," his aunt said. "How was your journey from Yorkshire?" she asked the lady.

"I came as soon as I got your letter," Lady Staffordshire said, not letting go of his hands or looking away from his face. "And I'm so glad I did."

They drank tea, discussed the badness of the weather and the warmth of the fire, and after a quarter of an hour they all rose to their feet.

"Staffordshire will support your claim," his grandmother pronounced. "What does the duke have to say?"

Lady Caroline shifted in her seat. "He's very unwell and refuses to meet with us."

"Insist upon it. You must not waste any time, Caro. It will look very bad indeed if the duke dies without acknowledging Montagu." She didn't stumble over the title, but Ash couldn't imagine ever getting used to it. "You must avoid the appearance of anything cloak and dagger. Besides, he may well wish to see his grandchild. I have half a dozen of my own, but he has none."

"If I had snarled and cursed, would she have declared me an impostor?" Ash asked his aunt after the older woman took her leave. Could he then have packed his bag, leaving behind his new coats and pantaloons along with this hateful title that people insisted on using, and returned to Holywell Street?

"Oh, no," she declared promptly. "That would only have made her even more certain you were a Talbot."

They caught one another's eyes and laughed. It was the first time Ash had truly laughed in the week he had been living at Arundel House. He felt the ache in his sides, and when he looked at his aunt, he saw that she was nearly doubled over in laughter. She, too, had gone a long time without laughing.

"If you had insulted her appearance and thrown a vase it would have quite sealed the matter. In fact, perhaps that's what you ought to do in the courtroom."

"I'll keep that in mind," he said dryly.

Ash had often felt unmoored without a family or a home. Without anyone or anywhere he belonged to, and with a body that sometimes seemed intent on killing him, he had often felt like a visitor everywhere he went—estranged from the living, dreading the moment the people he cared for would cast him off and the body he lived in would finally betray him. He hadn't let himself get too comfortable, hadn't let himself form connections that would trick him into thinking he belonged.

But looking at his aunt he knew he belonged here. It wasn't just the fact that her nearly black eyes were identical to his own, it wasn't just the family connection—one could share blood with any stranger on the street and not have it matter in the least. But Lady Caroline had shown him a duty. Maybe this was the answer to why Ash was here in this body, in this world, in the first place.

Or maybe he was here to simply be his aunt's nephew, to prove to her that her family wasn't entirely rotten, to prove that she had done a good deed twenty years ago by sending him away.

"When can we expect"—Ash still did not know what to call the man—"my uncle?"

Lady Caroline frowned. "As soon as tomorrow, depending on how muddy the roads from Leicestershire are."

"We ought to stay at a hotel," Ash said, giving voice to a worry that had been niggling at his mind since his arrival at Arundel House. "My uncle will not take my presence calmly." That was an understatement. He half expected his uncle to murder his aunt and Ash himself without delay. He did not seem to be a man who could be relied upon to make wise decisions.

"I will not leave this house," Lady Caroline said with more firmness than he expected. "It's my home as much as it is Robert's, and more so since I've had the running of it for the better part of two decades. *He* hurt *me*, Ash. I will not scurry away any longer."

"Quite," he said, unable to contradict her.

"Nor will I leave my father without protection. He's not a good man, but he's helpless. Speaking of which, Lady Staffordshire was quite right. We need to speak with the duke before Robert returns."

After a few hours of messages sent back and forth via the duke's grim-faced valet, the duke sent word that he would receive Lady Caroline and Ash.

"Over there is the portrait gallery," Lady Caroline said as she led Ash to the floor of the house that was reserved for the duke. "Most of our better art is at Weybourne Priory but we have a Reynolds and a Gibbs here, as well as a small pair of Gainsboroughs. Watch your step on that carpet."

Ash knew she was going on in this way to distract him from what was about to pass, but soon enough a liveried servant appeared to usher them through a sitting room and into a large, darkened bedroom. The curtains were drawn, the air was close, and on a large bed hung with velvet curtains lay a small, wizened figure.

"Father," Lady Caroline whispered. "Here's the man I told you about."

The old man's skin was pale and papery, but his eyes were

bright and unclouded by age. He looked at Ash. "Jamie," he said in a voice rusty with disuse.

"No, Papa, not Jamie."

"Course not," the duke said, his eyes focused now on Ash. "Jamie's son. The one you got rid of."

"I didn't get rid of him," Lady Caroline protested.

Ash stepped closer to the old man. "Your grace," he said.

"She got rid of you because you had fits," the duke said.

Lady Caroline made a sound of protest. "I didn't—"

"She"—he gestured to his daughter—"paid off some poor woman whose son died in a rookery, laid out the body herself, said it was you, and had the child buried the next day under the church floor with the rest of the Talbots. I was at a shooting party in Yorkshire and came home to find the house in mourning."

So that was how she did it. "How did you know, your grace? If you were away from London, I mean."

"I'm the duke," the old man said forcefully, and looked about to say more, but he was interrupted by a coughing fit. A servant stepped forward, but the duke waved him off. "I'm the duke," he repeated when he once again had breath. "The child's father told me. He wasn't going to do the bidding of a chit of a girl. Of course he told me."

"Got some money from you, too, I suppose," Ash said gently, not wanting to speak the word *blackmail*. "Why didn't you look for me?"

"The body had already been buried in the Talbot plot. I couldn't dig it up and expose my daughter's misdeeds to the world," the old man said. "Or my son's," he added darkly. "So you're to be the duke when I die. Won't have long to wait. Daresay you're pleased with yourself." When Ash didn't respond, the duke pointed a bony finger at him. "You'd rather my daughter return you to whatever hovel she found you in, then?"

"I'm not certain what kind of newspapers you receive here, but I didn't come from a hovel. I'm a tradesman, which you may well consider worse. And it doesn't seem that I have the choice to go back to where I came from, especially since where I came from was evidently here. So I mean to get on the best I can."

"Hmph."

"I hardly need to point out that if you don't like the looks of me, you could very well disclaim all knowledge of the dead urchin. On the other hand, if you wanted to speed things up, you could provide a sworn affidavit with the story you told me. As for me, I'd rather you do one of those things, because without a statement from you, your grace, I don't see any way around a long and costly legal battle between your son and me. I'd rather that money be spent on doing something about the chimneys in this house, but it's your choice."

The old man regarded him appraisingly. "Caro, get him out of here. I need to rest." As they left, they heard the sounds of his coughing.

Chapter Fifteen

Verity settled into something of a rhythm that first cold, damp week of December. She rose, she worked, she ate, she slept. She feared that the sense of calm and peace she felt in an empty house was certain proof that she was not meant to form a lasting partnership with anyone. In the evenings, she curled up on the sofa with a book while Ash's cat gave her murderous stares and repeatedly knocked over the inkwell.

"Yes, well, nobody said you had to stay here," Verity told the cat. Occasionally Verity left a dish of table scraps on the floor, and occasionally the cat left a dead mouse on Verity's pillow. Verity took this as a sign that they had reached a tentative détente; the cat sometimes even ventured to sit on the back of the sofa, but only if Verity pretended she didn't notice or care.

Predictably, the papers were making a meal of Ash's situation. In her line of work, she couldn't entirely ignore newspapers, but for the first few days she tried to at least avert her eyes from those articles about Ash. Whenever she walked into the workshop, however, she'd find the men hastily hiding the latest edition behind their backs, a pall of sudden silence falling over the room. She caught herself tip-toeing down the stairs, straining her ears to catch fragments of overheard conversation. At that point, Verity figured she might as well admit that she lacked the will to suppress curiosity about a person who had mattered—*did* matter—so much to her, when there was news of him right in front of her eyes, and began greedily reading everything she could about him.

Each edition of every paper had a story on "the long-lost heir of Arundel" or "the Commoner Duke" as they had taken to calling him, this latter sobriquet being a compliment from Whigs and an insult from Tories. Engravers took shameless advantage of having a subject they knew well enough to draw from memory, so every printshop from Grub Street to Hyde Park displayed ludicrous caricatures of Ash in the window. A notable example portrayed him carrying a common tankard of ale and betting on a cockfight, his ducal coronet askew, radical pamphlets tucked into his ermine cape. That would have amused Ash. He would have been less amused by the caricature of Lady Caroline Talbot absentmindedly dropping a baby in the gutter.

It was when she saw these engravings, done by his former colleagues, that Verity understood that there would be no going back for Ash. Whatever happened, he couldn't return to Holywell Street and work alongside people who had used him in this way. And what was worse, they were all lost to him. Ash had been alone too often, had been cast off by too many people too many times.

Then she grabbed her umbrella and cloak and made for the street.

"But what do I call these people?" Verity asked an hour later, pacing the floor of Portia's drawing room.

"I doubt you'll meet the duke, but if you do, simply call him your grace. Lady Caroline Talbot is either Lady Caroline, my lady, or madam."

"I meant what do I call Ash?"

Portia looked at her as if she were feverish. "Call him Ash," she said slowly, enunciating each syllable.

"I can't walk in the door and say 'Bring me to Ash.' Is he Lord Ash? He can't be Lord Montagu yet."

"Those who have declared themselves in support of his claim are already calling him Lord Montagu."

"Then what are they calling his uncle? The man who used to be Lord Montagu?" This was all dreadfully confusing, and exactly the sort of system one would expect from a class of people who regarded an accident of birth as more important than knowing who the devil one was speaking of.

"Lord Robert," Portia said. "It's very cold. You'll borrow my fox cape?"

"I can't very well wear your fox with my own dress. It'll look like I stole your cape. I'll get arrested."

"Then you ought to borrow one of Amelia's afternoon gowns as well."

"No," Verity said. "I'll go as I am." Still, as she lifted the heavy brass knocker on the door of Arundel House, she was very aware of the state of her gown, from its soiled hem to its frayed cuffs.

Well, she wasn't here to be pretty. She was here to see Ash, if he'd see her. She'd say her piece and then leave, which would have been a fine plan if she had the faintest notion of what her piece constituted. She knocked on the door, dearly wishing she had written a letter instead. But some things were better said face-to-face, and even though she wasn't entirely sure what she meant to say to Ash, she was fairly certain it fell into that category.

A footman opened the door. "I'm here to see Mr. Ashby," she said, unable to make her mouth shape his title. She clenched her fists around the handle of her satchel. "My name is Verity Plum." She realized that she was ready to stand her ground, to stomp her foot and insist upon seeing Ash. But the servant simply showed her inside to a small parlor and shut the door behind her.

The room was decorated in a subdued style, but scrupulously clean and well aired. Her mind, which for days had been flitting madly between topics, never alighting on any thought long enough to get comfortable, suddenly latched on to the particulars of this room, assimilating details as if they were of the utmost importance. She noted wine-colored whorls on the carpet and green stripes on the wallpaper. A very ugly painting of a horse hung above the hearth, and bits of bric-a-brac were arranged on a shelf. This seemed an extraordinary amount of effort to put into a room that likely served no purpose but the temporary storage of unwanted visitors.

Now that Verity was minutes away from seeing Ash, her hands were clammy and her heart racing. For the past week, she had allowed herself to think only about how annoyed she was—not with Ash, not with herself, but with the entire state of affairs that had ruined things between them. But now it sunk in that she was going to see him. She'd see his face, hear his voice, be near the body that had once been pressed against her own. She realized she was nervous about seeing him—about seeing *Ash*. That was the worst of it, that this predicament had taken away even the most basic foundation of their friendship. There, thank God, she was angry again, which was much better than the noxious brew of anxiety and contrition that had been with her for days.

Her thoughts were interrupted by the sound of a door slamming and a man's raised voice, followed by a woman's quiet pleading. Verity opened the door immediately. A large man, who looked very much like an older, angrier version of Ash, hollered at Lady Caroline while maids scattered.

"You have gone too far this time, Caroline," the man roared. "It doesn't matter what urchins you present with a claim to my title." He lowered his voice to a hiss that Verity could hear, but which the servants, who had retreated, would likely not. "It remains my title, and you would do well to remember that I'm the one with all the cards in this game." Lady Caroline looked like she was trying to disappear into the plaster of the wall, and Verity was put in mind of her mother cowering while her father slammed doors and shouted. "I ought to have sent you away at the same time Jamie was locked up. You were both always soft in your heads, him with his drawings and you with your plants. You've been living on my sufferance. Your bloody plants, your clothes, your entire manner of living, are all due to my generosity."

"I beg your pardon," Verity said. The duke spun towards her, his face somehow even redder. But really, she couldn't stand another minute of this. The world might teem with bullies and tyrants, and there might not be a damned thing she could do to stop them, but that didn't mean she couldn't try. "You no longer have any need to be generous, because Lord Montagu—" referring to Ash by his proper title actually tasted bitter on her tongue, but the look on this man's face was worth it "—has settled three hundred pounds a year on his aunt." This was pure invention—her goal was to draw fire from Lady Caroline. "So you can put that in your pipe and smoke it. In fact, he has more right to be in this house than you do, so why don't you take yourself off now."

Verity was not such a fool that she thought the man would meekly comply, but she succeeded in diverting the man's attention from Lady Caroline. However she did not expect what actually happened, which was for the man to roar like a toddler in the midst of a tantrum, and then take hold of the nearest vase, smashing it to the floor.

"You probably owe your father a hundred guineas for that vase," Verity said, because now the man was stalking towards her and that would give Lady Caroline time to collect herself. "All these years you've been carrying on thinking it all belongs to you, but it doesn't, you bloody oaf. Now why don't you fuck right off." She was going to get hit, and it was going to hurt, but this man was plainly going to hit somebody, and it was far better for it to be Verity than Lady

Caroline, because Lady Caroline looked like she had been through enough of that in her life. "I'm what, half your size? And you're going to hit me?" She held her hands out to her sides, as if inviting him.

"No, he will not," said a cool voice behind her. Out of the corner of her eye she saw Ash in the door that led to the street, idly lounging in the doorframe. Never before had Verity so vastly appreciated his talent for feigning boredom. "Good day, Uncle," Ash said. "I suppose we can dispense with the formal introductions."

Ash's first thought upon seeing the man who had wished him dead, committed his father, and waged a decades-long campaign of terror against his aunt, was that of course Verity would waste no time in flinging herself into the fray. Of course she wouldn't behave sensibly and run *away* from a man she knew to be a would-be murderer. His heart filled with a mixture of fondness and exasperation. Catching the eye of a nearby footman, he mouthed *constable* and watched the lad slip out the door.

Positioning himself between Verity and his raging uncle, Ash gestured with his chin to the sweeping staircase at the end of the hall where a few black-clad figures peered over a balcony. "I realize that this matter must be distressing to you, but surely you can't mean to make a scene in front of the servants." Ash did not care one jot about making a scene in front of servants or anyone else; as far as he cared, his uncle was free to embarrass himself in front of any audience he wished. But he needed to say something to buy time before the constable arrived, if a constable would even be of any use. In anticipation of Lord Robert's arrival, Lady Caroline issued orders for the servants to deny him entry, but Ash supposed they ought to have guessed that his uncle would bully his way into getting anything he wanted.

Now his uncle took a step closer. "These are all lies. I don't know or care who you are but I know you're no nephew of mine. My solicitors assure me that you and my whore of a sister have no evidence to support this cock and bull story you've cooked up between the pair of you."

"We can let the chief justice decide that next week," Ash said, wondering at the calm in his voice. "Meanwhile, I suggest you leave." A week ago, Ash would have felt preposterous, attempting to eject a man from his own house. But it wasn't his uncle's house—it was Ash's grandfather's house, and his aunt's home. Ash had every right to be here: he belonged here as much as he belonged in Holywell Street, as much has he had ever belonged anywhere. This was his birthright, and as vastly unfair as it was that some people inherited fortunes and others inherited nothing at all, he wasn't going to let this man do him out of what was his.

"It's an utter shame for a grown man to carry on like a baby who lost his rattle," Verity chided. "Are all men in your family like that, Lord Montagu?" Ash was fairly certain she'd sooner have her tongue cut out than call him by his title, so he guessed she intended it as a barb for his uncle.

"I'm afraid so, Miss Plum. I assume that in a fortnight I'll start throwing food at the table." Ash regarded his uncle dispassionately, with only a flicker of interest, because the more bored he acted, the redder and angrier his uncle became. If Ash kept going he might provoke the man into an apoplexy, and it likely spoke no good things about his conscience that he found this a consummation devoutly to be wished. "As illuminating as this has been, Uncle, I'm afraid we'll have to continue this at another time when there are no ladies present."

"This whore is no lady," Lord Robert growled. Evidently he was the sort of man who believed all women who thwarted his wishes were whores. How very predictable.

"Quite right," Ash said, catching Verity's eye and seeing something like amusement there. "I beg your pardon, ma'am," he said solemnly, then turned back to his uncle. "She'll take me to task for suggesting otherwise as soon as we're in private. Now, either this is going to come to blows with servants watching and newspapermen in the street outside, or you'll leave." He made up that last bit about the newspapermen, but it was plausible.

Lord Robert looked like he was seriously considering the first option. His hands were curled into fists and his expression took on an even more menacing cast.

"Robert," Caroline said, her voice quavering. "You are frightening the servants and making an ass of yourself. It will take generations to undo the shame you've brought on this family. Don't compound it by committing violent assault in the foyer of Arundel House and getting taken away by redcoats. I can only imagine what the judge would think of you then. Go stay at your club."

Glowering, the man looked between Ash and Caroline. Then he muttered an indistinct oath and returned to the street.

"I didn't think that would work," Caroline said. Her hands trembled. Behind her, her maid looked ready to run to her mistress, and Ash realized grimly that usually when this sort of scene played itself out, his aunt had wounds that needed tending to.

"Nor did I," Ash said. He didn't like it. That had been too easy. But his aunt seemed almost giddy with relief, so he merely reminded the servants to bolt the door and then headed for the library, gesturing for Verity to enter first. As soon as he shut the door behind them, Verity was in his arms. She didn't even kiss him, just flung her arms around his neck and held on for dear life.

"Ash, what the hell kind of situation have you gotten yourself involved in?"

"I'll tell you," he said into her hair, "until today I hoped my aunt was exaggerating. She's had a hard time of it, and I thought she might have overestimated his capacity for violence. Now, if anything, I think she was making light of it." She smelled like soap and ink and home and he tightened his arms around her. "How does a man get like that without being killed in a tavern brawl?"

"Not a lot of sons of dukes involved in tavern brawls," Verity said dryly, stepping out of his embrace. "Although, what do I know. I'm hardly an expert. Duels, maybe. And even then, I don't think they suffer any ill consequences." The man they had seen in the hall was manifestly not hampered by the forces that kept regular people from smashing vases whenever they felt stroppy. "One thing is clear, and it's that your aunt was quite right that he needs to be stopped. Was it true what your uncle said about there being insufficient evidence?"

"Oh, there's plenty of evidence that the grandson of the Duke of Arundel did not die, but was instead sent to be fostered in a village in Norfolk." He sighed and leaned against the door. "What's lacking is any information specifically connecting my history with that of Arundel's grandson. There are bits and pieces of circumstantial evidence—a letter signed by the first woman who fostered me, the scattered memories of an aging cleric, something vague whispered to the headmaster of my old school when I was brought there—but nothing firm and fast. The solicitor says it's enough to go on, but we'd all feel better with that one bit tidied up."

"You were dreadful in there," she said, making it a compliment. "I thought you were going to give that man an apoplexy."

"If I had ten more minutes I might have managed the trick," he said.

"You apologized to me for calling me a lady." She dissolved into laughter, resting her forehead against the door beside him, her shoulders shaking with mirth.

"It was remiss of me for even suggesting such a thing," he intoned gravely. "It's as if I learned nothing from you or Nate."

"So how are you?" she asked, resting her cheek on the door so she faced him. He turned towards her, and their mouths were inches away.

He studied her appearance. She wore no hat and at least twenty percent of her hair had abandoned all pretenses to being involved in anything like a coiffure. Beneath her cloak she had on what he recognized as the frock she wore to clean the soot from the fireplace. He did not know whether it was his imagination or whether her mode of dress had become more resolutely chaotic in the weeks since he had left Holywell Street, but he was certain he had never seen a more welcome sight. However, he was soon to be Lord Montagu, she was a pamphleteer and publisher of illicit novels, and when he looked upon her he ought to see that there could be no future between them. But he wanted to take hold of her wrist and never let it go, wanted to keep her in this house that would soon, appallingly, belong to him.

"I shouldn't have left you the way I did," he said.

"True, but that doesn't answer my question."

"How am I?" He shrugged and pushed himself away from the wall. "I wish I knew. I miss you and seeing you here is . . ." Confusing? Wrong? "I'll never regret seeing you, Plum, but it would have been easier to make a clean break of it. Why did you come?" He heard the weariness in his own voice.

She reached towards him then pulled back her hand. "I wanted to tell you that I'm still your friend. What I told you still holds. We're friends, with or without the rest of it."

"No," he said, shaking his head. "No. I don't want to hear it. I'm in love with you. I don't want your friendship. It would only remind me of what we aren't. Your *friendship*—" he spat the word "—would make me miserable. And goddammit, Verity, I'm incensed that it wouldn't make you miserable too."

"Then why the hell did you take me into your bed if you knew it would have to end?"

"I fooled myself into thinking it wouldn't," he admitted, furious with himself. "And, when I was being halfway rational, I thought I'd be able to part with you the way I've parted with everyone. I thought I'd be able to move on."

"And what in heaven's name did you think would happen to me? Did you think I'd just kiss you goodbye and forget that I had fallen in love with you?"

They stared at one another, the weight of her words hanging in the air between them. "I didn't expect you to love me back," he said finally.

"Then you're more prodigiously stupid than I had thought." And with that she stormed from the house, leaving Ash alone.

Chapter Sixteen

Verity closed the shop for the rest of the day so she could be furious in peace. She was curled on the sofa, sulkily drinking tea and breaking a piece of toast into angry little crumbs when Nan knocked on the door.

"There's a lady downstairs," the older woman said, handing Verity a calling card as if it were a holy relic.

"Mrs. Allenby?" Verity asked, perplexed as to why Portia would leave a card. Then she looked at the name on the ivory rectangle. "Good heavens, that's Ash's aunt. Show her up, will you?" She patted her hair, but it was a lost cause, so she jabbed some pins in it and hoped for the best.

"Lady Caroline," Verity said when the older woman entered the study. Seeing her in this room, where Ash had been such a familiar presence, Verity could see their resemblance to an almost eerie degree. "To what do I owe the honor?"

"It occurred to me that we've met twice now." She glanced around the room in a way that could not help but take in the worn carpet and cracked windowpane. "But under less than ideal circumstances for getting to know one another."

This was true, but Verity was at a loss as to why Lady Caroline would want to know her. "Indeed, ma'am," she said, gesturing at the sofa for her guest while she herself sat on the chair.

"I've heard so much about you."

"You have?"

A flicker of a wry smile darted across Lady Caroline's mouth. "You can't imagine that my nephew has been silent where you are concerned. You would be amazed at how often the conversation drifts in such a direction that he finds it necessary to mention what you would think or what you would do."

With a wave of irritation, Verity understood that Ash's aunt had come to warn her off. If so, she could spare herself the trouble.

"I'm a devoted reader of your new magazine," Lady Caroline said. "Do people truly send you those letters or do you make them up?"

Whatever Verity had expected from Lady Caroline, it had not been a conversation about the management of a ladies' magazine. "I made the first letter up. Actually, Ash made it up." She remembered that morning in her study with Nate and Ash, when they had all laughed and been momentarily carefree. "But in the other issues I answered letters that have been sent in. We get heaps of them," she said, not bothering to conceal her pride.

"This morning, I was so pleased to discover the December

issue on the breakfast table with my tea. But your answer to the letters . . ." She folded her gloves in her lap. "It was not your usual manner of advising correspondents."

That had been her response to the ladies with unfortunate marriages. "My first draft was a three-page screed on reforming the divorce laws."

A small smile flickered at the edges of Lady Caroline's mouth. "But what you actually wrote was quite . . . well, this is an inexcusably personal question but did you have my nephew in mind when you wrote of the great hope of love weathering obstacles?"

Verity refused to be embarrassed. "Yes. I wrote it in a moment of delusion. If you've come to warn me off Ash, there's no need. We parted on exceedingly bad terms."

"Unequal marriages are notoriously difficult," said Lady Caroline. "Everybody says so."

"Quite," snapped Verity, not needing the point driven home. "Neither of us is contemplating marriage."

"It's going to be bad enough for my nephew, trying to exist in the circles that his birth ought to have entitled him. Marrying a commoner will make it quite impossible."

"Ma'am," Verity said with rising exasperation, "you don't need to convince me. You, Ash, and I are all in perfect agreement on this matter."

Lady Caroline appeared not to have heard her. "On the other hand, it would not precisely be a marriage of unequals because he has been a tradesman and you are a tradesman's daughter."

"I'm a tradesman myself, I'll have you know," she said

before realizing that this was not at all the point. "Besides, Ash and I are equal, and you and I are equal, and—" Verity did not want to lecture this woman on Locke.

"Oh, I've read that Wollstonecraft book. But I'm not the one you need to convince."

"I'm not trying to convince you and I'm certain Ash needs no convincing on that topic," Verity said, bewildered as to how Mary Wollstonecraft entered the conversation.

"Precisely!" Lady Caroline said. "Indeed, there is something charming about a man who remains loyal to his childhood sweetheart despite a change in circumstance."

Verity's head was spinning. "I'm finding it difficult to follow the thread of this conversation, ma'am."

"Would you have married him if he were a commoner?"

Portia had asked her the same question in this very room, not a week earlier. "I never wanted to marry. I always thought the last thing in the world I needed was a husband."

"Very wise."

"My parents—" Verity shook her head in a way that she hoped the lady would interpret as *had a marriage one would not wish on one's worst enemies*.

"Mine as well, I'm afraid."

"And the letters I get only confirm my earlier beliefs."

"A very flawed institution, marriage is," Lady Caroline said.

"Quite," Verity agreed.

"A thoroughly difficult group of people, men," the lady added.

Verity nodded.

"Despite all of that, I believe my nephew is a good man."

"Certainly," Verity said.

"So you would have married him?" Lady Caroline asked.

Verity had lived long enough with Nate to know she was being argued into a corner. She thought again of the conversation she had with Portia not long ago. "If he had asked me, if he truly wanted that of me, maybe. Eventually, yes, I probably would have given in," she admitted. She was aware that this was not a stirring declaration of love, but the fact was that a month ago she would have rejected the possibility of marriage out of hand. That she was considering it, even so tepidly, was a radical shift, and, she feared, the thin end of the wedge.

"Do you not believe that he'd be as good a husband as a duke as he would have as an engraver?"

"That isn't the point," Verity protested.

Lady Caroline removed a piece of paper and a pair of spectacles from her reticule. "Do you not believe you and he are fundamentally equal and—" she read from the paper "—it is long past time to do away with meaningless distinctions of rank?"

Verity knew that phrase. That was from a piece she and Nate had written for the *Register* months ago. "We were referring to universal suffrage, not marriage."

"To be perfectly honest, Miss Plum, I don't care who he marries or who he takes as a mistress. I know I ought to, but I've spent twenty years wondering what happened to the child I tried to save, and now that I see him safe and sound I only want him to be happy. My nephew will make a good duke," Lady Caroline said, rising and shaking out her skirts. "And as long as this nation has dukes, it can only be for the best to have as many good men in that position as possible. He's kind and he's fair. He reminds me of his father, who was the best of brothers. And while I can't expect this to mean anything to you, it makes me proud to know that one day soon there will be a worthy Duke of Arundel."

"Why did you come here today?"

"You have a place in the world, something all your own. I envy you. Being anything at all to Ash—wife, mistress, even friend—will mean giving up some of that, and perhaps taking something from him in return. I wouldn't blame you for not wanting to do it. I came to remind you that the man you know hasn't changed. But he is rightfully the next Duke of Arundel, and if the court finds otherwise next week, it will be unjust. It is his place in the world and he's starting to accept that."

Verity felt the implied rebuke that at the very least she ought to do the same.

Ash had hoped that his uncle's absence would allow the servants to stop slinking about in terror lift the sepulchral gloom that blanketed Arundel House. When that didn't happen, he realized that the servants had as much at stake in the upcoming trial as he did: if Ash lost, his uncle would surely either dismiss the servants without references for their disloyalty or find some more dire way to retaliate.

With this in mind, he visited his grandfather's apartments for the second time.

"Do you enjoy dragging this family into disrepute, boy?" the old man croaked from his bed. The Duke of Arundel did not seem interested in forging a friendly relationship with his long-lost grandson.

Ash forbore from responding that any dragging into disrepute had occurred some decades since, and short of getting tried for treason and murder he could hardly outdo his uncle. "Exceedingly," he said. The duke let out a wheezy laugh. "But I came to ask you about the servants. They must be in your employ, not my uncle's. If I lose this suit, I want to know that you'll ensure they have references. And I want your promise that in your will you've left enough for my aunt to be independent."

A malicious gleam lit up the old man's eyes. "That's what you're worried about? Just goes to show you aren't a proper Talbot, no matter what blood you have in your veins."

"Because I exert myself on behalf of other people?"

"No, because references and incomes will be the least of their problems if you lose. If you win, too, come to that."

A shiver coursed down Ash's spine. "What do you mean by that?"

"Come now. You know what kind of man my son is. What do you think he'll do to you and anyone who has helped you? Do you think he's going to quietly disappear? He burnt down the conservatory at Weybourne Priory to punish Caro for allowing supper to be served cold."

Ash remembered the burnt pages of his aunt's herbarium. "How could you stand idly by while this happens? She is your daughter."

"And he is my son."

This man—possessed of title, fortune, and connections—had more power than anyone Ash had ever met, and he couldn't see his way to using it to protect his daughter. That amount of power was precious, rare, and the Duke of Arundel did nothing with it. He just let it molder and go to waste. Ash climbed the stairs to his own bedchamber and spent a sleepless night, thinking he heard footsteps in the darkened corridors or smelled smoke wafting from the attics.

Chapter Seventeen

In the windowless box room, Verity could see her breath and smell distinct signs of a mouse infestation.

"It's too cold to rummage through the attics," Nan said, clutching her apron in her hands. "You'll catch your death up there."

"It shouldn't take me more than a few hours," Verity assured her. "And if the trial is to begin next week, there's no time to spare." She had thought there would be months before the judge agreed to hear Ash's suit, and could only imagine that the duke had pressed the powers that be to expedite matters.

She stared at the pile of detritus in the box room. Nobody had ever cleared it out in the five and twenty years she had lived here; more and more things got added, shoved into spaces between trunks and cracked bedsteads and piles of what could only be rubbish. Before Roger left for Bath, he asked Verity to stow some of his belongings up here. Verity hoped to find a journal or perhaps whatever correspondence had existed between himself and the headmaster of Ash's school. She didn't like to think that Roger might have known the truth of Ash's origins and failed to tell Ash, but she had known Roger. The man had been fiercely protective of the boy who had come to him as a friendless invalid. If Roger had thought Ash was better off not knowing, if he had suspected—correctly—that Ash would be in danger should his identity become known, then he might have deliberately withheld that information.

It took hours to even find Roger's belongings, the contents of the room having gotten quite jumbled when Nate and Charlie rummaged through while packing for their journey. Eventually her eyes landed on a crate labeled in Roger's neat hand. She shoved it out onto the landing to examine it in better light. There was also a battered old trunk, too ratty to withstand an ocean voyage, and she dragged that to the landing as well.

Verity had hoped to find journals, but if Roger had ever kept a journal, he had not sent them to be stored in this attic. What she found instead were a pair of galoshes, an opera hat, several engravings that she would remember to send on to Ash, and a bible. This last object was perplexing, because Roger was as vehement an atheist as Nate was. It was a costly volume, bound in red calfskin with gilt on the edges. A red ribbon that had been intended for use as a bookmark was tied to another ribbon, and then wrapped around the entire book. Verity untied the ribbons, partly because she was loath to see a volume that had been produced with such care treated so badly, and partly because she had to know why

Roger—fussy, fastidious Roger—had done such a thing. She worked the knot loose and gingerly opened the cover, careful not to damage the binding. In between the front cover and the first page was a stack of letters, still folded. She delicately unfolded the top one and read the date. November 1799. And it was addressed to Roger from a man who signed himself Adrian.

It took only a single glance to determine why Roger had kept this letter. This was a love letter. There was nothing actionable, and if she hadn't known Roger well enough to be familiar with his inclinations she might not have noticed the sentiment, but it was a love letter nonetheless. She might have put the letter back into the bible, bound the book once again, and returned it to the shadowiest corner of the attic, if she hadn't seen the word *pupil* towards the end. Might Roger's Adrian have been one of Ash's schoolmasters?

She opened the next letter so quickly she nearly tore it. The date was two weeks after the first letter, and after a lengthy disquisition on the subject of chilblains, Adrian mentioned that his school had a new student who had arrived in the chaperonage of a rector from Ashby, in Norfolk. The clergyman had privately told the schoolmaster that the local rumor, passed on from a woman who fostered the child some years ago, was that the boy was the scion of a noble family who was put into hiding after his uncle made an attempt on his life. Adrian had asked whether the child knew of his origins, and the rector said that he did not. Adrian then asked what family the child belonged to, and the vicar said he did not know, but that it was one of the oldest in the land.

Verity realized she held in her hand the key to Ash's case, the piece of evidence that connected Ash with the child who had been brought to that village in Norfolk. She could throw it into the fire and hope that the Court of Common Pleas found Ash's claim to be without merit. But she knew she wouldn't. Ash had made his choice; he had found what Lady Caroline called his place in the world. Verity would support him in that, even if she didn't like it, even if it meant that any future they had together would bring about an irretrievable change for Verity.

She shook the dust out of her hair and sent a note to Arundel House.

Some hours later there came a knock on the shop door. She ignored it at first, but when the rapping persisted she ran downstairs, dressing gown wrapped tightly around her, ready to give a piece of her mind to whoever couldn't understand what dark shop windows meant. "We're closed," she called. "Been closed for hours. Bugger off."

"Plum," said a voice she would have recognized anywhere. "That's not how you run a business."

She flung the door open. Ash's hat was low on his forehead, the collar of his coat turned up high against his face, presumably so he'd avoid notice. "Come in before we have newsmen at the door," she said, and let him up to her office. "I didn't expect you to come in person," she said.

He stepped into the shop and she closed the door behind him. "You said you found papers in Roger's belongings that shore up the evidence for my suit, and you thought I wouldn't come in person?"

"I meant to send them to your solicitor."

"I came in person to see if you had taken leave of your senses," he clarified. "You're going to aid and abet me becoming a duke?"

"I'm going to aid and abet you, full stop," Verity retorted.

He regarded her for a long moment. "Thank you, Plum."

Upstairs in the study, she took the letters out of her desk and waited for him to read them.

When Ash finally looked up, he frowned. "Why wouldn't Roger have told me?"

"Ash, he thought you were in danger. You *were* in danger, and you still are. Or maybe he thought you were better off not knowing. For heaven's sake, you were better off not knowing, and so was I." She set her jaw. "But things are different now. You're the only thing stopping your uncle from doing a great deal of harm. So all that's left is to ensure that you win next week."

She hoped he recognized this for what it was: an overture, a concession, a tiny sign that she was willing to accept Ash's new role.

He stepped towards her. "Is that all that's left, Plum?"

She shook her head.

He peeled off his greatcoat to reveal a tailored coat that suited his broad shoulders and a pair of pantaloons that gave her thoughts an obscene turn. His linens were whiter than she had ever seen them, his hair smoother, his boots polished to a mirror shine. On his hand was a ring that gleamed red in the firelight.

"You look terrible," she said.

He raised an eyebrow. "I've missed you, too, Plum." It had been only a day since they had seen one another at Arundel House, but she knew what he meant.

"I hate your coat and your stupid ruby ring."

He tossed his hat onto the sofa. "I think you're glad to see me."

"Whoever did that to your hair ought to be shot out of a cannon." She was saying all the wrong things, but it seemed that as long as she kept saying them, he kept moving closer, stalking towards her. She must have been moving towards him, too, because now they stood toe to toe and she could smell the new costly soap he used. "You smell bad too," she whispered.

He took her chin in his hand and looked down at her. She didn't move away, but held his gaze steadily. When he bent his face towards hers, he paused when their mouths were an inch apart. When he finally brushed his lips across hers, the contact sent a shiver coursing up her spine, a breath stuttering out of her lungs that made a sound mortifyingly close to a whimper. She stepped away, dragging her body from his.

"If you want me to leave, I'll go," he said. "But I don't think you do. I think you want me here, like this, as much as I do."

"What happened to making a clean break of it?"

"I was a fool. I tried to tell you yesterday but it came out all wrong."

"I hate all of this." She poked a finger at his ring. "And this." She indicated the gold watch chain that dangled from the pocked of his well-cut silk waistcoat. "And this." She smoothed a hand down the soft wool of his coat. "I hate all of it."

"Why?"

"Because—" Her voice nearly broke, and she took a steadying breath. "Because it took you away from me."

He put his hand to her cheek, as if there was something he could do or say to make things right. "It doesn't have to be that way."

She grabbed his wrist. "Don't lie to me. Don't you dare." She looked into his dark, dark eyes, and for a moment she thought she might be able to tell the truth. But not yet. "Take it off," she commanded.

"Pardon? Take what off?"

"All these things I hate." She pointed at his clothes.

He blinked. "Sometimes I hate them too."

"Get rid of them."

"Well, Plum." That moment of raw honesty between them was gone and they were once again Ash and Plum, him cool and detached, her hard and angry. But he was already unwinding his cravat. "Far be it from me to deny a lady's—"

In a moment of inspiration she took hold of his cravat and pulled him close, a quick jerk, a meaningless show of force against a man whose very power was the force that kept them apart. She heard him suck in a breath of air, watched his eyes darken impossibly further. Then she tugged his head down to hers and took his mouth in a kiss.

Ash's heart slammed against the walls of his chest as Verity led him to her bedroom, then pulled him close for another kiss. The linen of his cravat was harsh and taut against his neck, and he wanted it tighter. He wanted a bite of pain to take away from everything else he was feeling.

"I said take it off," she whispered into his skin.

Willing his hands not to tremble with anticipation, he pulled off his cravat, but she kept hold of one end, passing the length through her hands again and again, contemplatively, as if coming to a plan. He shivered.

Coat, waistcoat, shirt, trousers: he flung them all into a pile and stood naked before her. He wanted to go to her, to pull the dressing gown off her shoulders and get rid of whatever shabby shift she had on beneath it. But plainly she wanted to be in charge tonight, and he wanted that, too, so he waited, watching as she pulled that strip of linen through her hands.

"Get on the bed," she said, and so he did. He lay back against the bolster and cushions, never taking his eyes from her. "Hands over your head," she said, approaching him, wielding that cravat as if it were a weapon.

He hesitated only a fraction of a second, not from fear or indecision but from the blunt force of the realization that this thing he had scarcely let himself imagine, this fantasy that had dwelt only in the most secret corners of his mind, was about to come true. Then he raised his arms. She rewarded him by kneeling on the bed beside him, her weight causing the mattress to dip slightly, angling his body towards hers. He felt the fabric wrap around his wrists: a threat and a promise. As she leaned over him, binding his wrists to the bedframe, her breasts, uncorseted beneath her shift and dressing gown, brushed across his lips.

"Plum," he whispered, his voice strangled.

"Shh." She tested her knot and ran her fingers down the length of his bound arms. The touch was equal parts soothing and agonizing. He was naked and tied up and completely at her disposal, and surely that thought should not be half as appealing as it was. But she was looking at him with an expression of frank appreciation, almost wolfish desire, and whatever perversions they were about, at least they were about them together.

"Look at you," she said, caressing his shoulders and then rubbing a thumb along his stubbly jaw. "All for me."

"All for you," he said, as if it were his part in the litany. He had known for ten years, for the entirety of his adult life, that he and Verity fit together, belonged together, and there was no dukedom, no title, no inheritance that could change that. And like this, at her mercy and under her gaze, he hoped she could see that. Her fingers trailed lower, over the muscles of his chest and the sensitive skin of his nipples. He suppressed a groan.

"Don't," she said. "I want to hear it." She pulled off her dressing gown and then she was only in her threadbare shift, as insubstantial as cobwebs, as translucent as a cloud. He wanted to touch everything the shift hinted at: the heavy curve of breast, the swell of her hips, the nip of her waist. He wanted to put his hands all over her, but she wasn't letting him, and that, for whatever backward reason, made it even better, made the sight of her sharper, more acute. He pulled at his bindings, trying to get his mouth closer to hers.

She responded by pulling the shift over her head and

bending forward, letting her breasts skim his lips. He took a nipple into his mouth, heard her sigh of relief as he swirled his tongue around the pebbled flesh. His cock, painfully hard, got only harder when he realized there was nothing he could do about it. He couldn't touch himself, and Verity was kneeling over him in such a way that even when he bucked his hips, he couldn't do anything to achieve even the slightest friction. He groaned, and she gave him an approving smile.

"Poor Ash," she said, crawling down his body. "Poor, poor Ash. Here you are, about to get a fancy title and an entire estate, and there's nothing you can do about your own cock." She crawled lower, then shoved his legs apart. He could feel her breath on his skin, could see her nipples brushing the fabric of the quilt. Following his gaze, she brought a hand to her breasts, toying with them, as if weighing them in her hands. He pulled at his bindings, mainly to reassure himself that he really couldn't get free. He couldn't; he was tied fast and sure, going nowhere, at her disposal. *Hers.*

Then she bent her head and licked the head of his cock, her tongue warm and wet and different from anything he had imagined.

"Verity," he groaned. "Oh God." Her hand was wrapped around his shaft, and she was regarding him with the intent curiosity she would devote to a new book or an interesting argument. Then she sucked lightly on the head and he cursed. There was nothing for it but to swear himself blue. He couldn't touch the soft strands of hair that fell onto his thighs, he didn't dare move his hips to bring himself further into the sweet warmth of her mouth. He held himself impossibly still and gritted his teeth as her lips closed around his length.

"You like this?" she asked innocently, raising her head to face him. Her eyes were bright with amusement.

"It's tolerable," he said, because that was the game. "I'll endure." He let loose another volley of profanity as she drew him into her mouth again, because he could take the game only so far. He gave himself up to her, let his mind be consumed by pleasure, by sensation, by Verity.

When his muscles started to hurt with the effort of not thrusting into the slick warmth of her mouth and his wrists chafed against the crisp linen, she pulled off him and came to straddle his thighs. Her lips swollen and her hair a mess, she looked at him carefully, as if to assess whether he wanted this as much as she did.

"Be my guest," he offered, gesturing with his chin in the direction of his cock and speaking with as much sangfroid as a man could while bound to a bed and tortured to within an inch of his life by the woman he loved. "Have at it."

She teased the head of his cock against her soft, wet center and he let out a strangled groan. Finally she had mercy on him and sank onto his length, enveloping him in that velvety heat. He watched where their bodies joined, watched his cock disappear inside her, watched the sway of her breasts as she sighed when he was fully seated. She moved her hips and moaned and that was the end of his self-control. He bucked his hips up into her, because even with his hands tied and the unspoken rules of this game between them, he could not hold back any longer. He needed relief, he needed more.

She responded by leaning forward, her hand braced on his shoulder, her breasts tantalizingly close to his mouth. He reached up and captured a nipple between his lips, and was rewarded when she made a sound of undiluted pleasure. He kept going, kissing and thrusting and doing everything in his power to wait, just another minute, just a little more.

"Ash," she breathed. "Ash, I can't. I need more," she said.

"Touch yourself," he said, and then she was clenching around him. The force of her climax nearly brought on his own. "Now, Verity," he said, urgent. She lifted off him and he watched himself spill in her hand.

"Plum," he groaned when his breathing returned to normal. "You are going to kill me. I think you might already have done."

"Pity," she said, leaning over him to untie his wrists. His hands, once free, felt light and strange, as if they didn't belong to him. She wiped her hands on the cravat and threw it aside. "I think I could go again."

"Come here." When she didn't move, he tapped his chest. She got the message then, and crawled up his body, kneeling over his chest. He pressed his mouth to the apex of her legs, swirling his tongue around the place where she had touched herself. Her taste, her scent, her wetness against his lips, the soft whimpering sounds she made as she tangled her hands in his hair—he felt unspeakably grateful to be this close to her, to be able to show her with his body some fraction of what she meant to him. At that moment, he knew he'd never choose to be apart from her, he'd do whatever it took, whatever she needed. He stroked inside her, slow and deep, and something he did must have been right because she swore.

"Do that again," she breathed. "Please, please." She was begging him. And the idea of Verity Plum begging for anything was enough of a novelty to make him smile against her skin as he moved his fingers inside her, drawing another litany of oaths from her.

Afterward, she collapsed beside him, her head pillowed on his shoulder and one leg flung across his hips. She had pulled the bed quilt over them, and they were cocooned together, warm and close in a single drafty room within a house that maybe, once upon a time, had been their home.

Later, after they had dressed, and were standing by the door of the cold, darkened shop, making lazy conversation to avoid saying good-night, she reached into her pocket and produced a folded sheet of paper. "I've been meaning to give you this. Nate left it on my desk before he left, along with a note saying I could print it if I wanted. You'll see straight away that I couldn't do anything of the sort. But it's Nate at his most Nate-like. It felt good to hear his voice. It'll be a while before we can expect a letter, and I thought you might like to be reminded that you have friends."

It was too dark in the shop to read, so he tucked the paper into his coat pocket. "Thank you." He brushed his lips across her forehead. She knew him well enough to understand that he had, despite his attempts to be reasonable, experienced Nate's leaving as an abandonment, and she was doing what she could to mitigate that.

"When will I see you next? Will you keep coming back to me?" she asked.

His first instinct was to tell her that of course he would, that he wanted nothing more. But this wasn't only about his desires; he needed to know that she wanted this as much as he did. "Are you asking me to?"

"Yes," she said, after only the smallest hesitation. "I . . . hell, Ash, I think I need you." Her gaze was fixed at some point over his shoulder, as if the words had cost her a lot. And, knowing her, they probably had.

He drew her closer to him. "I love you, Plum. I don't know how to stop coming back to you and even if I did I wouldn't want to. Marry me."

"You're deluded." She pulled away to arm's length, her face pale and outraged in the moonlight. "You and Portia both. And your aunt. One, you'd be a pariah." She ticked it off on her fingers. "Two, my skin crawls at the idea of having a title. Three, I would rather eat worms than live in that house."

He tugged her back to him. "One, if Portia Allenby and my aunt are already contemplating our marriage, then I don't think we'd be utterly friendless. Two, so does mine but I'm bearing up. Three, we could live elsewhere."

"We could carry on like this," she countered, gesturing between them.

He wanted to argue the point, but knew that the outcome of this discussion didn't matter. "Look, I want to marry you, Verity. It's the thing I want most in this life. But if you don't want to marry, then we won't. I'll take you on any terms you offer. Weekly visits. Monthly visits. I just need to know that you're a part of my life."

"Really?" She sounded surprised, but happy. "Even if I fell pregnant?"

The prospect of having an illegitimate child filled him with something twisted and shameful. But he knew that it wasn't an insurmountable problem. "We would care for any child we had under any circumstances," he said. "I trust you, and you trust me. We'd make it right." Because that was the truth. No matter what, marriage or no marriage, children or no children, negotiating a life together required a lot of blind faith in the goodwill of the person beside you.

Her only answer was to kiss him in return.

Chapter Eighteen

"Anything you do will reflect on him," Portia said, dropping an armful of dresses onto Verity's sofa. "If your names aren't already connected, they will be after this. You must dress the part."

"What part?" Verity asked.

"Don't be obtuse." Portia said, frustrated. "People will be assessing you as a potential duchess. If you're suitable, they'll say little. If you're unsuitable, they'll have a lot to say. Even if you only intend to be his lover, I can tell you that a mistress of a well-known man comes under similar scrutiny. I'm not suggesting you array yourself in peacock feathers and a sable coat. You could wear Amelia's brown velvet pelisse and promenade gown, or we could take in my dove gray sarsnet round dress with the black pelisse. Both are discreet but visibly costly. In fact, you ought to take both ensembles, and keep them, because you'll need to look above reproach every time you leave your house."

Verity clenched her teeth. There would be other places

where she had to give way, bits of herself that would be eroded by the force of this thing Ash had brought upon them. But for Ash, she'd do it. She'd do that and more and somehow she'd be glad for the chance to help him. "Fine," she said. "I can do that."

"Another thing, Verity dear," Portia said, her words careful and measured. "If I could have married Ned, I would have." Verity was startled to hear Portia refer to her late lover as anything other than Lord Pembroke. "In a heartbeat. You'll make your own choice, but if I had had the chance to marry Ned, I wouldn't have whistled it down the wind, not for the world."

Verity tried on the brown velvet gown and let Portia tame her hair with a pair of tortoiseshell combs. She drew the line only at a pair of pearl earbobs that pinched dreadfully.

"Brave girl," Portia said, surveying her one last time before leaving. "It's hard to let a little bit of yourself go."

Equipped with a wedge of cheese and a brand-new copy of the latest volume from the author of *Waverley,* Verity curled up on the sofa. But the novel failed to hold her interest. She didn't want to read about doomed highlanders or failed rebellions. She rooted around in her pocket for a much folded and creased issue of the *Examiner*; she had been carrying it around for days on the theory that she might finally get around to reading in it a poem that everyone from Portia's girls to the lads in the shop had been talking about. But when she thumbed through the pages, she found that she could read the words, see that they assembled into something beautiful, but they meant nothing for her. What use did she have for the sculptors of crumbling statues, dead kings, or travelers—all of them men, all of them gone, all of them with their heads lodged firmly up their backsides. The poem seemed to rebuke the hubris of leaders without realizing that it, too, fed into that cycle of pride in which men celebrated the deeds of other men, generation after generation. When Verity thought of a toppled monarchy, the statue of a tyrant half-buried in sand, she felt none of the melancholy that the poet seemed to want his reader to feel; instead she was filled with hope that maybe this tyranny, too, would pass, that maybe she would live to see a world in which the deeds of men were not the only measure of accomplishment.

She took off her spectacles and abandoned her reading. She thought of her mother and Lady Caroline, both of their existences shaped by the whims and demands of the men they depended on. She thought of Portia, who had fought hard for a degree of independence, only to wager the lion's share of her savings on finding men to provide for her daughters. She thought of nearly every letter written to the *Ladies' Register,* all asking variations of the same question: how was a woman to live her own life when she was dependent on the men nearest to her. Verity herself had jealously guarded her independence, refusing help lest it spill over into control.

She thought of Ash, and the way they felt for one another. It was the height of madness to love someone and be loved in return, and to throw that away as if it didn't matter. But they had both done it—he by leaving her, her by going to him with what must have seemed a tepid offer of friendship. They were now cobbling together some sort of understanding, but she still didn't know if the final result would be anything either of them could live with. And yet, for Ash, she thought she could live with almost anything that let them be together.

She dropped the *Examiner* and reached for the small hand mirror that Portia had left beside the sofa. Inspecting her appearance at arm's length, she expected to be alienated by what she saw, she expected to feel like she was participating in some kind of mummery. But all she saw was herself, rendered acceptable for Ash's world. She could do that. She would do that.

It was a dangerous thing, this being in love.

"You look pretty," said a voice in the doorway. "Is that my dress? It suits you better."

"Amelia!" Verity nearly dropped the mirror. "How did you get in here?"

"I sort of sailed past your shopman and he didn't know what to do. He was hardly going to tackle me. I'll apologize on my way out."

"If you're looking for your mother, she left an hour ago."

"If I were looking for my mother, I could have remained at home. I waited until she was closeted with the cook before slipping out. It's you I wanted to see." The girl twisted her hands in her fur muff and Verity raised an eyebrow. "It's about the book. I need to know—have you printed it?"

"You'll need to be more specific," Verity said, narrowing her eyes.

"I can't believe you're going to make me admit this." Amelia sank into the chair that Verity thought of as Ash's. "*The Princely Pretense*, which I wrote with your brother. Have you printed it? I thought I could just take the money and be done with it, but a third of the fee you paid me was meant for Nate and now I don't know what to do with it. Also if the book is actually"—she sketched out a vague rectangle with her hands—"a *book* then I want to see it."

"Well." Verity stared at the girl. "I suspected as much—"

"Of course you did." Amelia rolled her eyes. "How many people do you know who would write a book about Perkin Warbeck?"

"What possessed you?"

"I have to do something to earn a bit of money. Otherwise I stay up all night thinking of penury and Mama says that's bad for the complexion. Sleeplessness, that is. Not penury. Although, that too, I expect. So I wrote the book and was thinking of sending it off to a publishing house. But when you mentioned the possibility of printing . . . *that* sort of book. I talked to Nate and we, ah, collaborated. No, that isn't a euphemism."

"It doesn't need to be! My brother wrote an obscene book with a child of seventeen—"

"Eighteen, now," Amelia said grandly.

"Collaboration, indeed! I assume he wrote the, er, bedroom scenes? I knew I recognized his penmanship, or lack thereof."

"Well, it's done, so are you going to let me see it?"

"I suppose the illustrations aren't that explicit," Verity mused.

"Illustrations!" Amelia all but shrieked, clapping her hands together. Verity gave up any semblance of protest and went downstairs, returning with the first volume and the proofs of the second and third.

"Are people actually buying it?" she asked as she paged through the first volume.

"Yes," Verity assured her. "We're doing the next two volumes at the same time. It's a very engaging story, Amelia. You could do it again, even without Nate's contributions. If you're looking for a way to support yourself, that is."

Amelia went pink, more from happiness than embarrassment, Verity thought. "Thank you," she said. "I've already started a novel about Isabella of France."

"Or you could write a book about somebody who isn't . . . dreadful."

"Why on earth would I want to do that?" Amelia asked, scrunching her nose in distaste.

Only after Amelia left did Verity realize she had conducted the entire conversation in a velvet gown and with tortoiseshell combs in her hair. It was a reminder that fine gowns or tatty frocks, she was still herself. Maybe this was a chance for her to decide what parts of her life she wanted to keep and which she wanted to leave behind. She was so used to digging in her heels and fighting to keep things that were hers, that she hadn't thought of letting go as an option, let alone an opportunity. But whether she wanted to or not, things were going to change for her, and she could take advantage of that, but only if she trusted Ash enough to ask him for help.

It took three footmen to clear the way for Ash and his aunt to enter Westminster, and once they reached the courtroom themselves they found it packed nearly to the rafters with noisy spectators. Only when the judge pounded his gavel and the barristers began making their speeches did the cacophony settle into a restless whisper.

Ash felt hundreds of eyes on his back as his uncle's barrister described him as a grifter and a cheat, an impostor and a liar. He kept his face impassive, only reaching out to hold his aunt's hand when the lawyer's invective turned to describing Lady Caroline's betrayal and hinting at a hereditary insanity. They had expected as much, but hearing it said in a packed court, in front of people who knew them, made Ash feel exposed and ashamed. It was a reminder that there would always be those who believed he was every inch as bad as his uncle's lawyer insisted. Ash's mind turned to what his uncle would do when the trial was over. Regardless of the outcome, Ash didn't doubt that his uncle would retaliate against Ash, Caroline, and even the duke. He was a violent man, accustomed to getting his way.

When the court recessed, he took a surreptitious glance at the crowd on the way to an antechamber with his aunt. On the balcony he saw Verity sitting next to Portia Allenby. She shot him a small smile and waved discreetly. She was wearing a hat, which was so singular a circumstance he could only stare. He mouthed *hat* and gestured at his own head, and he would swear on his life that she actually blushed.

Later, his aunt took the witness stand, telling of how, after witnessing her brother push her orphaned nephew down a set of stairs, she had sent the injured child away with her lady's maid and a purse filled with coins. His uncle's lawyer asked all the questions Ash's solicitor had told them to expect: if she knew for a certainty that her brother had attempted to take the life of an innocent child, why not inform her father? Her answer—that she expected her father to support her brother's murderous efforts—made the courtroom explode into a buzz of conversation.

"The child was epileptic," Lady Caroline clarified. "As was his father before him. I knew my father and brother to have a prejudice against those afflicted with that condition."

Now Ash knew to a certainty that every eye in the room was fixed on him, as if waiting for him to have an episode right on the spot. Out of the corner of his eye he saw his uncle's malevolent gaze.

The judge then read the statement of the Duke of Arundel admitting that he knew his nephew had not died. This, the judge instructed the jury, was to assume even greater gravity given the duke's perilous health and the fact that the declaration was against his own self-interest.

Then the rector of Ashby testified, a tiny old man with sparse white hair and thick spectacles. Ash tried to remember him but came up with nothing. He had thought that perhaps the trial, with its orderly progression of evidence, would awaken some memories. But that period of his life before Roger was as lost to him as it ever was, leaving him with nothing but fragmented images that failed to coalesce into anything he could understand.

When court adjourned for the day, Ash and his aunt stayed back, waiting for the crowd to thin before attempting to summon their carriage. They sat in the judge's antechamber, barely making conversation while they drank the tea that appeared before them.

Ash did not want to go back to Arundel House. He would have preferred to walk along the river, to shake loose some of the restlessness that had settled in his limbs that day. But when the carriage was called, he went with his aunt. On the street, a somberly clad figure waited for them beside the carriage.

"Miss Plum," Lady Caroline called, before Ash quite got his bearings. "Let us drive you home."

"It's out of your way," Verity said, at the same time Ash flung the carriage door open and said, "Get in, Plum, before you get abducted by a newspaperman in search of a good story."

Verity cracked a smile and climbed in. There ensued a polite but wordless dispute over seating arrangements, which ended somehow with Ash's aunt occupying the entire front-facing bench while Verity and Ash sat opposite her.

"I'm going to give testimony tomorrow," Verity said once she had arranged her skirts.

Ash frowned. When his solicitor had told him as much, Ash had protested heartily. But Verity had been the one to find the letter, so she must take the stand. "I apologize for that."

"Don't," she said. "I told you that I want to help you. Besides, after hearing your uncle's barrister publicly slander you and Lady Caroline, I want a chance to look him in the eye." She said this viciously enough that Ash wouldn't have liked the barrister's odds if he met Verity Plum in a darkened alley-way. He very much wanted to take her into his arms but they were in a carriage with his aunt.

At close distance, Ash could see that Verity's unfamiliar garments were speckled with more than a little cat hair. "I gather you and the cat are getting along."

"She has a charming new habit of scratching me bloody if I stop petting her. Also, her name is now Isabella of France."

When the carriage stopped at Holywell Street, Verity tried to tuck a stray piece of hair beneath the brim of her bonnet.

"Here," he said, staying her arm. "Hold still." He retrieved a pin from his pocket to tie back the loose tendril.

"I'd like to know whose hair you're dressing these days to warrant still carrying hairpins around," Verity said over her shoulder as she stepped down from the carriage.

"Only you, Plum. I'm ever optimistic that I'll have a chance to put you to rights."

"Until tomorrow," she said, and Ash knew a moment of confidence that no matter what, they would look out for one another.

Chapter Nineteen

Verity arrived in the courtroom the next morning wearing a bonnet that was even more demurely enormous than the previous day's. She truly hoped Ash recognized two days of consecutive bonnets as the public declaration of love that it was. From where she sat, Ash seemed weary and on edge, and she wished she could have sat by him. But she had a different role to play this morning.

With her hands—sheathed in Amelia's finest kidskin gloves—folded in her lap, she watched as the judge read a letter from a trustee of St. Gerald's School in King's Lynn, Norfolk, stating that Adrian Lewes had been employed by that institution from the year 1792 until his death ten years later.

Then, accompanied by a din that rose to a roar, the judge announced Verity's name and she made her way to the witness stand. For the last two days the papers had talked about how one of their own, the publisher of the *Ladies' Register* and sister to Nathaniel Plum, had come into possession of an item of evidence that was crucial to the fate of the Forgotten Heir. This was too good a story to resist, of course. Every word she spoke would be transcribed in newspapers and distorted in broadsheets. She'd be lucky if she didn't have a ballad written about her.

Answering the barrister's questions in a loud, clear voice, she spoke about how she had come into possession of the letter, who Roger Bertram was, how she knew the plaintiff, and other questions as to her knowledge of Ash's life dating from his arrival in London.

She then answered Ash's uncle's barrister in tones of bland indifference. When the barrister asked whether it was true that she was the defendant's lover, and had cooked up this scheme in order to make herself a duchess, she let out a peal of laughter. The judge warned her to answer the question that was posed.

"Sir, if you're in the least familiar with my magazines, you'll know precisely in what regard I hold the aristocracy. For my brother's dearest friend and the companion of my childhood to now count himself among the most highly ranked men of the land is a grievous professional embarrassment." The court exploded into laughter, and no amount of gavel pounding brought order until Verity had descended from the stand and disappeared through the crowd. On her way from the stand, she met Ash's eye and he responded with a slight, grateful smile.

And then—oh, to hell with it. Instead of returning to her seat upstairs, she sat beside Lady Caroline. She didn't know if this was even allowed, and as someone who had been raised to have a healthy fear of the organs of the law, she half expected a bailiff to haul her off to a prison cell. But nobody even seemed to notice, because Ash was taking the stand and all eyes were on him.

He looked like the grandson of a duke and she hated it. She made plans to divest him of every stitch of snowy white linen, to make him pay for that cravat pin and signet ring. But beneath all those despicable trappings of class that was Ash up there, and she loved him, whatever he wore, whatever he was.

As Ash spoke, she knew she wasn't the only one who thought he looked the part. The court was silent, every person's attention on him. In a tone that conveyed a sense of acute embarrassment that he had found himself in this position, he told the court what little he remembered of his early life and the circumstances under which he had discovered his origins.

"Do you wish you had never found out the truth?" asked his solicitor.

"Yes," Ash answered without hesitation. "If I were still an engraver, I think I'd be halfway to convincing the woman I love to become my wife. Or maybe a third of the way." Verity heard soft laughter even as her cheeks heated. "But with things as they are, I doubt that will come to pass."

He was a fool. She had worn this bonnet. Did he not understand the significance of that? She was in love with an idiot. But she saw two members of the jury smile fondly at him, and even the judge brought a hand to his mouth to conceal what must have been a grin. That, she knew, was the moment he had won the case.

It was also, it seemed, the moment his uncle realized it, because while Ash was being cross-examined, his uncle, who until that point had been a dark and sullen presence on the opposite side of the room, rose to his feet. The courtroom fell silent, and then once again exploded into sound as the man pushed his way out of the room.

"I know that look," Lady Caroline said. Her face was ashen, and when Verity reached for one of her hands, she could feel the chill even through both their sets of gloves. "I need to stop him." The older woman rose to her feet. The judge pounded on his gavel, and Verity sought out Ash, who was still on the stand. He gave her a pleading look.

"All right," Verity said, standing. "Lead the way."

Lady Caroline's carriage was nowhere to be found, so Verity hailed a hack.

"Where are we going?" Verity asked.

"Arundel House. If we aren't too late."

"Too late for what, exactly?"

"I expect he's going to tear up my plants. He's always been a petty man." She sounded so resigned to this, and Verity remembered her mother's similar state of mind with respect to her father's temperamentality.

When they arrived at Arundel House, the front door was slightly ajar. The foyer was empty, the house utterly silent.

"Perhaps I was wrong," Lady Caroline said. "Perhaps he didn't come here at all, but went off to his club."

That was when Verity smelled smoke. "I think he's here," she said unnecessarily, as Lady Caroline was already dashing up the marble stairs. Verity sighed and followed her. This was probably the stupidest thing she had ever done, rushing farther into a building that might well contain both a killer and a fire. But for all she knew Lady Caroline was being murdered at that very moment. Or the duke might be being killed—no, on second thought she didn't care much about him. He was a villain and entirely welcome to die, as far as she was concerned. But Lady Caroline had been good to Ash and had suffered enough for a couple of lifetimes.

When she reached the top of the stairs, there was no sign of Lady Caroline. The smoke seemed to be thicker than it was in the foyer, but still she couldn't tell where it was coming from. Before she could debate whether to go downstairs and shout for the fire brigade, she was jerked backward by a strong arm around her neck. The man—presumably Ash's uncle—had apparently never witnessed a street brawl, because he was utterly surprised when Verity twisted her head and bit his hand. She stepped out of his grasp, searching the landing for anything she could use to bludgeon him with, her eyes alighting on a very solid-looking urn. But before she could reach it, Lady Caroline appeared behind her brother and hit him on the head with a newel post that appeared torn from the bannister. He hit the ground with a thud.

"Are you all right?" Verity cried. Lady Caroline had blood on her face and the sleeve of her dress was badly singed, hinting at damage beneath.

Lady Caroline ignored her. "He's not dead, is he?"

"I don't think so," Verity said, nudging the man with the toe of her boot. He rolled over, and the two women stared at him, and then at one another. He was inches from the broken segment of banister. Several posts were missing, as if they had been kicked out in anger, with the result that there was a gap of more than a yard.

"He tried to kill my father," Lady Caroline said. "He set a fire outside his bedchamber."

"It looks like he tried to kill you too," Verity pointed out, gesturing towards the blood on the other woman's face and the burn marks on her dress. "He certainly seemed intent on killing me. I do believe he tried to kill Ash once too. While we're tallying up his crimes, that is," Verity added, knowing she was rambling.

Lady Caroline stared at her brother, then took a deep breath. Then she braced her foot against his back and shoved him off. A moment later, they heard an ominously wet sound from below.

"What a pity that he fell by accident," Verity managed. "What a shame."

Lady Caroline stared in mute horror over the railing, as if unable to comprehend what she had done.

"I'll never forget how you rescued me from an assault and then my attacker fell to his death completely by accident," Verity recited, not taking her eyes from the older woman. There were advantages to spending some time on the windy side of the law. "Witnesses?"

Lady Caroline shook her head. "The servants are gone,"

she said after a moment. "The house is empty except for my father and his manservant. Ash must have given them the day out."

"Well. Let's go downstairs and see if we can find a constable." She looped her arm through Lady Caroline's and they headed for the street, two women who had made their own justice.

When Ash walked in the front door of Arundel House, he was greeted by the sight of Verity and his aunt bonding over the corpse of his uncle. As he had spent the harrowing trip from Westminster imagining the grievous injury of either Verity or his aunt, it was a pleasant surprise, all things considered.

"Perhaps we ought to get a constable," he suggested, shoving his hands in his pockets and deciding that he was not going to ask what had happened.

"We've already done that," Verity said. "Now we're waiting for the coroner." She outlined the facts, with enough emphasis on how it was a terrible accident to make him resolve never to ask any questions about the details. Ash had been afraid his uncle would retaliate against the duke and the household staff, which was why Ash had quietly sent the servants away for the day. He found that he was pleased to learn that his grandfather had slept through the entire episode, and that the house suffered only minimal damage.

In the end it was past midnight by the time the body was removed, the coroner's inquest scheduled, the servants returned, and the foyer cleaned of blood. Verity stayed with him the entire time.

"You still have on your bonnet," he remarked when they were collapsed on the sofa in the library, Lady Caroline having retired to bed.

That must have been the wrong thing to say because she sat up straight and pointed a menacing finger at him. "Perjurer," she declared. "A third of the way. Not likely to come to pass. Fabrications and falsehoods. As if I'd wear a bonnet for a man I didn't love with every fiber of my being."

He swallowed hard. "I don't doubt your love for me, Plum, although it's always gratifying to hear you remind me. But loving someone and marrying them are two different things entirely, as you've pointed out more than once."

She set her jaw and regarded him in a way that was all too familiar. This was Verity steeling herself. "I've been thinking about those letters Roger saved," she said, surprising him. "They were in love, weren't they? Roger and the schoolmaster?"

"He never said as much, but I think so."

"It must have been his friend's bible. And I thought to myself, Roger must have remembered his friend every time he looked at that careless knot. He didn't look at it as the text of a religion he rejected, but as a book that was dear to his friend. The ribbon was worn ragged, Ash." He could picture Roger worrying the knot, running the ribbon between his fingers. "I dare say they would have married if they could have. Instead Roger must have only found out about his friend's death weeks after it occurred. Ash, I don't want to read about you in the paper. I want to be by your side."

His arms were around her, hauling her into his lap. "That's a yes?"

"It's a yes."

Verity was in the back of the courtroom when the jury announced that they had found in Ash's favor. She wanted to see it happen, wanted to watch the moment Ash officially became a duke, as if the transformation would happen before her eyes. Ash was not present: a week after the death of his son, the old duke's health had taken a turn for the worse and he died in the night. Ash remained with his aunt at Arundel House. When Verity arrived home, she found a note from Ash to the effect that he would call on her the following day, special license in hand, and haul her before the clergyman of her choice at a time convenient to herself. He also wrote that if she would consider where she might like to reside, he would be grateful.

This baffled Verity. It hadn't occurred to her that Ash had been serious about living anywhere other than Arundel House. The Holywell Street house was out of the question, because it would be exceptionally awkward for the workers to have a duke poking his nose into their business, not to mention how it would throw Nan into apoplexies. But there could, apparently, be a middle ground between Holywell Street and Arundel House.

It occurred to her that what she really wanted to do was

continue the *Ladies' Register.* And that she could do from a distance, sending in material to be printed and then sold. The shop foreman could continue to publish the *Register* with minimal oversight. It made her feel slightly sick, the idea of giving up control of the rest of Plum & Co. It was hers, she had made it, and now she was going to need to step away from it. But Ash had stepped away from his own work in order to take on his duties. Even Nate had stepped away from his work when Verity had needed him to. Verity could do the same. Sometimes love required sacrifices; she had known this since her earliest days.

She responded to Ash's note with one of her own, stating that she would be at home the following morning, and he could arrive with settlement documents in hand. Her cheeks flushed as she wrote the words, but if she was giving up her livelihood, then he could ensure that she was provided for. It was fair. And it was something more than fair—it was just.

The following morning, she found Nan in the kitchen, reading what appeared to be a pamphlet, her brow furrowed and eyes narrowed.

"What's the matter?" Verity asked.

"It's just . . . if I didn't know better, I'd think this was written by Mr. Nate. Have a look for yourself."

Verity glanced at the front page and for a moment went quite dizzy. In large type were the words "On the Dangers of a Shackled Press" and below it an engraving in a style she would have known anywhere. It depicted the body of a man in chains, with buzzards in red coats picking at his bones, while jackals looked on in hungry anticipation. Sketched in the background was a gibbet, emaciated children, and soldiers holding out tin cups. An assortment of men in shiny boots and evening dress looked everywhere but at the dead man. Ash had drawn himself as one of the distracted bystanders, including himself among those who needed to pay closer attention. In case there was any confusion, he had signed his name to the bottom, a signature she had seen hundreds of times, but this time it read *Arundel*.

On the next page was a short paragraph: "What follows is an example of what is lost when the press fears for its safety. I, James Talbot, Duke of Arundel, set the type and printed these pamphlets with my own hands and no assistance. In the event that the Home Office finds these materials seditious, my direction is Weybourne Priory, Notts." Below was the entirety of Nate's last essay, in which he wrote about the dead of Pentrich, arguing that only the direst desperation would drive a man to take arms and revolt, because the chance of success is so minuscule and the cost of failure so high; a person would have to believe his death to be worth more than his life, and for a government to tacitly agree to that statement is to concede its failure and acknowledge it should be overthrown. It was a perfectly good essay, and made points Verity had been hearing for years, but to see them laid out starkly on paper, and by Ash's doing, moved her to speechlessness.

"Miss Verity?" Nan asked. "You all right?"

Verity realized she was crying. "Very much so." Other people might like love poems or posies; Verity's heart could be won only by outright sedition, and Ash had known it. Within hours of inheriting his title, he had declared himself against the government, and for Verity. "But I need to go to Arundel House immediately."

"If you could spare a moment before leaving, perhaps?" came a voice from behind her.

She spun around to find Ash leaning against the door that led to the shop.

"Nan, here's a couple of florins, go buy the finest cheese in the land, leave it on the kitchen table, then take the rest of the day off."

The older woman took the coins and left, throwing a wink at Ash over her shoulder.

"Who are you to dismiss my servant?" Verity asked, stalking towards him. "Overstepping and imperious." She took hold of his cravat and pulled him close so she could breathe in the scent of his shaving soap and skim her lips across the faint stubble of his jaw.

"I'm the man you're going upstairs with, Plum. Shocked you need this spelled out for you, always thought you cleverer than that. After that, I plan to go to Weybourne, but thought you might like to come with me. Caro says it's in an appalling state of dilapidation, so you don't need to worry about being subjected to a life of luxury."

This, she suspected, was his way of asking her to marry him in his ancestral home. She twisted her hand in his cravat and saw the mingled alarm and desire in his dark eyes. "Did you really print it with your own hands? How did you operate the press by yourself?"

"Ah, I did have an accomplice for that part."

"Your aunt?"

"Madam, I am not informing on my aunt."

She bit back a laugh and kissed him hard. God help her, she had missed this, missed having him by her side. "Upstairs," she said, her lips still against his. "Now. Then we'll go to your poxy house."

They got only as far as the study, Ash pressing her against the closed door. She promptly wrapped her legs around his waist as he reached for the fall of his trousers. She slid her hand between them, pushing his hand away and drawing him out, stroking him in her hand. "I'm feeling maudlin, Ash, but I missed this."

"It missed you," he said earnestly.

She snorted with laughter and then groaned as he slid inside her. "I meant that I missed *this*," she breathed. "Being close with you, doing this with you. I ought to have known from the first time we kissed that we needed to be together. Stupid of me."

"I knew before then," he said, driving into her. "And I'll spend the rest of my life reminding you, as often as you need."

"Please," she said. "Please." He was hitting a spot inside her that made her feel perpetually on the brink of climax, and while it was sweet torture, she needed more. She insinuated a hand between them, felt the place where they joined, where he thrust inside her again and again, and then she was gone, toppling over the brink, with only Ash to hold her.

Could it be that easy? As simple as two people deciding to be together regardless of every reason why they shouldn't?

Verity was willing to believe that it was, because the alternative was a life without Ash, without love, without hope. And hope, Verity was learning, wasn't just idly positing the truth of some fanciful notion. It was taking that truth and letting it be your lodestar, guiding your movements, providing your direction.

Whatever the next months or years might hold, Verity would go through it with Ash, and that was enough.

Epilogue

In the end, they wound up staying at Weybourne Priory for longer than either of them had contemplated. There was an entire village of houses with bad roofs and worse chimneys, which kept Ash quite busy and provided a way for him to dispose of reckless amounts of money. Verity, meanwhile, offered her shop foreman an extra six shillings a week and lodgings in the Holywell Street house in exchange for him handling the day-to-day business of Plum and Company until Nate returned. This gave her time to work exclusively on the *Ladies' Register.*

Staying in the country gave London a bit of time to get over the shock of having a new duke who had made a disgraceful marriage. While Lady Caroline declared herself content to weather the storm, Verity thought it could wait until some of the furor had died down. She hated the country much less than she thought she would.

A letter from Roger arrived after they had been in the country only a few days. He was well and the climate agreed with him. Verity watched as lines of concern smoothed from Ash's forehead and he seemed to drop a burden she hadn't entirely known he was carrying.

In the first weeks of spring, when the ground was still frozen and the trees were still bare, a letter finally came from America. Verity had burst into tears at the sight of her brother's handwriting, and Ash had needed to read the letter aloud to her.

Then, when the summer was in full swing, a peculiar letter arrived from Amelia. "Salutations on becoming a grandmother," she wrote to Verity. "Your demonic cat has had an appalling number of kittens, all very sweet, which leads me to believe they take after their father, whoever he might be. Also, it may interest you to know that there's a new scandal du jour. My brother—both my brothers, in fact—have made ill-advised marriages. Mother is delighted. The good news is that when you return to London you will no longer be the most outrageous aristocratic spouse, and that is all I'm going to say on the matter. I finished the Isabella of France manuscript (please find it enclosed) and have commenced a biography of Joanna the Mad."

"What's that look on your face?" Ash asked. He stood in the door of the room Verity had adopted as her study. His sleeves were rolled up and there were bits of hay or some other vegetation in his hair. A smudge of dirt sat under one eye. He looked very flushed and very happy. She would never have guessed that the country would suit him. She certainly wouldn't have guessed how well it would suit her, but she was coming to understand that it mattered very little where she was, compared to who she was with.

"The Marquess of Pembroke has outdone us in scandal, apparently."

"Damn. We'll have to take up as highwaymen to reclaim our spot," Ash said.

"I was thinking we could try piracy."

"That's the spirit." He grinned. "So do you want to go back to London? We could hire a house if you don't fancy staying where there's been a mur—totally accidental death."

"What kind of house?" Verity asked.

"Oh, I don't know. Someplace with gold leaf all over the water closets and enormous Corinthian columns in the foyer, so everyone will know we have no class."

And so everyone would know they weren't trying to play by the rules. "The ton will be disappointed if we don't have a replica pyramid in the garden."

"You make a good point." Ash came forward and sat on the edge of her desk. He twisted one of her loose strands of hair and fixed it in place with a pin he drew from his pocket. Which was pretty rich coming from a man who had the better part of a hay stack tangled in his hair, but Verity wasn't complaining.

"Come here," she said, pulling him down by the collar for a kiss.

"Anything for you, Plum," he said, and brought his lips to hers.

Author's Note

Ash's illness is a type of seizure disorder that would likely be diagnosed as epilepsy both today and in 1817. Before the advent of seizure control drugs, many people with similar conditions had their lives cut short or severely curtailed by illnesses and injuries related to their seizures. But there were also people with seizure disorders who lived full and happy lives. Writer and illustrator Edward Lear is a notable example, and a near-contemporary of Ash. I'm indebted to the friends who helped me come up with a realistic depiction of Ash's symptoms, although his situation is not meant to be universal.

For anyone who is wondering whether it would be appropriate or realistic for an unmarried man to lodge with an unmarried woman, we have a historical precedent that neatly echoes Ash and Verity's case. During the late Georgian era, caricaturist and printmaker James Gillray lodged for many years with Miss Hannah Humphrey, his publisher.

Several women in the publishing and print-selling industries owned and operated thriving businesses during the

Georgian era, so Verity's proprietorship of Plum & Company would hardly be remarkable to her peers. You may recognize the address of Verity's bookshop: Holywell Street is primarily famous as the epicenter of Victorian pornography. Before that, however, it was a hotbed of political radicalism. Literature, political radicalism, and erotica were intertwined in this period; indeed, the poem that Verity struggles with in Chapter Eighteen is Percy Shelley's "Ozymandias," which was first printed in a radical weekly paper, and some years later reprinted by famous pornographer and radical William Benbow.

Perkin Warbeck, while seemingly a bizarre choice for a lady novelist of the early nineteenth century, was the topic of a novel by none other than Mary Shelley. For many years, there was some confusion about whether Warbeck's wife, Lady Catherine Gordon, was the granddaughter of the king of Scotland. We now know that she was not, but I let the author of our novel labor under that misapprehension.

In considering what Ash's solicitors might do to advance his claim as speedily as possible, I borrowed some details from the case of the Tichborne Claimant. In the 1850s, the heir to the Tichborne baronetcy died in a shipwreck; ten year later, a man claimed to be that presumed-dead heir. I have to confess that I expedited the proceedings in a way that I'm afraid is sadly unrealistic by 19th century legal norms.

Don't miss the rest of
Cat Sebastian's Regency Imposters series!
Keep reading for an excerpt from

UNMASKED BY THE MARQUESS

Available now from Avon Impulse

The one you love . . .

Robert Selby is determined to see his sister make an advantageous match. But he has two problems: the Selbys have no connections or money and Robert is really a housemaid named Charity Church. She's enjoyed every minute of her masquerade over the past six years, but she knows her pretense is nearing an end. Charity needs to see her beloved friend married well and then Robert Selby will disappear . . . forever.

May not be who you think . . .

Alistair, Marquess of Pembroke, has spent years repairing the estate ruined by his wastrel father, and nothing is more important than protecting his fortune and name. He shouldn't be so beguiled by the charming young man who shows up on his doorstep asking for favors. And he certainly shouldn't be thinking of all the disreputable things he'd like to do to the impertinent scamp.

But is who you need . . .

When Charity's true nature is revealed, Alistair knows he can't marry a scandalous woman in breeches, and Charity isn't about to lace herself into a corset and play a respectable miss. Can these stubborn souls learn to sacrifice what they've always wanted for a love that is more than they could have imagined?

Chapter One

Alistair ran his finger once more along the neatly penned column of sums his secretary had left on his desk. This was what respectability looked like: a ledger filled with black ink, maintained by a servant whose wages had been paid on time.

He would never tire of seeing the numbers do what he wanted them to do, what they *ought* to do out of sheer decency and moral fortitude. Here it was, plain numerical proof that the marquessate had—finally—more money coming in than it had going out. Not long ago this very library was besieged by a steady stream of his late father's creditors and mistresses and assorted other disgraceful hangers-on, all demanding a piece of the badly picked-over pie. But now Alistair de Lacey, eighth Marquess of Pembroke, could add financial solvency to the list of qualities that made him the model of propriety.

This pleasant train of thought was interrupted by the sound of an apologetic cough coming from the doorway.

"Hopkins?" Alistair asked, looking up.

"A person has called, my lord." The butler fairly radiated distress. "I took the liberty of showing her into the morning room."

Her? It couldn't be any of his aunts, because those formidable ladies would have barged right into the library. Alistair felt his heart sink. "Dare I ask?"

"Mrs. Allenby, my lord," Hopkins intoned, as if every syllable pained him to utter.

Well might he look pained. Mrs. Allenby, indeed. She was the most notorious of his late father's mistresses and if there was one thing Alistair had learned in the years since his father's death, it was that the arrival of any of these doxies inevitably presaged an entry in red ink in the ledger that sat before him.

And now she was sitting in the morning room? The same morning room his mother had once used to receive callers? Good Lord, no. Not that he could think of a more suitable place for that woman to be brought.

"Send her up here, if you will, Hopkins."

A moment later, a woman mortifyingly close to his own age swept into the library. "Heavens, Pembroke, but you're shut up in a veritable tomb," she said, as if it could possibly be any of her business. "You'll ruin your eyes trying to read in the dark." And then she actually had the presumption to draw back one of the curtains, letting a broad shaft of sunlight into the room.

Alistair was momentarily blinded by the unexpected brightness. Motes of dust danced in the light, making him uncomfortably aware that his servants were not doing an adequate job with the cleaning, and also that perhaps the room had been a trifle dark after all.

"Do take a seat," he offered, but only after she had already dropped gracefully into one of the chairs near the fire.

The years had been reprehensibly kind to Portia Allenby, and Alistair felt suddenly conscious that the same could not be said for himself. She had no gray in her jet-black hair and no need for spectacles. The subdued half mourning she had adopted after his father's death made her look less like a harlot who had been acquired by the late marquess on a drunken spree across the continent some eighteen years ago, and more like a decent widow.

"I'll not waste your time, Pembroke. I'm here about Amelia."

"Amelia," Alistair repeated slowly, as if trying that word out for the first time.

"My eldest daughter," she clarified, patiently playing along with Alistair's feigned ignorance. *Your sister,* she didn't need to add.

"And which one is she?" Alistair drummed his fingers on the desk. "The ginger one with the freckles?" All the Allenby girls were ginger-haired and freckled, having had the great misfortune to take after the late marquess rather than their beautiful mother.

Mrs. Allenby ignored his rudeness. "She's eighteen. I'd like for her to make a proper come out."

So she wanted money. No surprise there. "My dear lady," he said frostily, "you cannot possibly need for money.

My father saw to it that you and your children were amply provided for." In fact, his father had spent the last months of his life seeing to little else, selling and mortgaging everything not nailed down in order to keep this woman and the children he had sired on her in suitably grand style.

"You're quite right, Pembroke, I don't need a farthing." She smoothed the dove-gray silk of her gown across her lap, whether out of self-consciousness or in order to emphasize how well-lined her coffers were, Alistair could not guess. "What I hoped was that you could arrange for Amelia to be invited to a dinner or two." She smiled, as if Alistair ought to be relieved to hear this request. "Even a tea or a luncheon would go a long way."

Alistair was momentarily speechless. He removed his spectacles and carefully polished them on his handkerchief before tucking them into his pocket. "Surely I have mistaken you. I have no doubt that among your numerous acquaintances you could find someone willing to invite your daughter to festivities of any kind." The woman ran a monthly salon, for God's sake. She was firmly, infuriatingly located right on the fringes of decent society. Every poet and radical, not to mention every gently born person with a penchant for libertinism, visited her drawing room. Alistair had to positively go out of his way to avoid her.

"You're quite right," she replied blithely, as if insensible to the insult. "The problem is that she's had too many of those invitations. She's in a fair way to becoming a bluestocking, not to put too fine a point on it. I hope that a few evenings spent in, ah, more exalted company will give her mind a different turn."

Had she just suggested that her own associates were too serious-minded for a young girl? It was almost laughable. But not as laughable as the idea that Alistair ought to lend his countenance to the debut of any daughter of the notorious Mrs. Allenby, regardless of whose by-blow the child was. "My dear lady, you cannot expect—"

"Goodness, Pembroke. I'm not asking for her to be presented at court, or for vouchers to Almack's. I was hoping you could prevail on one of Ned's sisters to invite her to dinner." If she were aware of what it did to Alistair to hear his father referred to thusly, she did not show it. "The old Duke of Devonshire acknowledged his mistress's child, you know. It can't reflect poorly on you or your aunts to throw my children a few crumbs."

So now, after bringing his father to the brink of disgrace and ruin, she was an expert on what would or would not reflect poorly on a man, was she? The mind simply boggled.

"Of course I wouldn't expect to attend with her," she continued.

He reared back in his chair. "Good God, I should think not."

Only then did she evidently grasp that she was not about to prevail. "I only meant that I would engage a suitable chaperone. But I see that I've bothered you for no reason." She rose to her feet with an audible swish of costly silks. "I wish you well, Pembroke."

Alistair was only warming to the topic, though. "If I were to acknowledge all my father's bastards I'd have to start a charitable foundation. There would be opera dancers and housemaids lined up down the street."

At this she turned back to face him. "You do your father an injustice. He was not a man of temperate desires, but he and I shared a life together from the moment we met until he died."

"I feel certain both your husband and my mother were touched to discover that the two of you had such an aptitude for domestic felicity, despite all appearances to the contrary." Mr. Allenby had been discarded as surely as Alistair's mother had been.

Was that pity that crossed the woman's face? "As I said, I'm truly sorry to have bothered you today." She sighed. "Gilbert is a regular visitor at my house. I mention that not to provoke you but only to suggest that if you're determined not to acknowledge the connection, you ought to bring your brother under bridle."

She dropped a small curtsy that didn't seem even slightly ironic, and left Alistair alone in his library. He felt uncomfortable, vaguely guilty, but he knew perfectly well that he had behaved properly. His father had devoted his life to squandering money and tarnishing his name by any means available to him: cards, horses, women, bad investments. And he had left the mess to be cleaned up by his son. Alistair, at least, would leave the family name and finances intact for future generations.

He paced to the windows and began pulling back the rest

of the curtains. It annoyed him to admit that Mrs. Allenby had been right about anything, but the room really was too dark. He had been working too hard, too long, but even now with all the curtains opened, the room was still gloomy. The late winter sun had sunk behind the row of houses on the opposite side of Grosvenor Square, casting only a thin, pallid light into the room. He went to the hearth to poke the fire back to life.

His plan had been to double check the books and then go out for a ride, but the hour for that had come and gone. He could dress and take an early dinner at his club, perhaps. Even though the Season had not quite started, there were enough people in town to make the outing worthwhile. It was never a bad idea for Alistair to show his face and remind the world that this Marquess of Pembroke, at least, did not spend his evenings in orgies of dissipation.

As he tried not to think of the debauchery these walls had contained, there came another apologetic cough from the doorway.

"Another caller, my lord," Hopkins said. "A young gentleman."

Alistair suppressed a groan. This was the outside of enough. "Send him up." He inwardly prayed that the caller wasn't an associate of Gilbert's, some shabby wastrel Alistair's younger brother had lost money to at the gambling tables. He glanced at the card Hopkins had given him. Robert Selby. The fact that the name rang no bells for him did nothing to put his mind at ease.

But the man Hopkins ushered into the library didn't

seem like the sort of fellow who frequented gambling hells. He looked to be hardly twenty, with sandy hair that hung a trifle too long to be à la mode and clothes that were respectably, but not fashionably, cut.

"I'm ever so grateful, my lord." The young man took a half step closer, but seemed to check his progress when he noticed Alistair's expression. "I know what an imposition it must be. But the matter is so dashed awkward I hardly wanted to put it to you in a letter."

It got worse and worse. Matters too awkward to be put in letters inevitably veered towards begging or blackmail. Alistair folded his arms and leaned against the chimneypiece. "Go on," he ordered.

"It's my sister, you see. Your father was her godfather."

Alistair jerked to attention. "My father was your sister's godfather?" He was incredulous. There could hardly have been any creature on this planet less suited to be an infant's godparent than the late Lord Pembroke. "He went to church?" Really, the image of his father leaning over the baptismal font and promising to be mindful of the baby's soul was something Alistair would make a point of recalling the next time his spirits were low.

"I daresay he did, my lord," Selby continued brightly, as if he had no idea of the late marquess's character. "I was too young to remember the event, I'm afraid."

"And what can you possibly require of me, Mr. Selby?" Alistair did not even entertain the possibility that Selby was here for the pleasure of his company. "Not an hour ago I refused to help a person with a far greater claim on the estate than you have."

The fellow had the grace to blush, at least. "My sister and I have no claim on you at all. It's only that I'm in quite a fix and I don't know who else to turn to. She's of an age where I need to find her a husband, but . . ." His voice trailed off, and he regarded Alistair levelly, as if deciding whether he could be confided in. Presumptuous. "Well, frankly, she's too pretty and too trusting to take to Bath or Brighton. She'd marry someone totally unsuitable. I had thought to bring her to London, where she would have a chance to meet worthier people."

Alistair retrieved his spectacles from his coat pocket and carefully put them on. This Selby fellow didn't seem delusional, but he was speaking like a madman. "That's a terrible plan."

"Well, now I know that, my lord." He smiled broadly, exposing too many teeth and creating an excess of crinkles around his eyes. Alistair suddenly wished that there was enough light to get a better look at this lad. "We've been here a few weeks and it's all too clear that the connections I made at Cambridge aren't enough to help Louisa. She needs better than that." He shot Alistair another grin, as if they were in on the same joke.

Alistair opened his mouth to coolly explain that he could not help Mr. Selby's sister, no matter how good her looks or how bad her circumstances. But he found that he couldn't quite give voice to any of his usual crisp denials. "Have you no relations?"

"None that suit the purpose, my lord," Selby said frankly. This Mr. Selby had charming manners, even when he met with disappointment. Alistair would give him that much—it would have been a relief to see Gilbert develop such pleasant ways instead of his usual fits of sullenness. "Our parents died some years ago," Selby continued. "We brought an elderly aunt with us, but we grew up in quite a remote part of Northumberland, and if we have any relations in London, we've never heard of them."

Northumberland? Now, what the devil could Alistair's father have been doing in Northumberland? Quite possibly he had gotten drunk at a hunt party in Melton Mowbray and simply lost his way home, leaving a string of debauched housemaids and misbegotten children in his wake.

That made something else occur to Alistair. "There's no suggestion that your sister is my father's natural child?"

"My—good heavens, no." Selby seemed astonished, possibly offended by the slight to his mother's honor. "Certainly not."

Thank God for that, at least. Alistair leaned back against the smooth stone of the chimneypiece, regarding his visitor from behind half-closed lids. Even though there was nothing about Selby that seemed overtly grasping, here he was, grasping nonetheless. There was no reason for this man, charming manners and winning smile, to be in Alistair's library unless it was to demand something.

"If you want my advice, take her to Bath." He pushed away from the wall and stepped towards his visitor. Selby was a few inches shorter than Alistair and much slighter of build. Alistair didn't need to use his size to intimidate—that was what rank and power were for—but this wasn't about intimidation. It was about proximity. He wanted a closer look at this man, so he would take it.

Selby had tawny skin spotted with freckles, as if he were accustomed to spending a good deal of time outside. His lips were a brownish pink, and quirked up in a questioning sort of smile, as if he knew what exactly Alistair was about.

Perhaps he did. Interesting, because Alistair hardly knew himself.

Alistair dropped his voice. "Better yet, go home. London is a dangerous place for a girl without connections." He dropped his voice lower still, and leaned in so he was speaking almost directly into Selby's ear. "Or for a young man without scruples." The fellow smelled like lemon drops, as if he had a packet of sweets tucked into one of his pockets.

For a moment they stood there, inches apart. Selby was ultimately the one to step back. "I knew it was a long shot, but I had to try." He flashed Alistair another winning smile, more dangerous for being at close range, before bowing handsomely and showing himself out.

Alistair was left alone in a room that had grown darker still.

"What did he say?" Louisa asked as soon as Charity returned to the shabby-genteel house they had hired for the Season.

"It's a nonstarter, Lou," she replied, flinging herself onto a settee. She propped her boots up onto the table before her. One of the many, many advantages of posing as a man was the freedom afforded by men's clothing.

"He turned you away, then?" Louisa asked, looking up from the tea she was pouring them.

"Oh, worse than that. He asked if his father had gotten your mother with child, then advised me that if I allowed you to stay in London, you'd end up prostituting yourself."

Louisa colored, and Charity realized she had spoken too freely. Louisa had, after all, been raised a lady. "Oh, he didn't say that last thing quite outright, but he dropped a strong hint." She hooked an arm behind her head and settled comfortably back in her seat. "Besides, what does it matter if he thinks we're beneath reproach? He's never even heard of us before today. His opinion doesn't matter a jot."

"Maybe he's right, though, and I shouldn't stay in London." Instead of looking at Charity, she was nervously lining up the teacups so their cracks and chips were out of sight.

"Nonsense. As soon as these nobs get a look at you, you'll take off like a rocket."

Louisa regarded her dubiously. But it really was absurd, how very pretty Robbie's little sister had turned out to be. Her hair fell in perfect flaxen ringlets and her skin was flawless. Other than her blond hair she looked nothing like Robbie, thank God, because that would have been too hard for Charity to live with.

Charity shook her head in a futile attempt to dismiss that unwanted thought, and then blew an errant strand of hair off her forehead. "I only have to figure out how to make them notice you in the first place, and if that prig of a marquess isn't willing to help, then we'll find another way."

"Was he really that bad?"

Charity put her hand over her heart, as if taking an oath. "I tell you, if he had a quizzing glass he would have examined me under it. He seemed so dreadfully bored and put upon, I nearly felt bad for him. But then I remembered all his money and got quite over it."

That made Louisa laugh, and Charity was glad of it, because it wouldn't do for the girl to worry. Charity was worried enough for both of them. Going to Pembroke had been a last resort; he was such a loose connection of the family, but he was the best Charity could come up with. Louisa needed a husband, and she needed one soon, because Charity wasn't sure how much longer she was going to be able to keep up this charade. Dressing like a man didn't bother her—quite the contrary. But pretending to be Robbie when the real Robbie was cold in his grave? That was too much. It was a daily reminder of what she had lost, of what she would never have.

Louisa put down her teacup and clasped her hands together. "I'd be glad to go to Bath for a few months. Remember that the Smythe girls found husbands there."

Charity remembered all too well. One of them had married a country clergyman and the other had gotten engaged to an army officer on half pay. She'd be damned if Louisa threw herself away like that. Hell, if she had gone through with this farce for Louisa to wind up marrying a curate she'd be furious.

She had to forcibly remind herself that her feelings were immaterial. This was her chance to see Louisa settled in the way Robbie would have wanted. It was only because of the Selbys that Charity was here in the first place, clean and fed and educated, rather than . . . Well, none of that bore thinking of. She was grateful to the family, and this was her chance to take care of the last of them.

"Listen, Charity. When I think of the expense of this London trip—"

"You mustn't call me that," Charity whispered. "Servants might hear." And if Charity knew anything about servants, which she most certainly did, it would only be a matter of time before one overheard. And then their ship would be quite sunk.

"Oh!" Louisa cried, clapping a hand over her mouth. "I keep forgetting. But it's so strange to call you Robbie."

Of course it was. Not everyone was as hardened to deceit as Charity had become. She had been assuming this role for years, from the point when the real Robert Selby had decided that he did not want to go to Cambridge and would send Charity in his stead. She, at least, was used to answering to his name. But since Robbie had died two years ago, she increasingly felt that she no longer had his permission to use his name. The deceit was weighing heavier on her with each passing day.

All the more reason to get Louisa set up splendidly. Then Robert Selby could fade gracefully out of existence, leaving his Northumberland estate free for the proper heir to eventually inherit, while Charity would . . . Her imagination failed her.

She would figure that out some other time. First, she'd take care of Louisa.

"If all else fails, we'll go to Bath or a seaside resort. I promise." And she flashed her pretend sister her most confident smile.

About the Author

CAT SEBASTIAN lives in a swampy part of the South with her husband, three kids, and two dogs. Before her kids were born, she practiced law and taught high school and college writing. When she isn't reading or writing, she's doing crossword puzzles, bird watching, and wondering where she put her coffee cup.